CALENDAR GIRL

Praise for Georgia Beers

Blend

"You know a book is good, first when you don't want to put it down. Second, you know it's damn good when you're reading it and thinking, I'm totally going to read this one again. Great read and is absolutely a 5-star romance."—*Front Porch Romance Book Reviews*

"Georgia Beers hits all the right notes with this romance set in a wine bar…A low angst read, it still delivers a story rich in heart-rending moments before the characters get their happy ever after. A well-crafted novel, Blend is a marvelous way to spend an evening curled up with a large glass of your favorite vintage."—*Writing While Distracted*

"The leads are very likeable and the supporting characters are also well developed. A really enjoyable novel, and one that leaves the reader longing for a glass of wine!"—*Melina Bickard, Librarian, Waterloo Library (UK)*

Right Here, Right Now

"The angst was written well, but not overpoweringly so, just enough for you to have the heart sinking moment of 'will they make it,' and then you realize they have to because they are made for each other."—*Les Reveur*

Right Here, Right Now "is full of humor (yep, I laughed out loud), romance, and kick-ass characters!"—*Illustrious Illusions*

"[A] successful and entertaining queer romance novel. The main characters are appealing, and the situations they deal with are realistic and well-managed. I would recommend this book to anyone who enjoys a good queer romance novel, and particularly one grounded in real world situations."—*Books at the End of the Alphabet*

"*Right Here Right Now* is a slow-burning sweet romance between two very different women. Lacey is an accountant who lives her life to a plan, is predictable and does not like change. Enter Alicia, a marketing and design executive who is the complete opposite. Nevertheless they click...The connection is sexy, emotional and very hot."—*Kitty Kat's Book Review Blog*

Lambda Literary Award Winner *Fresh Tracks*

"Georgia Beers pens romances with sparks."—*Just About Write*

"[T]he focus switches each chapter to a different character, allowing for a measured pace and deep, sincere exploration of each protagonist's thoughts. Beers gives a welcome expansion to the romance genre with her clear, sympathetic writing."
—*Curve magazine*

Lambda Literary Award Finalist *Finding Home*

"Georgia Beers has proven in her popular novels such as *Too Close to Touch* and *Fresh Tracks* that she has a special way of building romance with suspense that puts the reader on the edge of their seat. *Finding Home*, though more character driven than suspense, will equally keep the reader engaged at each page turn with its sweet romance."—*Lambda Literary Review*

What Matters Most

"There's so much more going on, from the way they flirt to how they each learn who the other really is, the way their feelings come about to how the conflict is resolved and where the relationship is at by the end of the book. All the right romantic elements are there, packaged in a way that kept me interested, surprised, and often smiling."—*The Lesbian Review*

A Little Bit of Spice

"As always with Ms Beers's novels, this is well written and edited, well paced and flowing. Definitely one for the reread pile…in fact, one of my favourites from this author." —*The Lesbian Reading Room*

Mine

"From the eye-catching cover, appropriately named title, to the last word, Georgia Beers's *Mine* is captivating, thought-provoking, and satisfying. Like a deep red, smooth-tasting, and expensive merlot, *Mine* goes down easy even though Beers explores tough topics."—*Story Circle Book Reviews*

"Beers does a fine job of capturing the essence of grief in an authentic way. *Mine* is touching, life-affirming, and sweet." —*Lesbian News Book Review*

Too Close to Touch

"This is such a well-written book. The pacing is perfect, the romance is great, the character work strong, and damn, but is the sex writing ever fantastic."—*The Lesbian Review*

"In her third novel, Georgia Beers delivers an immensely satisfying story. Beers knows how to generate sexual tension so taut it could be cut with a knife…Beers weaves a tale of yearning, love, lust, and conflict resolution. She has constructed a believable plot, with strong characters in a charming setting."—*Just About Write*

By the Author

Turning the Page

Thy Neighbor's Wife

Too Close to Touch

Fresh Tracks

Mine

Finding Home

Starting from Scratch

96 Hours

Slices of Life

Snow Globe

Olive Oil & White Bread

Zero Visibility

A Little Bit of Spice

Rescued Heart

Run to You

Dare to Stay

What Matters Most

Right Here, Right Now

Blend

The Shape of You

Calendar Girl

CALENDAR GIRL

by

Georgia Beers

2018

ISBN 13: 978-1-63555-333-8

THIS TRADE PAPERBACK ORIGINAL IS PUBLISHED BY
BOLD STROKES BOOKS, INC.
P.O. BOX 249
VALLEY FALLS, NY 12185

FIRST EDITION: NOVEMBER 2018

CREDITS
EDITORS: LYNDA SANDOVAL AND STACIA SEAMAN
PRODUCTION DESIGN: STACIA SEAMAN
COVER DESIGN BY ANN MCMAN

Acknowledgments

So much goes into a book besides the words. And while it seems like I thank the same people novel after novel, that doesn't change the fact that I couldn't do what I do without them.

Thank you to Radclyffe, Sandy, and everybody at Bold Strokes Books for making this journey fun and stress-free. I appreciate that more than I can say.

Thank you to Lynda Sandoval, my editor extraordinaire, who never fails to make me look better than I actually do. She's become a pro at pointing out my issues while making me laugh, and she's made editing a task I no longer dread. I've learned so much from her, and I expect I'll continue to do so for many years (books) to come.

Thank you to my writer friends who help me each day, whether by giving an opinion on a cover or title or holding me accountable on word count or asking me to hold them accountable on word count. We are all working together, and that makes this solitary writer feel less alone each day.

Thank you to my family and my non-writer friends who always support me…even if they're not quite sure what I do for a living. I'm surrounded by amazing, loving people, and I know it.

Last, but never, ever least, thank you to my readers. Your comments and emails keep me going, I hope you know that. I am eternally grateful.

CHAPTER ONE

"I don't understand this." Kyle Bannon's expression mixed confusion with the beginnings of anger and a sprinkling of disbelief. Addison watched them swirl together and begin to color his face a deep scarlet.

"What don't you understand, Kyle? Our sexual harassment policy is very clear." Addison kept her tone steady, her face neutral, when in reality, she wanted to smack him. He knew better. He knew *much* better, and to be frank, she hated that he'd put her in this position.

"But it's not sexual harassment if we're together, right?" Jerrika Marshall's voice was small, hesitant, as if she thought speaking might disrupt something in the atmosphere.

"Exactly," Kyle said, pointing at her, but clearly not on the same page as she was with regard to tone. "She's my girlfriend. So how am I harassing her?" He was pissed; that much was clear.

Addison felt her own ire rising, her increased heart rate making it feel like her heart suddenly took up too much space in her chest. "Do you think I want to do this, Kyle? Do you think this is fun for me?" She shook her head. "You touch her ass when you walk behind her. You flirt with her. And don't get me started about the make-out session in the supply closet. You put us here. The two of you."

He stood in front of her large mahogany desk, hands on his hips, and stared her down through his wire-rimmed glasses, his dark eyes flashing behind the lenses. He had a lot to say, Addison could see it all over his face. He said none of it. Next to him, Jerrika stared at her shoes.

"We are an arm of a very large, very well-known company. If I make an exception for you, I'll have to make them all over the place and that will bleed into the rest of Fairchild Enterprises, which I cannot let happen. You've left me without a choice. Have you seen the news lately with regard to sexual harassment? One of you has to go. I'll let you decide which." She folded her hands on the desk and waited, schooling her features, staying completely neutral even though her stomach felt like a giant pool of acid.

"I'll go." Jerrika's voice was so quiet, Addison wasn't sure she'd even spoken until Kyle jumped in.

"No. I'll go." And then he grabbed her hand and entwined their fingers, pulled it up to his mouth, and kissed it. The gesture felt much more intimate than it was and Addison had to fight the urge to look away as if she was intruding.

Jerrika looked up at him for the first time since they'd been called into Addison's office. "No, you've been here longer than I have and the Maintenance Department needs you. You should stay. I can find another job." Her eyes welled up and Addison got the impression that made her angry. When Jerrika turned her gaze on her, Addison knew she was right. A little crackle of fire sparked as Jerrika pulled off her clearance pass and tossed it onto Addison's desk. "I'll go pack up my things."

Kyle let go of her hand and watched her leave the room, stayed looking at the door long after she'd disappeared through it. When he looked back at Addison, she wondered if the fire had spread when he and Jerrika had held hands. The same anger glowed on his face. "You know what?" he said to Addison, as he yanked off his own pass. "I'll pack up my things, too." His pass joined Jerrika's on the desk.

"Come on, Kyle," Addison began. Things had gone exactly as she'd expected up until this moment. "You've got a good job here. You don't really want to do this."

"No. I don't." He narrowed his eyes as he tossed her words back at her. "You've left me with no choice."

With that, he stormed out of her office, not quite slamming the door behind him, but not being gentle. Addison stared at it, at her coat gently swinging from the hook mounted on the back, while she wondered how she'd miscalculated the outcome of this so badly. She'd expected them to protest. She'd expected Jerrika to be the one to quit, based on the meekness Addison had seen so far. She had not expected Kyle to follow suit. That was going to cause extra stress for Addison, and it was as though the acid in her stomach heard the thought and agreed, churning extra horribly. Addison gripped the edge of her desk and willed herself not to throw up as a now-familiar pain squeezed her abdomen. When the willing didn't work, she had no other option but to hurry to the ladies' room down the hall from her office.

Ignoring the judgmental looks from others in the open office setting was something she was used to. She could hear her mother's voice in her head. *"You're not here to be their friend. You're here to run this company."* Still, Kyle was popular, and it was obvious from the veiled unhappy glances that news of his departure—and Jerrika's—was already spreading. She wouldn't hang her head—she had nothing to be ashamed of, but that didn't mean it wasn't uncomfortable to know how her employees felt about her.

As was her regular course of action, she did her best to shake it off.

Not for the first time, she wished she had her own private bathroom attached to her office. There was one woman in the ladies' room, but thankfully, she was washing her hands and finishing up. Addison managed to hold it together until she left before bolting into a stall and throwing up what little lunch she'd eaten.

It was the third time this week.

"Son of a bitch," she said quietly as she waited it out, head in her hands, not wanting to leave the safety of the porcelain bowl until she was sure she was finished. She flushed and then sat there, noting the surprising cleanliness of the floor, the grout between the tiles. She squeezed her eyes shut, then opened them again, her gaze falling on tiny lettering next to the toilet tissue dispenser.

Fairchild is such a bitch.

"Immature, totally uncreative, and shows a stunning lack of originality," she muttered. Realizing it was written in what looked to be Sharpie, she shook her head, making a mental note to get a maintenance guy in to scrub it off somehow. She pressed her fingers to her temples and moved them in a slow circle. She'd always been prone to headaches, but lately, she seemed to have one constantly. On very bad days, it would bloom into a migraine, which was the worst because she could lose an entire day. She fought them hard, but they rarely let up until hours had gone by.

Four more minutes on the floor was all she allowed herself before she slowly stood, hand on the metal stall wall for balance. Her head felt a bit light and she waited out a wave of dizziness. The pain in her stomach was gone, though, and that was a good thing. With a slow intake of breath, then a slow release, she exited the stall and headed to the sink to rinse her mouth and wash her hands.

The reflection in the mirror startled her.

There was zero color in her face. She looked like a corpse, her skin pale and carrying a tint of gray. Dark circles underlined her eyes, announcing to the world just how little sleep she'd been getting. Her brown hair, which normally shone with gentle red highlights, hung limply, no wave to it, no happily curling ends to skim her collarbone. Just...hair. Hanging there. Lifeless. She braced herself on the counter with both hands and leaned in close to the glass, squinting at her own face.

She didn't look healthy.

"Shake it off, Addie," she whispered as she scratched the side of her neck, leaving angry red lines. "You're fine. Just tired. Get your shit together and finish this day."

The pep talk bolstered her just enough to straighten her posture and get her to walk, head high, steps typically quick, back to her office. Then she collapsed in her chair as if she'd just run a sprint. Not good. As she gave herself a moment, she gazed out the window, watched as Kyle—box under his arm—chatted with another employee while standing next to his car. Both sported the red winter jackets with the Fairchild Rentals logo embroidered on the front and khaki pants...the official uniform of the maintenance crew.

Fairchild Rentals was Addison's baby, one arm of the enormous Fairchild Enterprises, a commercial real estate company her mother had started nearly twenty-five years ago. There were three offshoots, each run by a Fairchild sibling. Addison was in charge of Fairchild Rentals, the company that operated and maintained five apartment complexes across the county. Her younger brother, Jared, oversaw the running of four malls in two counties. Her younger sister, Katrina, was the CEO of the Fairchild Research Hospital and Cancer Center.

Recently, her mother had been hinting about retirement. She'd worked hard for a long time and turned a company she'd started from the ground up into something huge and well-known, with a sparkling reputation for treating its employees wonderfully and giving a boatload of money to charity each year. But she was tired. She wanted to enjoy the fruits of her labor. And she had three children, any one of whom could take over for her.

Addison wanted that job so badly, she could taste it.

She picked up her mug as she watched Kyle get into his car and took a sip of very cold coffee, which hit her stomach like liquid fire. She grimaced and set it back down. She'd had more than enough caffeine today—she could almost hear Sophie, her best friend since college, scolding her about how much coffee she drank. *"Jesus, Fairchild, you're already wound tighter than anybody I've ever met. There's this new thing called decaf. You should try it some time."*

Addison managed half a smile at the thought, but it was curtailed by the throbbing in her head, which seemed to suddenly increase. With a quiet groan, she opened her desk drawer and pulled out the jumbo-size bottle of Motrin, which had recently become her constant companion. She shook four pills into her hand and washed them down with the same awful coffee, just as the phone on her desk began to ring.

Back to the chaos, she thought as she snatched up the handset.

❖

"I was beginning to think you weren't going to make it. Again." Sophie Bennett sat at a table for two in Vineyard, her favorite wine bar. She did her best to school her features and not look all that annoyed, but Addison knew her well.

"I told you I'd be here." Addison shed her coat and glanced surreptitiously at her watch as she did. Yeah, she was nearly half an hour late, which wasn't like her. She prided herself on being punctual, but lately, things seemed to be getting away from her. She felt the grimace cross her face, felt the frustration ripple through her.

"You told me that the last time, too." Sophie sipped from her glass of some kind of red. "And you blew me off."

"And I apologized." Addison didn't want to get annoyed, but she felt it bubbling low in her gut. With a sigh, she sat. "I'm sorry this time, too. Rough day."

Addison and Sophie had been best friends since they were matched up as suitemates in college. There had been four of them in the suite, but the other two girls were friends from high school and did everything together, leaving Addison and Sophie on their own. They had similar interests and equal drive, and it just seemed natural for them to pair up. Sophie had been pre-law, Addison had a dual major of economics and business management, and together, they'd helped each other graduate with honors.

Sophie, now thirty-one, was one of the best-known attorneys in the city, and if Addison had to pinpoint her best weapon, it would be her appearance. Small in stature, blond with big blue eyes, prominent cheekbones, and a voice that registered a bit on the high side, Sophie tended to snow just about everybody. Nobody ever expected her to be a badass. She was the epitome of cute, and people had a way of making instant assumptions based on appearance. It was only when Sophie was ripping out their jugular while they were on the stand that they realized what a fatal mistake they'd made in assuming her appearance had anything to do with how she did her job.

The waitress came over with a glass of red. She was friendly, her dark ponytail swinging behind her, an inviting smile on her face. She grinned at Sophie as she set the glass in front of Addison, and with a cock of her head in Addison's direction, said, "She made it."

"She did," Sophie replied. "Thanks, Bridget."

Addison blinked as the waitress left. "What just happened?"

"I ordered a glass of wine for you ahead of time so you wouldn't have to wait. Or make a decision." With a nod toward the wine, she said, "Drink. You'll like it."

The only reason Addison didn't argue was because Sophie knew her that well. One sip proved her right: the wine was delicious, a rich blend of cherries and pepper on the front…something earthier on the back. She hummed her approval.

"So." Sophie propped her elbow on the table and her chin in her hand. "You look like shit, Fairchild. What's going on with you?"

"Jesus, are we doing this again?"

The stand-off across the table was not their first and it certainly wouldn't be their last. Sophie usually backed down first. Ninety percent of the time, Addison won these things. But not this time. Sophie's blue eyes held hers and she let her head tilt a bit to the side—a gesture she used on juries all the time when making a salient point.

"Come on, Soph. Not after the day I've had. My phone rang off the hook. I expected to fire one employee and I lost two instead, one that will be hard to replace at this time of year. And I threw up in the ladies' room while reading about what a bitch I am on the stall wall."

"Again?"

Addison saw her mistake too late. She shouldn't have mentioned the part about getting sick and tried to backpedal. "No big deal. I think I ate something that didn't agree with me."

"Yeah, I'd believe that if you ever ate." Sophie narrowed her eyes. "You need to see a doctor, Addie. Get checked out. You've lost weight. You never feel well. You're getting sick on a regular basis. You don't eat. You don't sleep. You live on coffee. None of this is good. You know this, yes?"

The bubbling in her gut began to boil. The wine didn't help. "I don't need this today, Sophie. I already have a mom, thank you."

Sophie's right eye twitched. That was the only way Addison could tell she'd hit a nerve, and she was immediately sorry but couldn't bring herself to say so. Sophie looked away and took a sip of her wine, while Addison used the moment to calm her heated blood and choose her words.

"Look. I appreciate your concern. I do. I love you for it. But it's not necessary. I'm fine. Am I stressed out? God, yes. What else is new? We're rewriting the leases, Hammerhead needs new roofs on all the buildings, maintenance has a skeleton crew right now, and my mom is going to retire after the first of the year."

Sophie's head snapped back around at that news. "She is?"

Addison nodded, sipped.

"Finally. I didn't think she ever would."

"Me neither."

Sophie brought her glass to her lips, drank without taking her eyes off Addison. Addison hated when she did that. Sophie Bennett had crazy intense eye contact, which she used on witnesses for her opposition when she thought they were lying on the stand or when she was trying to suss out something they weren't saying. It took every ounce of energy Addison had to keep from squirming in her chair and looking away in guilt. She saw the moment Sophie figured it out; her eyes widened just a touch and she sat back in her chair, folded her arms across her chest.

"One of you is taking over for her."

She didn't need clarification, but Addison gave it anyway. "Yes. Most likely me or one of my siblings. I suppose there's an off chance she'll tap one of the guys who has been with her since the beginning—maybe Jack or Robert—but they're both the same age as her, and I imagine they want to retire as well."

Sophie leaned her forearms on the table. "So it's most likely you, Katrina, or Jared."

Addison nodded.

"And you want it to be you."

"Absolutely." Addison sat back, sipped her wine. "It should be me. I'm the oldest. Jared doesn't have enough experience. Katrina..." She let the sentence dangle. Her little sister was her real competition, and while she was reasonably sure the job would be hers, she couldn't deny that Katrina was a savvy businesswoman. She shrugged in an effort to highlight how very nonchalant about it she was. Yup. Totally cool. No big deal. "People like her."

Sophie looked like she was going to delve into that. She actually opened her mouth, apparently thought better of it, closed it again. After a sip of wine, she completely changed the subject. "Tell me about your terrible day."

Grateful for the shift, Addison rehashed her issues with Kyle and Jerrika. "I looked the other way for a while, but when they got caught in the supply closet..." She shook her head. "A couple people complained, and with all the headlines about sexual harassment lately, there was no way I could get away with doing nothing."

Sophie grimaced. "So, she went, I assume? She's only been there a short time, right?"

Addison blew out a breath. "Yeah, that's how I thought it would go. But then Kyle went all Knight in Shining Armor and quit on me."

"Huh." A ghost of a smile played across Sophie's lips.

"What?"

Lifting one shoulder, Sophie asked, "Don't you think that's kind of romantic, though? That he stood up for his girl like that?"

Addison rolled her eyes. "Now is not the time for chivalry. He had a good job. Decent pay. Benefits. Christmas bonus coming up in a month."

"He was following his heart."

"Or his dick."

Sophie snorted a laugh. "My best friend, the pessimist."

"I'm not a pessimist. I'm a *realist*. Big difference."

"Po-tay-to, po-tah-to," Sophie said and finished her wine. "Think he'll be back?"

"I don't. He was pretty pissed." Addison wasn't looking forward to replacing him, but she'd figure it out.

They caught up on the rest of life over a second glass of wine and a shared cheese board, and when Sophie glanced at her iPhone, her eyebrows went up. "I've gotta get home," she said. "I've got depositions tomorrow I'm not ready for. You good?"

Addison nodded and decided not to mention that over the past several minutes, she'd felt that same pain in her stomach and a light-headedness that was new in its intensity. She hoped it would just pass, as such things usually did, but when she stood from her chair, it was as though she'd lost all feeling in her legs and she collapsed to her knees before she even knew it was happening. Vaguely, she heard Sophie say her name, but it seemed so far away, and like she was underwater. She wasn't sure which of them was underwater, though. Was it her? Was it Sophie? Why couldn't she seem to answer this simple question?

And then the answer didn't matter because everything went black.

CHAPTER TWO

I'm telling you, Jack, that girl is going to be the death of me."
Samantha couldn't see Meredith Fairchild, but she could hear the concern in her voice even from the other side of the office wall. It wasn't the concern of a boss or even that of a friend. It was the concern of a mother, and Samantha could detect the tiniest bit of panic in the worried tone.

Samantha Morgan was the direct admin to Jack Saunders and had been for the past two years. Jack had worked for Meredith for nearly twenty years, and when his long-term secretary had finally retired, Sam had somehow, against all odds, gotten the job. She'd wanted it badly; working for Fairchild Enterprises was a big deal. And a good one. Excellent pay. Even better benefits. A management team made up of good, hardworking people who did a ton of charity work in the name of their employer. Sam worked her ass off to prove herself worthy of her position, and luckily, she excelled at her job. Over the past twenty-four months, she'd made herself indispensable, and in the process, she and Jack had become almost friends. He was like a second father to her… or maybe a favorite uncle. His trust in her grew and he gave her more and more responsibility, which she took on happily. Now? Jack barely knew what day it was without Sam to remind him.

As she sat at her desk outside Jack's office, she listened through the wall and the open door.

"What did her doctor say?" Jack's deep voice. He, too, sounded concerned. Not surprising, as he'd known Meredith's children since they were all still in school. He was probably like an uncle to them, too.

"Not her doctor. The emergency room doctor. Sophie had to take her to the damn hospital. She's got an ulcer. She's way too stressed. Her heart rate was through the roof. She's lost another six pounds..." Meredith's voice broke and Sam felt her own heart constrict at the sound. "She works so damned hard, Jack. I don't know how to get her to ease up."

"Addison's always been this way, Mere."

"I know."

There was silence for several moments, and Samantha prayed the phone wouldn't ring. She felt slightly guilty eavesdropping. But only slightly.

"I think we revisit the personal assistant idea," Jack said.

"We tried that. She refused." Meredith was obviously annoyed by that. "You know how damn stubborn she is."

"Like mother, like daughter." The affection in Jack's voice was easily heard.

"Ha ha. She'll never agree to it."

"So we make it mandatory."

A beat of silence passed before Meredith said, "You mean... require it?"

"You're the boss."

"I am, aren't I?" Jack must have nodded because Meredith went on. "How do you suggest we find such a person?"

That was all Samantha needed to hear.

The school bus pulled up to the bus stop and, not for the first time, Katie Cooper marveled at how much bigger it seemed than she remembered. She knew it was an illusion because of how very small Simon and Noah were, but still, she found herself thinking, *were they always such behemoths? Even when I rode one?* She knew the answer was yes, but she asked the question every day anyway.

She felt Noah's little hand tighten its grip inside hers. He was nervous again, and Katie tightened her own fingers to reassure him. Squatting down to meet his blue eyes—which were slightly wider than usual—she brushed his white-blond hair off his forehead.

"Hey," she said quietly. "You're going to be fine. You're going to have a great time at school. Remember how much fun you had yesterday?"

He nodded but looked uncertain.

"It's going to be like that again, but probably even better. You'll make stuff and you'll play with cool toys and I can't wait to hear all about it tomorrow. Okay?"

He nodded again, and it was obvious how hard he was trying to be brave, tears welling in his big blue eyes but not spilling over. Holding his other hand was his twin brother, Simon, who had no qualms whatsoever about getting on the bus. "Come on, Noah," he said, trying to be patient and failing as he gave his brother's hand a tug.

Katie shifted her stance so she could grab Simon's face with both hands. She placed a kiss on his cheek, then whispered in his ear, "Do me a favor. Go easy on your brother, okay, buddy? Look out for him. Can you do that for me?"

Simon nodded enthusiastically because he loved being given things to do for Katie and she knew it.

She did the same thing with Noah—took his little, frightened face in both hands and kissed his cheek. "You're going to have such a good day."

He nodded once more—Katie had learned it was his go-to when he was trying not to cry—and allowed his brother to tug him onto the bus.

The bus monitor, a woman in her sixties, gave Katie a reassuring smile and mouthed *I've got them*, which Katie greatly appreciated.

The twins found their seat and waved out the window at Katie as the bus pulled away. She waved back, her heart squeezing in her chest as if the boys had come from her own womb. They'd been going to pre-K for nearly two months now, but she still got teary as she watched them head off on their own.

A ding sounded from her back pocket, indicating a text, and she was glad for the distraction.

Still looking for a second job?

It was from Sam. Katie typed back.

Yep.

Sam's reply came almost instantly, as if she wasn't even waiting for Katie to answer.

Can you meet me tonight at 5:30? Jade's. I think I can help.

Well. That was intriguing. Katie sent back a reply saying she'd be there, then headed into the Anderson house to clean things up before she left.

The scent of peanut butter still hung in the air in the gourmet kitchen, remnants of the twins' lunch they'd had just before school. They were in the afternoon class, which worked better for Katie because, once she got them onto the bus, she was able to go home and help her mother for a while. She'd had a job she loved as an account executive at a tech company, but when she'd inquired about shifting her position to part-time in order to help her parents when her father became ill, she'd been denied, which had surprised her. And stung, if she was being honest. Evidently, they didn't love her in her job as much as she liked being there. She'd started nannying the twins in July, their mother working in the mornings and then relieving Katie in the afternoons. Now that they were in school for half a day, she missed them, which was a bit puzzling, as she hadn't missed them when their mother came home and she left them during the summer. Maybe it was actually putting them on a bus, sending them off to school, out into the real world, that felt so very different from leaving them with their mother. She wasn't sure. All she knew was that watching the bus drive away with them each day was more emotionally wrenching than she'd expected it to be.

Gathering her things, she locked the house and drove her eleven-year-old Honda home. Well, to her parents' house. No, home. She still hadn't gotten used to that. She'd left the apartment she'd shared with Samantha a month ago and moved back to her parents' house in order to help out, financially as well as physically.

Dementia was a horrible, horrible thing.

It had only been a year, but David Cooper had developed early-onset dementia caused by Alzheimer's and Katie was often shocked by how quickly her father seemed to be…disappearing. He'd gone from being a gentle, funny, loving man to somebody who was anxious, confused, or angry much of the time, often all three at once. Sometimes he was fine. Almost his usual, normal self. Other times—and often mere minutes after seeming to be fine—he would explode in anger. Or worse, he'd dissolve into tears. Katie was often left feeling like her head was spinning and she had no clue what to do. This was their new normal. And it was devastating most of the time.

In the driveway, parked behind her father's Toyota that he no longer drove, Katie turned off the engine and sat. Collected herself. It was new and necessary, this pause before entering the house she grew up in. This steeling herself. Bracing. Because that's what it was: bracing. Katie had learned to brace herself before going inside because the reality was, she never knew what she was going to walk into. Would he be sleeping peacefully? Had he had a good morning, and therefore, Katie's mother would seem the tiniest bit less stressed out than usual? Or had it been a horrendous morning that left her mother haggard and frazzled, her father violent and angry? Would he be happily watching television? Or throwing things across the living room?

It was getting to the point where she never knew.

Deep breath in. Slow breath out.

Katie headed inside.

"Mom?"

Liz Cooper appeared from the kitchen, a dish towel in one hand, the other holding her forefinger to her lips in the universal request for silence. Then she pointed to the recliner in the living room where Katie saw her father, eyes closed, apparently napping.

Liz waved her into the kitchen.

"How's he been today?" Katie asked, barely above a whisper. She knew how much these breaks—when her father crashed into a nap— were a necessity for her mother. And her mother's sanity.

"Eh. Not great. Not awful." Liz shrugged as she folded the dish towel in thirds and hung it over the handle of the oven. "Want some tea?" she asked Katie, as she put the kettle on the front burner and turned it on.

"Absolutely."

She pulled out a chair at the small kitchen table and watched as her mother busied herself with mugs and tea bags. Katie didn't get a lot of time alone with her mother anymore. There was some, but most of the time, Liz was so utterly exhausted that she took whatever breaks she got to grab a nap or go for a quiet walk. They didn't really talk like they used to, either. Katie missed that. Her mother had always made the best sounding board. Even in school, her friends were amazed by the relationship she had with her mom. Disagreements between them were rare; Katie liked to think that was because she was a good girl and her mother was a reasonable parent. As a teenager, she actually *wanted* to spend time with her mom. When most of her friends heard that, their eyes bugged out in disbelief and they wondered why in the world she'd want to do such a ridiculously lame thing.

Life was different now. Changed. Altered. Not that she didn't want to hang out with her mom any longer, just that it was harder and harder to find time for just the two of them. Her father, who used to be the guy to bring light and energy into any room, now seemed to suck out all the air more and more often. God, it was hard to watch.

Liz set two mugs of steaming tea down on the table, then doctored her own with cream and sugar. Katie grinned, as she always did when she did the same thing to her own tea.

"Like mother, like daughter," Liz said quietly, her standard comment when they had tea together. "How were the boys today?"

This felt almost normal, this type of conversation, and Katie was thankful for that. Every snippet of normal she could grab, she snatched at, held it as tightly in her grip as she could. "Noah is still a little ball of nerves. I feel so bad for him. He's trying so hard to be brave, but he's just scared. Simon is pretty good about helping him along, but he's got zero fear, so I'm not sure he gets what the big deal is."

"You were like Noah."

"Was I?"

"For kindergarten, yes. You were terrified. And so was your mother." Liz covered her sheepish grin by taking a sip of her tea.

"You were? Why?"

"You had no siblings and not much in the way of extended family. It had been just you and me for four years. Part of me was worried about how you'd do, surrounded by other kids, because that would be so new for you. The other part of me wondered what I was going to do without you."

"Aww, Mom." Katie reached across the table and squeezed her mother's forearm. "You never told me that. What happened?"

Liz chuckled. "You met Samantha, that's what happened."

"And the rest is history."

"It sure is."

"Speaking of Sam, I'm supposed to meet her tonight when she gets out of work. I think she might have a line on a job for me." Katie squinted at her mom. "Are you okay if I scoot for an hour or two later?"

Liz nodded.

"I won't stay out long. I can give you a break now for a couple hours and I know you'll need another one by tonight."

"Sweetie, it's fine. Go have a drink with your BFF and don't worry about me. I can handle things here."

Katie forced a smile onto her face for her mother's benefit. Liz needed Katie to know she was handling things, even when she was barely holding on. Katie understood that and played along, but she was always watching out of the corner of her eye. She worried almost as much about her mother as she did about her father, as she was reasonably sure that either one of them could topple at any given moment. Katie had to be ready to catch them. She had to.

Yeah, this new normal? Katie was *not* enjoying it.

❖

"She's so tired, Sam." Katie shook her head, then took a swig of her beer. "She's got dark circles under her eyes. She's stopped wearing makeup because she doesn't have time to put it on. She's constantly in sweats because she's too exhausted to put an outfit together."

"God, that sucks." Samantha sipped her Cosmo. "How's your dad?"

Katie tipped her head one way, then the other. "Depends on the day. Today wasn't bad. He was napping when I got home, and he stayed that way for over an hour. I sent my mom out to the store. I don't think we needed anything, but she barely leaves the house unless I insist."

"This has to be so hard for her." A sheepish look crossed Sam's face as she averted her eyes so she was staring at the pink liquid in her glass. "I want to call her, to check in, to say hi, but…" She frowned as she looked up at Katie.

"You don't know what to say."

A small nod. "I do text her."

"It's okay, Sammi. I get it. Keep texting. She likes hearing from you."

"Yeah?"

Katie nodded. "She doesn't talk to people very often. Dad takes up so much of her time and energy." She didn't like to think about it, about how lonely her mother had become. She and Katie's father were the epitome of soulmates. He was her air, and she his. Katie couldn't begin to fathom the depths of the cracks that must be forming in her mother's heart over this.

A beat went by before Sam said, "Okay, let's talk about something happier." Her smile was gentle and tender, making it clear she wasn't brushing aside what Katie and her family were going through. She'd never do that; Katie knew it. They'd been best friends for twenty-four years and nobody knew her better than Sam. She set down her martini glass, put her forearms on the table, and leaned forward. "I have a proposition for you."

"Why, Samantha Morgan. And all this time you've been telling me you don't play on my team."

"Ha ha. You're hilarious." Sam's green eyes twinkled as she brushed a hunk of red hair off her forehead. "I like my own team just fine, thank you, and I have a *job* proposition for you."

Katie cocked her head, definitely curious. "I'm listening."

"I know your hours have been cut with the twins heading off to school. I also know you need as much money as you can get to help out at home."

A grimace crossed Katie's face. "My dad's medical bills are getting crazy. I think my mom's close to panicking but won't tell me that. I have to sneak peeks at the mail."

"I figured. So, here's the deal." Sam gave a brief rundown of the conversation she'd overheard earlier. "I talked to Jack afterward and he told me they're getting Addison a part-time personal assistant until she's back to a hundred percent. Which means it's temporary, but the pay is beyond generous. I told him about you, that I've known you since we were kids, that you have a business degree, that you're crazy organized. I told him you'd be great for the job, and he trusts me. He wants to meet with you first, but if you want the job, it's yours. He's already told Mrs. Fairchild, and she trusts him, so..." She let the sentence dangle.

"Wow," Katie said, because it was all she could manage in the moment. She took a beat with the information, let it absorb into her gray cells. "So...how temporary are we talking?"

Sam shrugged. "I don't know for sure, but Jack and I thought at least three months. Possibly four." She named a figure that had Katie's eyes opening wide.

"Wow. For three months?"

"Maybe four."

Katie nodded slowly. "What happened to her? To Addison?"

"I've never met her, though I've seen her several times. She works herself to the bone, according to Jack. She's constantly overstressed, and apparently, it caught up with her last week. She was out with a friend and fainted. She tried to brush it off, but the friend insisted on taking her to the emergency room where they ran a bunch of tests. She's got an ulcer, high blood pressure, an endless headache, she's too thin. Lots of issues." Sam paused to sip her drink and Katie saw a shadow cross her face.

"What? What aren't you telling me?"

Sam shook her head. "Nothing. Just that…she has a reputation for being kind of a…" She pursed her lips, pushed them to the side of her face as she searched for the right word.

"Whirlwind? Amazing boss? Bitch?"

"Yes." Sam pointed at her. "That last one."

"Awesome."

"Come on. You've handled four-year-old twin boys for over a year. I think a type-A personality businesswoman would be a piece of cake for you."

Katie narrowed her eyes. "You make a fine point, my friend."

"And as I said, I've never actually met her, I'm just telling you what I've heard. So this could all just be rumor and innuendo. She could be lovely."

"That *is* something to take into consideration."

"As is the money."

"As is the money. Yeah. So there's that."

"Just talk to Jack. How about that? Come by tomorrow after you put the boys on the bus and see him. I'll sit in if you want."

Katie realized in that moment how silly she was being. "No need. I'm a big girl. I can talk to him myself. Okay." She slapped a hand down on the table. "Let's do that."

They set up a time and then shifted focus to talk about other things. In the back of her mind, though, Katie was keeping track of the time, knowing her mother was going to need to be tagged out.

Half an hour later, on her drive home, Katie felt herself getting excited about the possibility of a new job, about being able to contribute more to help with the bills that seemed to be piling up despite her parents' insurance coverage. About being able to use her degree. She loved being a nanny, loved Simon and Noah like they were her own. But nannying wasn't what she wanted to do with her life. She hated that her parents had spent all the money on college and she wasn't using her degree at all. That fact sat under her skin and niggled at her uncomfortably. Maybe this personal assistant job was just what she needed until she could find something more permanent.

Maybe it would change her life.

A small snort of a laugh pushed out of her as she grinned at her own melodramatic thoughts. It was a job, though. One that would use her degree and pay her generously, two things that made her very happy in that moment.

And just like that, she was looking forward to tomorrow.

She had a good feeling about working for Addison Fairchild.

CHAPTER THREE

N o." Addison was adamant. She made sure of it in the tone of her voice, in the steeliness of her eyes. She held her mother's gaze—not an easy feat—and was pretty sure she'd made her point clear. This was a definite nope. A not happening. An absolutely not. No.

"Yes."

Damn it. Meredith's eyes were just as steely. No, they were more so. After all, Addison did get hers from her mother. Apparently, she needed another twenty years to perfect the steel before she was in the same league as Meredith Fairchild.

"Mom, come on. I don't need a babysitter."

They were in Addison's loft apartment, and she was under a thick afghan on her couch. The freezing rain teemed outside, hammering the balcony and drumming against the floor-to-ceiling windows in the living room. The sky was gray and dull, much like Addison's mood.

She was tired. *So* tired. She couldn't remember ever having been this tired in her entire life. She felt like she had no bones left, like her limbs were made of rubber and just flopped around uselessly, spaghetti. Lifting an arm to reach for her water glass felt like an ordeal. Her head was foggy—from the medication still in her system, she was sure—and she didn't like dealing with her mother when she wasn't 100 percent.

"She's not a babysitter," Sophie said, from where she stood in the corner of the room.

"You shut up." Addison pointed a finger at her, the traitor. "I'm not speaking to you."

Sophie responded by rolling her eyes, completely unfazed, as usual.

"Sophie's right. She's not a babysitter. She'll be here to lighten your load, take some of the extras off your plate."

"If you could keep an admin instead of chasing them all away by insisting on doing everything yourself, you wouldn't be in this boat." Sophie tilted her head as if daring Addison to argue with her.

Addison responded by holding up her hand, palm toward Sophie, and turning her head away. "Talk to the hand."

"Yeah, 1998 called," Sophie said, with a snort. "It wants its catchphrase back."

"You are stressed beyond belief, Addison." Meredith sat on the couch next to her and laid a warm hand on her foot, squeezed it through the blanket, obviously wanting to steer the conversation back on track. "You have a bleeding ulcer. Your blood pressure is through the roof. You don't eat well. You don't sleep well. All you do is work. Sophie says she hardly sees you."

Addison shot Sophie another glare.

"That's right. I ratted you out." Sophie shrugged.

"I'm worried about you." That last line from Meredith was delivered softly and punctuated by an audible swallow. Addison looked into her eyes and saw it. Underneath the put-together exterior, the expensively tailored slacks and silk top, the perfectly colored and styled blond hair, the don't-mess-with-me demeanor, there was worry. Even some fear.

With a clearing of her throat, Addison explained, "Yes, but I just need a little bit of recovery time and I'll be able to get back to—" She didn't get to finish her sentence because suddenly, that soft, concerned tone of Meredith's vanished.

"Addison Elizabeth, *that is enough*."

Addison's eyes widened in surprise, and one thing was crystal clear: Meredith Fairchild was *not* messing around. Her blue eyes flashed with anger and she pointed an accusatory finger at her daughter. "You are the most pigheaded, stubborn woman I have ever met. And I've been in the real estate world for more than two decades, so that says a lot. You, young lady, take the cake and I've had just about enough of your inability to listen to reason. You'd do well to remember that despite what you may think, you still work for me. I call the shots around here, and if I say you're getting a personal assistant, then you're getting a personal assistant, goddamnit."

Addison stared. Blinked. Stared some more.

Her mother rarely, *rarely* swore. She liked to use tone and a large vocabulary rather than foul language to get the attention of her peers. So this was big. This meant Addison had very possibly pushed too hard on this subject. A glance toward the corner showed her Sophie, biting down on her lips and trying to smother a grin—which she failed at.

Addison opened her mouth to say something, thought better of it, and closed it again. She was in sweats, on the couch, under a blanket, in the middle of a workday. It went against everything she'd worked so hard to achieve, and it all suddenly hit her like a punch to the stomach.

"I hate this," she finally whispered, defeat settling over her, pressing her shoulders down. She was mortified to feel her eyes well up, and she scratched at the side of her neck in frustration.

"I know, honey." Meredith softened again, and not for the first time, Addison marveled at how good she was at shifting moods. "I know you do." She squeezed Addison's ankle again. "It won't be forever. The assistant is temporary because your condition is temporary. Okay? Think about that. A few months, tops. You heard the doctor. You just need to take it easy for a while, let your body rest when it needs to. I don't want you working such ridiculous hours. There's no need. You have a staff, and now you'll have an assistant. Let her do the work while you relax. Watch a movie. Read a book. Eat a decent meal. You know, do things that normal people do." She winked, taking any sting out of the words. "And let this person help you. Jack said he was impressed with her. She came recommended by his admin, and you know how much he adores her."

Addison nodded, the lump in her throat making it hard to form words.

"He interviewed her. Said she was smart and quick and organized. She's got a job in the mornings, so she'll be here at one o'clock tomorrow."

"Here?" Addison echoed, sitting up to launch a protest.

"Yes, here." Meredith silenced her with a look. "I don't want you going into the office for the rest of the week. And when you do go, you're to take her with you, let her help." When Addison didn't respond, Meredith narrowed her eyes, repeated herself. "Let. Her. Help. And be nice."

"Okay. Okay. Fine." Addison sat back with a loud sigh and folded her arms across her chest, totally aware of how childish she must look. And not caring. "What's her name?"

"Katie Cooper."

Addison snorted. "Of course it is."

It was another half hour before they finally left her to wallow in peace. She spent the next hour annoyed and feeling sorry for herself before deciding she'd had enough of that.

"Katie Cooper." Addison scoffed. Apparently, that was going to be the sound she made any time she had to say the name of her new personal assistant, because seriously? Was there a more cheerful, more annoyingly happy name in the English language? "Katie Cooper," she said again. Then scoffed. Again.

When her phone rang a little after seven that night, Addison glanced at the screen and considered not answering. She was still irritated with Sophie and told her so as soon as she hit the green button. "I'm mad at you. What do you want?"

"Please. Get over yourself." Sophie never did take any of Addison's shit, and she apparently wasn't about to start today. "Your mother asked me to be there for moral support."

"She needed it."

"Moral support for you, dumbass." Sophie's sigh was loud and spoke of years of being put-upon. "Anyway. When Meredith Fairchild asks me to show up someplace, I show up."

"She always did like you better than me," Addison said, feeling herself softening toward her best friend. She fought it. She lost.

"Can you blame her? Everybody likes me better than you."

"True story."

"How are you feeling?" And just like that, they were back to normal.

"Tired. Not bad, but tired." It was the truth. The most prominent symptom Addison had experienced since being in the ER was fatigue, which the doctor told her wasn't unexpected. "I feel like I've been run over by a truck. Or a train. Or maybe both. First one, then the other."

There was a beat of silence before Sophie spoke again, and this time, her voice was small. Smaller than Addison had ever heard it. "You scared me, Addie."

"I know." Addison swallowed. "I'm sorry."

"I'm aware that this is all annoying for you. Inconvenient. That you just want to get back to work. But…" Sophie cleared her throat and Addison had a moment of wondering if Sophie was about to cry before remembering that Sophie didn't cry. "I really need you to take better care of yourself. Okay?"

"Okay."

"Because if something happened to you, I'd have to do interviews and then train a new best friend and I don't have the fucking time or energy for that."

Addison smothered a smile even as she felt a warmth in heart. "Understood."

"Good." They were both quiet for a moment, as if each of them needed some time to regroup. "Do you want me to come by tomorrow when the assistant arrives?"

Addison shook her head. "No, it's fine. I can handle it."

"You're sure."

"I am."

"Let her help, Addie."

"Why does everybody keep saying that?" Addison whined.

"I'm not even going to dignify that with an answer about how stubborn you are." Sophie's chuckle was low and throaty. "All right. I just wanted to check on you. Need anything?"

"I'm good."

"Get some rest. In the bed, not on the couch."

"God, you're bossy."

"I am bossy as fuck. And don't you forget it."

They hung up and Addison felt the tiniest bit better. Still not thrilled with the idea of some "assistant" getting in her way and interrupting her workday, she decided to set that aside for the time being. She at least had tomorrow morning to work on her own, as Katie Cooper wouldn't arrive until after noon. That would give her some time.

She sighed as she turned to watch the rain. It ran down the windows in long rivulets, creating wavy shapes and light on the hardwood floor. She should go get her laptop from the second bedroom she used as an office and at least answer her email.

Instead, in a completely uncharacteristic move, she readjusted her butt in the couch, slid down a bit, and continued to watch the rain. There was something mesmerizing about it, the gentle rumble on the balcony, the streaks of water reflecting the streetlights on her windows. It was almost relaxing, and she felt her eyelids grow heavy, her muscles relax.

She'd worry about tomorrow when it came.

❖

When the elevator opened and Katie stepped out, she found herself facing two antique-looking tables that bookended a full-length mirror. On each table was a vase filled with colorful flowers in gorgeous fall hues of orange and red. She leaned toward one bouquet and was surprised to find they were real and fresh, their petals not nearly as scented as spring flowers, but they still gave off an earthiness that, combined with the smell of the two coffees she carried, made for a very pleasant aroma.

Standing in front of the mirror, the wood frame thick and heavy, something dark—cherry, maybe? Mahogany?—she gave herself one last once-over. The tech company Katie'd worked for had a business casual dress code, so she didn't own a ton of what would be considered strict business clothing, but she did have a couple pairs of black dress pants. She'd put one of them on, added a simple white capped-sleeve T-shirt that she'd dressed up with a black-and-white patterned scarf just like Sam had taught her. *"The beauty of a scarf is that it allows you to class up a seven-dollar T-shirt."* She'd also attempted to teach Katie several different complicated knots to achieve different looks, but Katie only remembered one. Now she smoothed it while looking at her reflection, tucked her dark hair behind an ear, adjusted the black laptop bag hanging from her shoulder, and took a deep, nervous breath.

Looking one way, then the other, she chose the direction to apartment 5E and headed toward it, her ballet flats making almost no sound on the thick, burgundy carpet that blanketed the long hallway. Everything about this building screamed "expensive." The carpet, the crown molding along the ceiling, the ceiling itself, which was white tin. The light fixtures were elaborate without being ornate, both the sconces on the wall every few feet and the small chandeliers hanging above her head. Even the doors to each apartment—tall, made of heavy wood, and accented with deep bronze handles, hinges, and peepholes. They had knockers rather than doorbells, which somehow made them seem even more elegant rather than pretentious.

Katie couldn't imagine what the rent in a place like this was.

Apartment 5E was at the end of the hall, making it what Katie assumed must be an end unit.

"Nothing to be nervous about," she whispered to herself. "Nothing at all. You've done your research. You're perfect for this job. Nothing to be nervous about. You're totally ready." With a puff of her chest, she shifted both coffees to one side, reached up, and used the bronze knocker on the door. "You're totally ready," she repeated to herself.

And she was. She was ready for the organization. She was ready for the phone calls and the scheduling and the emails. She was ready to file and to fetch coffee and to pick up dry cleaning if necessary, although she hoped that wasn't what her job entailed. Just the idea of getting back into the fast-paced world of business had her psyched. Oh, yeah, she was so ready for this job.

What she was *not* ready for when the door opened was Addison Fairchild.

Specifically, how much the online photos had *not* done her any justice. Because, good God, even probably tired and coming off a hospital visit, Addison Fairchild was stunningly beautiful.

Addison stood in the doorway, one hand on the edge of the door, her blue eyes deep and intense, if a little tired looking. Her hair was light brown but with a hint of red, a very flattering color combination that set off her creamy skin and distractingly full lips like she was a work of art and the colors were chosen solely for that purpose. It fell a bit past her shoulders in gentle waves that Katie imagined were silky soft. *I mean, probably, right? Look at them.* Katie did her best to take in Addison's outfit without giving the impression she was ogling—which was exactly what she wanted to do. Badly. Black pants, emerald-green long-sleeve shirt that might have been silk, black heels.

"You're Katie?"

Addison's voice—deeper and huskier than Katie expected—startled her back to reality. "I am."

"Come in." Addison stepped aside and held out an arm, inviting Katie to enter.

"I was told you were under the weather and that's why I was hired. I thought you'd be in sweats or something." A nervous laugh rippled out of her before she could catch it. Damn it. Beautiful women always made her anxious and jumpy.

"You thought wrong."

Those three words told Katie pretty much all she needed to know about this situation. Mainly that Addison didn't want her here. Samantha had told her that might be the case, that Addison Fairchild was as stubborn and high-strung as they came. Katie had prepared for that possibility. Sort of.

"Apparently, I did." Katie smiled widely—too wide? With the intention of shaking Addison's hand in a proper introduction, she shifted the coffees again.

And promptly dropped one on the floor where it hit the hardwood with a slap and splattered all over Addison's hardwood floor, entryway rug, and probably super-expensive shoes.

"Oh, God!" Katie cried, working hard to tamp down the approximately seventeen swear words that ran through her head in that moment, each more offensive than the last. Instead, she quickly set the other cup on a nearby side table, dropped to her knees, and whipped off her scarf. Using it to mop up the coffee—not ideal, as there's a reason they don't make towels out of nylon—she shook her head. "I'm so sorry. God. I'm such a klutz sometimes." Her hair fell in her face and she put up with it for about 3.5 seconds before using the elastic band she always had on her wrist and pulling it into a messy bun on top of her head. Addison's shoes hadn't moved and finally, Katie ventured a look up.

Addison was gazing down at her, her expression unreadable.

"Um. Do you have some paper towels or something?"

Addison nodded as she turned to go.

"No, no, just tell me where," Katie said, as she held out a halting hand, stopping Addison. "You're supposed to be recovering."

"In the kitchen near the sink." Addison pointed to her right.

Katie pushed herself to her feet and went in search of the kitchen. Which wasn't hard to find, as the entire apartment was open-concept, and the kitchen was of the enormous gourmet variety. Pushing past the desire to stand and stare, mouth agape, at the exquisite cherry cabinets and deep gray granite counters, she found the paper towels propped on a brushed nickel holder. "Do you have any cleaner?" she called.

"Under the sink," came the response.

Back in the living room, Addison had sat, her head visible over the back of the couch. In the entryway sat her shoes, right where she'd been standing, as if she'd simply stepped out of them, left them there, and gone on her merry way.

Katie dropped back down to her knees and finished cleaning up the mess. Everything came clean except the edge of the rug, and Katie cringed at the thought of how much it must be worth. "Um...I'm happy to pay to have your rug cleaned. The coffee stained the edge a little bit. I'm so sorry about that."

Addison waved a hand without looking, focused instead on the laptop perched on her thighs. "It's fine."

Katie carried the dirty towels and cleaner back to the kitchen, then grabbed her messenger bag off the floor where she'd dropped it. The other coffee still sat on the small table near the door, so she snapped that up, too, but carefully. Venturing toward the couch, she set the cup down on the coffee table, being careful to take a coaster from the pile—they had cuddly, happy puppies on them, which seemed incongruous with the rest of the room...and the personality of their owner—and use it. "I brought you a cup of coffee. I wasn't sure how you took it, so I just got it black." She reached into her bag and pulled out a handful of creamers and little packets of sugar, set them next to the cup.

Addison's icy blue eyes moved from the screen to the coffee and stayed there for a few seconds. "What kind?"

Katie cleared her throat. "French roast?"

With an almost imperceptible nod, Addison reached for the cup, leaving the additives untouched. Katie watched her hands, which were small and feminine, as she took the lid off and then lifted the coffee to her lips. She took a sip, closed her eyes as if savoring it. She took another, then glanced up at Katie. "Sit." Indicating the other end of the couch, she added, "Thank you for this." She lifted the cup a tad. "I needed it."

"You're welcome. And again, I'm so sorry." Katie took a seat, opened her bag, and took out a pen and a pad of paper.

When Addison turned to look, her gaze fell on the pad and lingered. "What's that?"

"I'm going to take notes?" Katie heard herself and cringed. She had a bad habit of framing statements as questions when she was nervous or uncertain of herself. It made her sound weak, and weak was the last thing she wanted to be in front of Addison Fairchild. She'd already made a terrible first impression, and she wasn't about to screw up the rest of the day.

"On paper?" Addison asked the question as if Katie had said she was chiseling notes into a piece of stone.

Katie cleared her throat, another bad habit that projected uncertainty. Forcing confidence into her voice, she told Addison, "I have a laptop in this bag, too. Don't worry. I just find it faster to jot notes on paper."

Addison nodded but said nothing further on the subject. "All right, let's get started." She patted the couch next to her. "Sit closer, so you can see my screen."

Katie did as she was asked, and the first thing she noticed about being this close to Addison was that she smelled like sunshine. How that was possible, Katie wasn't sure. All she knew was that, sitting next to Addison, she detected the scent of wildflowers and coconut and a summer breeze and it all combined to evoke sunshine in her mind. Again, the opposite of the demeanor Addison projected. Katie quietly inhaled. Deeply.

"God, look at all this email." Addison's voice was barely a whisper, so Katie assumed she was talking to herself. She scratched at the right side of her neck, leaving angry red marks on the delicate skin there. "I'm so far behind."

"Can I make a suggestion?" Katie asked.

Addison nodded as she reached for the coffee and took a sip. Katie could hear her swallow.

"I can help you with the email. Just give me a quick and dirty rundown of the basics of your job. I don't need crazy in-depth details, but a bit more than what I gathered from online research. Just an overview." She flipped the paper in her pad to a sheet covered with her own handwriting. "I actually have some questions about the business in general and your role specifically. If you can answer them this afternoon, I can go over stuff tonight, put a plan in place, and we can hit the ground running tomorrow."

Addison's gaze was focused on her computer screen, but Katie got the impression she was thinking, going over what Katie had said. "I'm not against that."

Okay, not exactly a ringing endorsement of her suggestion, but Katie would take it.

Addison set the cup back down, then turned to look fully at Katie, those blue eyes boring into hers with an almost palpable intensity. "Look, I don't know what you were told about this job, but let me give you some facts." Her tone wasn't angry or mean. It was simply…firm. Matter-of-fact. Emotionless. It was the tone of a woman used to being listened to. "It's temporary and you're only here because my mother— the CEO of Fairchild Enterprises—insisted. I can handle my job. I always have. And despite what she thinks or what you may have been told, I've simply had a minor setback, but I will recover in no time. I don't stay down for long."

"I understand." Katie gave one nod. "You allowed me in here under duress."

Addison squinted at her and the wind seemed to leave her sails, as if she suddenly realized how she'd come across. "Yes. Exactly."

"If it was up to you, I wouldn't be here at all."

Katie was pretty sure Addison Fairchild wasn't one to hesitate, but she seemed to right then. Barely noticeable, but it was there. "Correct."

"Got it. Understood." Fine. If that was how she needed to play this, that was how she would play it. The job may have been only temporary, but the pay was amazing, and Katie needed the money to help her parents. She wasn't about to give it up because Addison Fairchild's pride was a little banged up. Katie indicated her pad. "Shall we get started?"

❖

The Cooper house was so small and modest compared to the wide-open, expensive loft Katie'd spent the afternoon in. But it was also warm and cozy and inviting, and Katie always felt herself relax just a bit once she'd walked through the door. She hung up her coat, set her bag down, and headed into the small kitchen where she could hear her mother moving around.

"Mom, you look exhausted." It was true. Dark circles. Limp hair. A walk that seemed to have no energy or purpose. Katie pushed her chair back from the small kitchen table. "Let me make you some tea."

"No, no," Liz said, waving her off as she set the receiver to the baby monitor they used to listen for her father on the table. "Tonight calls for alcohol." She opened the refrigerator and took out a bottle of Riesling, held it up for Katie to see. "Join me?"

"Riesling? Isn't that sweeter than you like?"

"Hey, it's a *dry* Riesling. And it was on sale. And it's wine." She didn't wait for Katie's response, simply pulled two wineglasses down from the cupboard and filled them. She set one in front of her daughter, then sat down and held up her glass. When Katie touched hers to it, Liz asked, "So? How'd it go?"

"Let's just say my first impressions need work."

"What did you drop?" Liz raised her eyebrows in question, knowing her daughter well.

"Coffee."

"Oh, no."

"Oh, yes. All over her beautiful hardwood floor, her leather pumps, and what I have to believe is a very expensive rug."

Liz grimaced and held her glass up a second time for a second cheering. Katie obliged. "Other than that, how did it go? Was she mad? Was it what you were expecting?"

Katie blew out a breath, gazed off into the distance as she recalled the afternoon. "It was...different. She doesn't want an assistant. She made that clear."

"But the guy you talked to told you that."

"He did. So what she said didn't surprise me because I'd been warned." Katie sipped her wine. "Doesn't matter, though, because the fact is, she needs help. She has way too much on her plate. She just doesn't want to admit it."

"Control freak?"

"A major one. That's my guess. I'll find out tomorrow when I go over this plan with her and see how she takes it."

Liz swallowed some wine, then lowered her voice to conspiratorial levels. "She pretty?"

"Mom!"

"What? It's an innocent question."

"There is nothing innocent about that question."

Liz chuckled. "Well, is she?"

"Yes, she's pretty. In fact, she's gorgeous. Ridiculously so, given that she was in the hospital two days ago. But it doesn't matter. I'm there to do a job she doesn't want me to do, and she already hates me for ruining her rug."

Liz reached over and laid her palm against Katie's cheek. "Nobody could hate you, sweetie."

Katie snorted a laugh. "No? Give me something valuable of yours and let me spill some French roast all over it. See how you feel about me then."

Liz's laugh was interrupted by a yawn.

"Mom. Seriously."

"I'm fine. Just a rough day."

Katie's father had been angry when she'd gotten home. Swearing—something he rarely did—over the stew his wife had made for dinner, claiming she was trying to poison him. Katie could tell her mother was reaching the end of her rope when she muttered for him not to tempt her.

She looked at her mother until Liz met her gaze. Katie softened her voice. "Mom. How long can you keep this up?"

Liz looked away, emotion swimming in her eyes. "I don't know."

They were quiet for a beat, Liz lost in her doubts and Katie not knowing what to say. Finally, she reached for the baby monitor. "Look. I have more work to do. Why don't you get some sleep? I can listen for him." She expected a protest, so when her mother's eyes lit up hopefully, Katie had to hide her surprise.

"You don't mind?"

"God, no. That's why I moved back in. Go. You can't live on three hours of sleep a night." She held up the monitor. "I got this."

Liz downed the rest of her wine and stood. "Thank you, sweetie."

Katie nodded with a smile as she watched her mother shuffle slowly off toward the stairs, letting that smile fade once she was out of sight. Katie was worried. About her father, of course, but lately about her mother. There was no way she could keep up such a pace. She'd resisted having help come in at first. Then she'd relented to a visiting aide three times a week for two hours at a pop. Insurance had covered that, but Katie knew they needed to increase the visits. Her father was only going to get worse, and he wasn't a small man. When he had an outburst, it was loud and scary and they didn't always know how best to handle it. Having a professional around more often would help with that stress.

But everything cost money, and Liz had had to quit her job at a retail clothing store in order to have more time at home. So while the bills had gone up, the income had gone down. That's why Katie had insisted on moving in and contributing. Her mother hated it. Katie knew that. Hated needing her daughter's help. Hated needing her daughter's money even more, going so far as to flat out refuse it more than once. In response, Katie had taken to doing quiet things. Sneaking a bill out of the pile of mail here and there and paying it. Buying groceries before her mother had a chance to realize what they were low on. The baby monitor had been her idea—and her purchase—and after all the initial protestations, Katie's mother had embraced it, and now couldn't get along without it.

It was both a blessing and a curse to have money and pride take up so much attention. A blessing because it took their mind and attention off the deterioration of David Cooper. A curse because it took their mind and attention off the deterioration of David Cooper. The fact of the matter was, Katie was losing her father. Slowly and steadily. And the stress of caring for him was overshadowing that. The whole situation was horrifically cruel.

Katie felt the emotion threaten to well up, to form a lump in her throat, and she fought it. She'd gotten good at that: fighting emotion. She couldn't let it overwhelm her. There was too much to do. With a clearing of her throat, she refocused her attention on the laptop and notepaper in front of her and got back to work. Her plan was to knock Addison Fairchild's designer socks off tomorrow.

She hadn't realized she'd lost track of time until she heard a gentle rustling through the baby monitor. She blinked hard, her eyelids feeling lined with low-grit sandpaper, and a yawn cranked her jaw open wide. She stopped what she was doing and listened but didn't hear much else. Deciding she'd better get to bed, as she had two four-year-olds to deal with in the morning, she packed up her things and headed upstairs.

As she reached the top of the stairs, aided by the night-light in the hallway, she thought she heard the trickle of water running and wondered if somebody had forgotten to crank the handle on the bathroom sink tightly off. She stopped in the doorway of the bathroom when she saw her father.

He was standing at the toilet and glanced at her. She could make out the white of his teeth in the dim light and realized he was smiling at her. "Hi, honey," he said quietly as he held his penis with both hands and relieved himself into the toilet.

Katie's gaze snapped up to the ceiling on its own, as if she had no control. "Hey, Dad," she whispered, doing her best not to make a big deal out of the scene, lest he get angry. "You okay?"

"Yup. Just had to go." His voice was closer now, and the turning on of the water told Katie it was safe to look.

"I'll walk you back to your room," she offered as he washed his hands, then dried them on a nearby towel.

"Okay," he said cheerfully, joining her in the hall.

They walked the short distance to his room together, his arm thrown affectionately over her shoulder, and for a moment, she could almost forget how sick he was. These moments of near lucidity were becoming fewer and farther between, and Katie had learned she needed to grab them when she could.

"In you go," she said, holding the covers on his bed up. He slid in and got cozy and Katie tried to ignore the odd role reversal of parent and child. When she had him all tucked in, she asked, "You good?"

"I am."

"Okay. Good night, Dad. See you in the morning. I love you." She bent and kissed his forehead.

"I love you, too, Katie-cat."

She turned away quickly and left the room, not wanting him to see the tears that had welled up in her eyes at the nickname he'd given her when she was two. He hadn't called her that in nearly a year.

Another thing she'd been learning since her father's diagnosis was to embrace her emotions rather than fight them, and she tried to do that now. Safely in her own bedroom, she stood with her back against the closed door and allowed the tears to come, then slowly slid down the door to the floor.

She cried quietly—God forbid her mother hear her; she didn't need more to worry about. It wasn't often that she allowed herself this kind of release because, to be honest, there was always a small part of her that was afraid that once she started, she wouldn't be able to stop. That fear aside, though, she also knew she needed to let this stuff out. She needed to feel her emotions. Samantha was always telling her, *"You have feelings for a reason. Embrace them. Feel them. Then let them go."*

Katie felt like that was exactly what she was in the process of doing with her father. Very slowly. Torturously.

Embrace him.

Feel his presence.

Let him go.

CHAPTER FOUR

Thank God it's Friday.

That was the only thought running through Katie's mind as she got into her car in the Andersons' driveway after finally getting Simon and Noah onto the bus. She leaned her forehead against the steering wheel and simply focused on her breath—a little trick she'd learned from an old yoga instructor to help her relax when she was stressed. It worked, but Katie realized with gentle surprise that it wasn't out of the realm of possibility for her to fall asleep right then and there, sitting in the driver's seat of her car in a driveway that wasn't hers.

Exhausted beyond belief. That's what she was. She felt like a used tissue that had been tossed into the street, left out in the rain, and then run over by a car. Flattened, soggy, useless. She'd slept like crap, waking up at least once each hour. It hadn't helped that she'd stayed up as late as she had. Then the unexpected meeting of her dad in the bathroom had replayed in her mind on a loop as she tried to fall asleep. All told, she'd gotten maybe a full two hours. Maybe.

But.

She had a plan for Addison Fairchild. So there was that.

Lifting her head, she checked her reflection in the rearview mirror, ran a fingertip under each eye where her mascara was apparently also tired and had decided to take up residence on her face instead of her eyelashes, and blew out a breath. With a turn of the key in the ignition, she got herself on the road to get coffee, then headed to Addison's loft apartment. This was supposed to be the last time they met there. Addison intended to be back in the office on Monday, so Katie's route would be different and slightly longer. She'd have to make sure she didn't drag her feet once she got the boys off to school.

Twenty minutes later, she was knocking on the door of 5E and stifling a yawn as it was pulled open.

"Hi," Katie said.

Addison nodded and turned to walk into the living room, leaving the door open and Katie standing there.

"Okay, then," Katie mumbled and headed inside, closing the door with a foot. More loudly, she said, "I brought coffee. I promise not to spill it."

"I'd appreciate that." Addison sat down on her leather couch. Papers and her laptop were spread out on the wooden trunk that served as a coffee table. She looked almost as tired as Katie felt; that was the first thing she noticed. But her outfit was clean and crisp, her navy blue slacks looked freshly pressed—who did that anymore?—and her light-blue sweater made the color of her eyes pop. Some of her hair was pulled back; the rest hung down in soft waves of red-tinted brown. She picked up a pair of black-rimmed glasses and slid them onto her face. Katie swallowed hard.

"Here you go." Katie set the French roast down near Addison, who picked it up and sipped without looking. She set her bag down and unzipped her jacket. "So, I went over some things last night and worked out a plan—"

Before she could finish her sentence, Addison held up a hand like a traffic cop. "Don't take your jacket off. I have a couple errands for you to run."

"Oh. Okay." Katie slid her arm back in and rezipped.

Addison hit the Return key on her laptop. "There. I emailed it to you."

Katie bit her tongue as she pulled out her phone and scrolled to her email. She opened the one from "afairchild" and read it. It was simply a list with addresses where appropriate.

Pick up dry cleaning.
Go to post office.
Get car washed/fill tank.
Go to grocery store. (This one had its own separate list of items.)

Do this last: get dinner. (This one came with not only a restaurant and its address, but an order. Just one. A grilled chicken salad and a cup of clam chowder.)

"Oh," Katie said, because she could think of nothing else.

For the first time since Katie walked in, Addison looked up at her. Her blue eyes were accented by shadows underneath and her skin had a bit of a gray tint. "What?"

"Nothing." Katie squinted at her. "Are you okay?"

"I'm fine. Is there a problem with the list?"

Katie cleared her throat. "No. Not at all. It's just that…" She let her voice trail off, not sure how to put her thoughts into words.

Addison sighed in obvious annoyance. "It's just what, Ms. Cooper? I have a ton of work to do. What's the issue here?"

Katie mentally counted to five while she kept a ridiculously fake smile plastered to her face. "It's just that I spent a lot of time on a plan for my helping to take some of the load off you, which is the reason I was hired, I'm told. I'd hoped you'd at least look at it." She did her best to keep her voice light and hopeful rather than irritated and frustrated, which was how she was feeling in the moment.

"Look. According to my boss, you are my personal assistant. I have given you a list of personal things I could use a bit of assistance with." She held up a hand again. "Not that I can't handle them myself. I absolutely could. I'm appeasing my boss. So I'd appreciate it if you'd do what you're getting paid for." Katie stood rooted to her spot and blinked, having trouble processing the dismissal. Addison must have noticed because her expression softened slightly and she added, "Email me the plan, and I'll take a look."

"Okay." Katie swallowed down her aggravation. *Fine. All right. If that's the way she wants it.*

"My keys are on the table next to the door. It's a black Mercedes and it's in the underground garage."

With a nod, Katie picked her bag back up, slung it over her shoulder, and headed for the door, scooping the keys up as she went. Once safely ensconced in the elevator and two floors below Addison's, Katie allowed herself a scream of frustration. Then she glanced at the camera mounted in the upper corner of the elevator car, waved sheepishly, and mouthed an apology to the security guy probably watching. Then she pulled out her phone and emailed her plan to Addison, her faith that it would be even glanced at, let alone read, hovering somewhere around "never gonna happen."

When the doors slid open, she stepped out and stood there for a beat. "Why are parking garages always super creepy?" she asked aloud, her voice echoing as she looked around carefully, squinting at pillars and trucks, the part of her that had seen too many horror films totally expecting an ax murderer to jump out at any moment to hack away at her.

With a push of the button on the key fob, the car that beeped its location was only two vehicles away. Katie headed toward it, taking surprising note of the fact that this wasn't a sedan. It wasn't the Mercedes of a stuffy old white guy. Oh, no. Her steps slowed as she approached it, the little sport coupe. It was black, sleek, sexy and—as far as Katie was concerned—didn't need to be washed. It shimmered under the harsh fluorescent lights of the garage.

She pulled the door open, took a seat, and shut herself in, sinking into the unbelievably soft tan leather seat as she ran her hands over the steering wheel, which was also covered in cushioned, buttery leather. She inhaled deeply, the interior's scent a pleasing blend of New Car Smell and that sunshine thing that Katie associated with Addison. The Engine Start button lit up, waiting to be pressed.

"Don't mind if I do," Katie said, and started the car. She reached into her bag and retrieved a pair of sunglasses, which she slid on.

Maybe this wasn't such a bad gig after all.

"You don't look a ton better, Addie. Are you taking it easy like you're supposed to?" Sophie set her mug down on the coffee table and then leaned back against the couch to study her. The concern on her face was genuine. "How do you feel?"

"I feel fine," Addison said, trying hard not to sound churlish but pretty sure she missed the mark. "I just have so much to do, and I feel myself slipping further and further behind." She waved at the mess on the coffee table, which should've looked better at seven p.m. than it had at nine a.m. but didn't.

"Is the assistant not helping?"

"She is." Addison pointed toward the entryway, hoping to distract Sophie from asking any more about it. "She spilled coffee in the first five minutes she was here."

"She was probably nervous. Did you welcome her nicely? Or were you all Ice Queen with her?"

Addison widened her eyes. "Ice Queen?"

Sophie scoffed, waved a dismissive hand. "Please. Don't act like this is news to you." They kept eye contact for a beat before Addison looked away. "Seriously, though, how is she?"

"She's fine." Addison could feel Sophie's eyes still on her as if they were actually poking at her somehow but didn't look her way. It took every ounce of energy she had not to squirm in her seat.

"Are you letting her help?"

"Of course."

"Really." Sophie's voice was laced with skepticism. "What did you have her do today?"

"I gave her a list."

"And what was on that list?"

Addison sighed a sigh that clearly said she was becoming aggravated with the questions. Sophie, of course, was unaffected and simply waited her out. "Things to do. Errands."

"Errands."

"Yes, errands." Needing to busy her hands, Addison shuffled some papers around uselessly.

"Let me guess. Get you coffee? Pick up your dry cleaning?" Sophie pointed at the plastic-covered garments hanging from the coat tree near the front door. "Those types of errands?"

"She's supposed to be here to help me, so I gave her things to help me with."

"Jesus Christ, Addison. Why do you insist on thinking you're Wonder Woman? Is it your never-ending quest to please your mother?" Sophie's voice held a tint of anger now. "Your assistant is supposed to help you with *work*. With *your job*, which has gotten to be too much, obviously, as it gave you a bleeding ulcer and sent you to the hospital. What the hell is the matter with you?"

Addison shook her head, said nothing, felt scolded, frustrated.

"Addie." Sophie's voice had gone gentle as she slid closer. A hand on Addison's arm, she said, "Look at me."

Reluctantly, Addison did.

"People are worried about you." She held up a hand as Addison opened her mouth to interrupt and waited until it closed again. "*I* am worried about you. And you know me: I worry about very little."

It was true. Sophie was one of the most calm, laid-back people Addison had ever known. Next to nothing fazed her. She was excellent in a crisis because she didn't freak out.

"I need you to let her help. I need you to delegate some of your work to her. That's why your mom hired her, you know?"

Addison picked up her mug of decaffeinated tea, which Sophie had made for her, claiming she drank way too much coffee. Which was true, Addison knew. And terrible for her ulcer, which she also knew. She sipped, was surprised by the light cinnamon flavor. "I know."

"It wouldn't be hard to come up with a sort of plan. Like, just map out the things you're willing to hand over to her. I know you hate giving up one iota of control, but..." Sophie shrugged as if to say, *"Too fucking bad."*

"Actually, she did that already."

"Who? The assistant?"

With a nod, Addison reached for her laptop, called up the email Katie had sent, and turned it so Sophie could see it.

"Wow," Sophie said as she scanned the document. "She's got everything listed, when you meet about things, when she takes care of your emails and which ones. I love how it's all organized by date and by days of the week, right up until the end of her gig." She looked up at Addison with a grin. "You've got your own little calendar girl."

"Ha ha."

Sophie pointed at the screen. "Seriously, though. This is good stuff. It's a solid plan for how she can help you. She did this herself?"

Addison nodded.

"Yeah, let her help you." When Addison didn't respond positively, Sophie asked, "Okay. What's the deal here? I mean, I know you're a ridiculous control freak, but this is a) about your health and b) only temporary. Tell me what's going on."

Addison picked up her mug and sipped, using the time to gather her thoughts, to choose what she should say. One glance at Sophie, though, and she gave up. She could never pull a fast one on her best friend. Sophie knew her too well. She'd ferret out any disparities and pounce; it's what made her such a good trial lawyer. Addison blew out a breath. "My mom is going to retire at the end of the year."

Sophie's face remained neutral as she nodded. "Yeah, you told me that already." She waited for Addison to continue. When she didn't, Sophie prompted her. "Okay. So what does your mom's retirement have to do with—wait a second..." Addison grimaced. "Are you freaking out? About who she chooses? Still?"

Addison turned so her body was fully facing Sophie, feeling suddenly animated. "I'm the best qualified. Right? I mean, Jared's young. He does a decent job taking care of the malls, but it's pretty straightforward. Katrina..." She let her voice trail off as she thought about her younger sister and their rather complicated relationship.

"Is the competition. Right." Sophie inhaled slowly, then let it out as she focused on Addison. "None of this is news. I don't understand why you've let it tie you all up in knots. Your mom's gonna do what your mom's gonna do. She always has."

"Yeah..."

"Would she ever consider hiring from outside the company?"

Addison gave it some thought, but not much because she knew her mother well. "No. I don't think so. She built the company from the ground up. She's not going to want someone who's not a Fairchild running the whole thing."

"And you think that giving up some of your crap to the assistant—what is her name, anyway?"

"Katie Cooper." Addison deadpanned.

"Aw, that's cute. So, you think giving up some of your crap to Katie Cooper will...what? Eliminate you from the running? Give Katrina the advantage? Explain your logic, please."

Addison groaned. "I don't know! I can't explain it. It just...is."

Sophie stared at her for what felt like much longer than it probably was, and finally rolled her eyes. "You're such a damn weirdo."

They moved on to other subjects, thank God, but when Sophie left about an hour later, her parting words were, "Let Katie Cooper help you." And at Addison's impatient look, she added, "I mean it. Don't make me rat you out to your mother again. You know I would. In a New York minute."

Flopped back down on her couch after that, Addison took a moment and tried to simply breathe. Just breathe. She wasn't feeling great. Her heart had been racing and her stomach was killing her, but she hadn't told Sophie because she didn't want to be rushed to the hospital again. She was fine. It was fine. She just needed to relax a bit.

A glance at the coffee table didn't help, and she turned away from it pointedly, doing her best to focus on something besides work, at least for the few minutes she needed to calm her body down. She closed her eyes.

Deep breath in.
Slow breath out.
Deep breath in.
Slow breath out.

She kept that up for several moments until she felt her heart rate slow, her blood stop racing so fast. Her shoulders moved as a quiet chuckle escaped her. Meditating was not something she ever would have predicted herself doing. Too still. Too hokey. Too crystal-gazing-spiritual for her. She was a businesswoman who relied on numbers and reports and sales and *facts*, not chakras and energy. But when she'd been in the hospital and felt her stress climbing, a nurse had asked if she ever meditated. Addison wanted to roll her eyes, but she was too alarmed by her body's betrayal and didn't have the energy to shoo the nurse way. Instead, she found herself oddly riveted by the instructions the nurse gave her, and before she knew it, they were breathing in slow tandem, focusing on nothing but the filling and emptying of their lungs. Addison was shocked by how well it had worked.

In addition to the controlled breathing, Addison was supposed to also clear her mind. That idea still made her laugh because clearing her mind was not something she'd ever been able to do. Not as a kid. Not as a teenager. Not now. There was always something in her head. Mostly work, but sometimes other things. Point being, wiping her brain clean, even for a few minutes, was next to impossible.

But the breathing definitely helped.

When she felt a little better, she reached for her laptop without looking at the rest of the piles of crap strewn about. She needed to get to bed soon, but she wanted to take a last look at Katie's calendar. The phrase "calendar girl" zipped through her head again and she made a mental note to smack Sophie the next time she saw her because that name was going to stick now.

It wasn't bad, Katie's plan. In fact, it was quite good. It made sense. It was very organized. She didn't like to admit that—and she probably wouldn't out loud—but it had some salient points. It also had some suggestions that Addison mentally crossed off immediately, but...

Her phone interrupted her thoughts with a beep, indicating a text. It was Katrina.

How are you feeling?

Addison narrowed her eyes, wondering if her anxiety over who their mother would choose as a replacement had conjured Katrina up. She quickly fired back.

I'm great! Super! So much better. Thanks for asking.

She attached a smiling emoji and hesitated over the Send button. With a sigh, she deleted the message and typed out a less snarky one. Her panicked weirdness lately was not Katrina's fault. Addison had no idea if Katrina even wanted to take her mother's seat—because Addison hadn't asked her—but why wouldn't she? Addison certainly did. Plus, she was the big sister and the job should be hers.

Closing her laptop, she hauled herself off the couch and headed to the bedroom.

She had to prepare for Monday when she'd return to the office. She had to be 100 percent.

More than 100 percent, if she could.

CHAPTER FIVE

The main offices for Fairchild Rentals were smartly located in the center of the city. This made it easier for the maintenance guys, as well as the office personnel, to get to the five separate apartment/condo/townhouse complexes across the county at any given time. Each complex had its own on-site staff, but the next tier up was housed in the main office building.

Low and slightly peaked, the building looked to have been constructed in maybe the 1980s, Katie speculated. Freshly stained cedar siding and what looked to be a brand-new roof tugged it closer to present day, and Katie noticed how neat and tidy everything was outside. The lawn was perfectly manicured, the landscaping bursting with pops of color in the form of mums, large pots of them, even as fall was sliding toward winter. Yellows and oranges and deep brick reds. The windows were spotless and glinted in the occasional autumn afternoon sunlight as she pulled her car into the lot and parked next to Addison's Mercedes. She got out and threw a loving glance at the Benz.

"Hello, my old friend," she whispered, reminiscing about gliding along in the car last week as if she were gliding smoothly across a perfectly calm lake. It was effortless to drive, Addison's Mercedes, and Katie absently wondered if she should throw some dirt on it, mess it up so Addison might send her out to get it washed again. With a shake of her head, she pulled her focus back to the task at hand and tugged her coat more tightly closed against the chill in the air.

The first thing Katie noticed when she pushed through the glass double doors of Fairchild Rentals was the warmth. It smelled like fall, the scents of cinnamon, nutmeg, and crushed leaves hanging in the air, though she couldn't seem to locate a candle of any sort. The walls were a creamy ivory and decorated with tasteful paintings of outdoor scenes. Oak hardwood floors gleamed beneath a few scattered throw rugs with burgundy and baby blue accents. The ceilings were higher than Katie had expected when looking from the outside, and there were skylights and a couple of ceiling fans that turned lazily in the sporadic rays of sun.

A classy wooden desk was situated to Katie's immediate left, obviously meant as a welcoming station for visitors. Behind it sat a small woman in her sixties with salt-and-pepper hair and a slightly hesitant, yet somehow inviting smile.

"Can I help you?" she asked as Katie approached.

"Hi, I'm Katie Cooper. I'm working for Addison Fairchild. Can you point me in the right direction?"

An expression—something that looked an awful lot like sympathy to Katie—zipped across the woman's face before she seemed to grab it, tuck it away, and return to her usual, welcoming look. "Oh, sure." She pointed behind her and to her left. "Just follow this row and head to the back corner. She's in the last office on the left."

Katie smiled her thanks and headed that way, taking in the rest of the place as she did. The area was all open-concept, cubicles with low walls so the employees manning the eight desks could still see one another. Four desks were occupied, three of those people with telephone handsets against their ears. Four were empty, chairs pushed in neatly. Along the wall on Katie's left was an open space that looked like a large break room, complete with two tables, a soda machine, a fridge, and a coffee station. There may have been more, but that was all Katie could make out as she passed the open door and glanced in the window that looked out onto the rest of the office. Addison's office was laid out much the same way. Katie first passed a large window. The vertical blinds were drawn, but not closed, and through the slats, she could see Addison sitting at her desk.

When she reached the doorway, Katie knocked softly on the doorjamb.

Addison looked up, black-rimmed glasses perched on the end of her nose, those blue eyes snagging Katie's, and one eyebrow arched up.

She looked a bit better, more rested, and Katie had the sudden vision of a sexy librarian about to shush her. It was not unpleasant.

"Hi," Katie said. "How are you?"

Addison gave one perfunctory nod. "Fine. You?"

"I'm good." Katie hovered, not sure if she should enter, not sure if she should put her bag down, not sure if there was a spot for her in this office, though it was quite roomy, with a small, round conference table in one corner and a black leather sofa against the wall. As she let her eyes roam, Addison's voice yanked her back.

"You can work there." She indicated the round table with a jerk of her chin. "Just set yourself up and get comfortable."

"Okay. Great." Katie took off her jacket and draped it over the back of one of the wooden chairs. She set her bag down and pulled out her laptop, booted it up. "Is there Wi-Fi?" she asked.

Addison was focused on her computer monitor and several beats went by before she shifted her gaze to meet Katie's. *God, those blue eyes can look icy.* In that moment, it occurred to Katie that Addison and the rest of the office building were polar opposites in almost every way, the building being warm and inviting, Addison being cool and a little standoffish. It was too bad, really, because Addison had serious potential to be hot. If only she was, maybe, a tiny bit nicer. If only she'd relax a bit. If only she smiled once in a while.

"The code is at the front desk. Ask her for it."

Okay, then, Katie thought, noticing that Addison didn't even use the woman at the front desk's name. Did she even know it? Katie got up, carried her laptop with her back to the salt-and-pepper-haired woman, then held out one hand. "Hi, again. I didn't catch your name," she said.

"Oh," the woman said, surprised if her expression was any indication. She put her hand in Katie's, and this time, her smile wasn't at all hesitant. "I'm Janie. Katie, was it?"

Katie nodded and returned the smile. "I need the Wi-Fi information and I was told you're the queen for that. True?"

Janie's cheeks turned a gentle pink. "Well. I don't know about that." She opened a drawer and took out a laminated card. "Here you go. We change the password once every couple of weeks. Email me if you have any questions."

Katie nodded her thanks, set the card down so she could read it, and punched the info into her computer. She wondered if she'd get an email address. "I'm in." She handed the card back. "Thank you, Janie. It's really nice to meet you."

"Same here." Janie continued to smile, and for some reason, that made Katie very happy.

Back in Addison's office, Addison hadn't shifted her position at all, still focused on her computer screen, one hand on her mouse. Katie sat back down at her previous spot. *I'm a Temp of the Round Table*, she thought, then accidentally let a tiny giggle slip out. She glanced up and made a face, noticed Addison looking at her over the top of her glasses, and damn if it wasn't stupidly sexy.

"Hi," Katie said. "Sorry. Um, I was wondering. Will I get a company email address?"

Addison's brow furrowed.

"I mean, it would certainly make communication easier."

Addison scratched the side of her neck. "I suppose it would. That's a good point. Are you online now?" At Katie's nod, she instructed, "Go to the Fairchild Enterprises website, click on 'staff,' and scroll until you find Jose Garcia."

Katie found him in the I.T. category. "Got him."

"Click on his contact info and give him a call. Tell him what you need." That was, apparently, all she was going to get because Addison went back to her computer screen. Two seconds later, her phone rang, and she snatched it up with a clipped, "Addison Fairchild."

With a mental shrug, Katie reached for the handset of the phone on her little round table, dialed the number on the website, and waited while it rang. Waited and watched Addison as she spoke about a lease somebody wanted to break. She was animated, used her hands to talk, scratched her neck more than once as she spun left and then right in her chair.

"Garcia," came the voice on the phone, and for a split second, it startled Katie.

"Oh. Um, hi. Is this Jose?"

"Yep."

"Hi. My name is Katie Cooper and I'm a new hire working for Addison Fairchild. I'm supposed to talk to you about getting an email address."

The rest of the afternoon went quickly enough, but it also gave

Katie a pretty clear picture of how this temp job was going to go. She watched as Addison was pulled in several different directions. Phone calls, meetings, maintenance issues, email, and things that had to do with the umbrella company of Fairchild Enterprises all battled for her time and attention. And while Addison handled it all remarkably well, Katie could see the toll it took as she observed from her corner seat. Her skin tone seemed to get a bit duller as the day went on and she blinked rapidly and often, making Katie wonder if her eyes were bothering her. The amount of coffee she drank was staggering—she sent Katie to get it for her four times—and Katie never saw her put one crumb of food into her mouth, though she caught her grimacing a couple times as she laid a hand across her stomach.

"You okay?" Katie asked more than once.

"Yeah. I'm fine," Addison had replied each time with a quick nod.

While Addison ran around putting out fires, answering a million questions, and barking orders into her phone, Katie did very little, and it began to get frustrating. Jose Garcia got her set up with her own email address faster than she'd expected, so that was good, but the problem with being given little to do was that even five hours felt like they dragged on for ages. By four, Katie was ready to throw herself out a window. Which wouldn't have mattered, as they were on the ground floor, but still.

When her computer pinged, indicating a new email, Katie blinked at it for a moment, not quite comprehending. When she opened it, she grinned. It was from Samantha.

Saw your new email address come through and thought I'd say hello. Welcome to F.E.! How's it going over there on the rental arm of things?

Still grinning, Katie typed back, careful not to be too personal or too disparaging.

Going well so far. Getting the hang of things. Trying to learn the ropes.

She sent off her email and less than three minutes went by before her phone pinged, telling her she'd received a text. Samantha again.

Tell me the truth. Do you want to kill her yet?

Keeping her phone near her lap so Addison might not see—though why that would matter at this point, given the big fat nothing she'd been handed to do all day, was beyond her—Katie typed back.

No, but I'm bored out of my skull. She gives me hardly anything to do. #ControlFreak.

Sam, always one to see the bright side, responded with *Just keep thinking about the money...*

Katie hadn't told anybody but Sam and her mother how much this job was paying. She actually wondered if Addison even knew, as she hadn't been the one to hire her. Another email beeped through, and as if he'd sensed Katie's thoughts, it was from Jack Saunders—the one who *was* signing her paycheck. Like Sam, he'd noticed her email address pop through and wanted to see how things were going, though he was more to the point and less personal. He asked what Addison had given her to do so far.

Though she felt a bit like she was spying on Addison—or at least being a little bit sneaky—she understood that Jack was technically her boss, so she answered honestly. She'd gotten coffee several times—she didn't think reporting the exact number of times was necessary—she'd contacted I.T. to set up her email, she'd run off 500 copies of a flyer about upcoming parking lot sealing for one of the complexes and 250 of another regarding tenants cleaning up after their dogs. She'd also spent over an hour studying the Fairchild Enterprises website, which she'd already done in preparation for her interview with Jack, so she didn't tell him that. Instead, she proofread her list, signed the email in a professional manner, and sent it off to him, feeling oddly guilty about it, as if she'd tattled.

"You can go."

Addison's voice surprised Katie. She snapped her gaze up to find those icy blue eyes watching her. "I'm sorry?"

"It's after five. You can go home."

"Oh. Okay." Katie gave a nod of understanding and began gathering her things. Addison didn't look up again until Katie was good to go and said, "See you tomorrow."

Addison made a sound of some sort.

"Have a good night." She shrugged as, this time, there was only a nod. With a sigh, she left Addison sitting at her desk, just as she'd been five hours earlier when Katie had arrived.

"Good night, Katie," Janie said with a cheerful little wave as Katie passed by her desk.

Katie waved, glad to have a friendly face follow an entire afternoon of little to no eye contact and conversation that never consisted of more than three short sentences at a time, most of them directives of some sort.

Despite the overall pleasant atmosphere of the Fairchild Rentals offices, the crisply chilly fall air outside felt new and clean, and it washed over Katie like a gentle shower of refreshment. She inhaled and felt like it was the first full breath she'd taken since she'd gotten there. Standing next to her car for a beat, then two, she simply breathed. Took air in, let it out, and felt herself relax. Which was weird because she hadn't actually realized she'd been tense until that moment.

"Wow," she muttered as she rolled her shockingly stiff shoulders and then got in her car.

A text from her mother told her they needed milk and apples at home, so Katie stopped at the store. When she finally made it home, she knew immediately it had been a rough day for her mom, who greeted her, nevertheless, with a tired smile. Katie pretended not to notice that she was unshowered, her sandy hair hanging limp, and she was still in her morning sweats.

"Hey, Mom." She kissed Liz on the cheek, then flinched as she heard her father slam down a butter knife as he sat at the kitchen table. Her eyebrows went up, her gaze moving to her mother, who closed her eyes as if summoning strength.

"Take your time, honey." She picked up the butter knife and a slice of toast from the plate in front of her husband and spread raspberry jam on it. "See? Like this."

One of the things that Katie found hardest to absorb about her father's deepening illness was the speed with which his moods changed. He'd been angry as he slammed down the knife, his eyes flashing, four seconds ago. Now he looked like he might cry as his wife handed him a slice of toast with a tender, exhausted smile. He took it gently, moved it to his mouth, and took a bite, his eyes never leaving Liz's as they shimmered with unshed tears.

Katie swallowed hard as she watched the exchange, and not for the first time, she wondered how her mother did it, how she went through every day this way, knowing there was no relief, that it would never get any better, only worse. Her own eyes welled up and she quickly turned away, not wanting either of them to see.

"Mom," she said a few minutes later and cleared her throat. Her father was now calmly eating his toast and gazing off into the middle distance. "Why don't you go take a shower, relax a bit, and maybe go to a movie or something?"

Liz's expression registered several emotions, one right after another. First came protest, then surprise, followed by gratitude, relief, and finally, hesitation. "Are you sure?" she finally asked.

Katie smiled, dropped her bag, and shed her coat. "Absolutely. I bet Laura would love to have some time with you," she said, referring to her mother's best friend. "Give her a call. I got this." She pulled out a chair and sat down next to her father. "Right, Daddy?"

He continued to stare, to chew, and didn't seem to notice her presence.

She pretended not to notice *that*.

CHAPTER SIX

Tuesday morning did not welcome Addison with open arms. It was her own fault, she knew, but still. She'd prefer not to feel like warmed-over pea soup. She'd stayed up way too late and slept fitfully, and her stomach was giving her all kinds of signs that it was not happy with her. She knew she should eat something that wasn't made of chemicals, but she just didn't have much of an appetite. Nothing sat well. Instead, she poured her coffee into a travel mug and headed into the office, mentally listing all the things she needed to get done.

The morning flew by, as it always did when she was crazed, and before Addison even registered the time, Katie Cooper walked in the door, which meant it was already noon.

"Hi," Katie said with her signature smile, and for some reason, Addison found herself unable to look away. Katie's dark hair was down at the moment, but Addison knew there was an elastic band on her wrist and she could whip her hair into a ponytail or messy bun in the span of seven seconds. There was something kind of endearing about that. Her clothes were simple and not at all flashy: navy-blue pants and a pale yellow sweater. The energy she gave off was palpable, somehow invigorating and cheerful, and Addison found herself feeling a little melancholy around it, though she couldn't pinpoint why. Katie unpacked her bag, setting her laptop on the round table as she glanced up at Addison. "How was your morning?"

Shaking herself back to reality, Addison refocused on her computer screen as she replied, "It was okay."

"Good. Let me give my email a quick check and then you can let me know what I can do for you today."

The phone rang, saving Addison from any more small talk, which she despised. Or staring, which she apparently enjoyed a little too much. As she answered, a sharp pain hit her belly, as if some creature was trapped inside and trying to fight its way out. With a knife. Or maybe a sword. Possibly a machete. She grimaced and did her best to swallow a groan, noticed that Katie was looking at her over the top of her screen. Half listening as one of her complex managers told her in a panicked voice about a leaking roof, she clenched her teeth and willed the pain to subside.

The Universe, apparently feeling a sense of humor rather than sympathy, instead sent Addison's mother breezing into the office. She stopped in her tracks the second she was through the door.

"What's wrong with her?" Addison heard her ask Katie.

"I don't know. She just got really pale all of a sudden."

Addison squeezed her eyes shut, trying to follow the conversation in her office, the panic on the phone and her own pain proving to be too much. Through gritted teeth, she said, "Let me call you back," then replaced the handset without waiting for a reply. With one hand, she pushed her chair back from her desk so she could lean forward, doubling over against the stabbing in her stomach.

Her mother was by her side in an instant. "Addison. What is it?" Addison could feel the warm hand on her back, rubbing in soothing circles. "Your ulcer? Have you been taking the meds?"

She didn't answer, waited out the stabbing pain, and after a few more moments, it eased up. She opened her eyes and sat up. "I'm good. I'm okay now."

"No, you are not okay. Damn it, Addison, you need to take better care of yourself. I don't understand you."

While they'd had this same conversation more than once, Addison was again surprised by her mother's expression. It was in her eyes. Worry. Fear. Big-time concern. The snarky comment Addison had ready died in her throat and the fight went out of her like air from a leaky balloon.

"You should go back to the hospital."

"No," Addison protested, probably louder and more vehemently than necessary. Lowering her voice, she repeated herself as she scratched the side of her neck. "No, Mom, I'm okay. It's just a pain. I get them all the time. It'll pass. I just need a minute."

"If you won't go to the ER, then you're going home."

"Mom…"

"Do not argue with me, Addison Elizabeth." Meredith's tone left no room for interpretation, and Addison knew it. "Either you go home or I call an ambulance right now."

Addison clenched her jaw, irritated by the ultimatum even though, deep down, she knew that she hadn't rested quite enough after her hospital stay, and this relapse was most likely the result. "Fine."

"I want you to take her home," her mother said, and it took a couple seconds for Addison to realize she was talking to Katie. "Her things are over there. Her laptop is in her attaché. Once you get her there, you make sure she is in bed, not on the couch."

"Mom. Seriously?"

"I know you. If you set up on the couch, you'll sleep there." Meredith turned back to Katie. "The bed. Understood?"

"Absolutely." Katie widened her eyes for a split second, but then she gave a firm nod and zipped around the office, gathering up Addison's things as well as her own.

Addison's mother helped her into her jacket, and Addison felt like a child again. Which wasn't awful for a few seconds.

"Ready?" Katie asked.

With a nod, Addison followed her out of the office and through the open area. The handful of people at their desks stopped to look. Addison kept her head down, shame heating her face.

Before she could say anything to Janie at the front desk, Meredith spoke up. "Ms. Fairchild will be at home for the rest of the day, Janie. If you have any issues, direct them to Katie."

"Yes, ma'am," Janie said, brow furrowed. "Feel better," she called as they exited the lobby.

"My car or yours?" Katie asked, once they were in the parking lot. Before Addison could answer, Katie chuckled and said, "That was a dumb question. I have an eleven-year-old Honda, you have a new, sporty Mercedes, and your assistant is not a stupid woman. Yours it is." The lightness of her tone caused the corners of Addison's mouth to tug up just a bit as she stepped off the curb.

"Ready?" Katie asked, standing next to the driver's side door.

With a nod Addison moved to the passenger side, in no mood to argue about who would drive.

God, this was going to be a painful afternoon.

❖

Watching the dynamic between Addison Fairchild and her mother had proven beyond interesting to Katie. Not only because it was so different from her and her own mother, but because watching the woman who was used to barking orders have orders barked at her was almost surreal. And oddly satisfying.

That being said, Addison was in obvious pain, and Katie didn't like seeing it. She might not have registered it if she hadn't already spent some time with Addison, but Katie was a pretty observant person. Addison's normally determined stride was just a touch slower today, her not-so-healthy pallor even less healthy, drained of almost all color until her complexion was the same hue as the skim milk Katie had poured into her cereal that morning. She said very little as they made the trip from the Fairchild Rentals office to Addison's loft—even failing to grunt or make her usual noncommittal sounds in response to things Katie said—and the elevator ride up was a silent one.

The loft was warm and cozy, and yet again, Katie was surprised by how somebody so cool and remote could have a space that was the exact opposite. She set everything down and shed her jacket, hanging it on the coat tree. She held out her hand for Addison's jacket and put it on top of hers, then watched as Addison kicked off her heels, walked across the thick area rug to the couch, and plopped down with a huge sigh. Head in her hand, she massaged the forehead with her fingertips.

Damn it.

"Um…you're supposed to go to bed." Katie did her best to keep her tone strong but wasn't sure she was successful.

"The couch is fine."

"That's not what your mother said."

Addison shifted her gaze to Katie's, and if she'd felt better, Katie was pretty sure her voice would hold a lot more venom. Instead, she just sounded irritated and tired. "I'm a grown woman."

"I'm aware of that. You're also in pretty bad shape today." Katie did her best to stay matter of fact. "Your mother—"

Addison stopped her sentence with an upheld hand, a habit of hers that was getting on Katie's nerves. "Like I said. Grown woman. I no longer have to do what my mommy tells me to, okay?" This time, there was a definite bite to her words.

Katie bristled, and she felt her anger bubble up. "That is totally true. I, however, am not a daughter but an employee who gets paid not by you but by her and her people. If she tells me to do something, I do it. Know why? Because I need this job."

They stayed like that for what felt like several very long minutes to Katie. Addison on the couch, icy blue eyes flashing, Katie standing in the entryway, one hand on her hip. A standoff of sorts, which Katie had never been good at, so she blinked in shock when she actually won.

"Fine," Addison said with another sigh, and it was obvious that, more than feeling Katie was right, she was simply too tired to argue. She pushed herself to her feet. "Give me ten minutes to change and then come on in with my bag." She padded off toward the other end of the apartment without waiting for a response.

Katie stood still for a beat, absorbing her victory, and finally allowed the smile to creep across her face and make itself known. As she was taking things out of her own bag, Addison called to her from the bedroom.

"There's a bottle of Chardonnay in the fridge. Can you bring a glass for me when you come?"

"Sure," Katie called back, and headed into that enormous, beautiful kitchen. The wine was easy to find, the glasses, not so much. It took her five tries opening different cupboards and taking in the set of heavy, stoneware dishes in all its pieces. They were all a deep, rich blue with black bottoms, somehow both elegant and simple at the same time. Plates, smaller plates, bowls of three different sizes, coffee mugs, all stacked neatly in the roomy cabinets. Katie envisioned a dinner party featuring them laid out on the large dining room table, tall candles in the center, wineglasses sparkling in the light of the overhead fixture that hung from a black cable.

Wineglasses.

Katie snapped out of her reverie and found the wineglasses, took one down, filled it. Then she carried it back into the living room, scooped up her things, and headed slowly down the hallway toward where she assumed the bedroom must be.

Addison's loft actually contained three bedrooms. The first one Katie passed she assumed was a guest room. It held a queen-size bed, a dresser, and a TV, but nothing personal of note…at least not from what she could see as she walked past. The second bedroom contained exercise equipment. A treadmill, a stationary bike, a yoga mat, some free weights. Katie had a quick vision of Addison running on the treadmill, reddish-brown hair in a cute ponytail that flounced back and forth with her strides, face and chest glistening with perspiration…

A quick shake of her head dislodged that image quickly and Katie cleared her throat loudly as she reached the third bedroom. "Okay to come in?"

"Yeah."

Addison's bedroom fell into the same category as every other setting in her life that Katie'd been allowed to see. Warm, inviting, comfortable. The walls were a relaxing color Katie had trouble describing…sort of a light purplish gray. The bed was enormous and covered in a deep purple down comforter with cream-colored accents, the headboard and footboard twisty pieces of art made from wrought iron, incredibly elegant to look at. The same hardwood floor in the living room ran through the entire loft, and a huge, thick area rug was laid out at the foot of the bed, part of its ivory-colored softness disappearing underneath.

On one side of the bed, Addison was perched, several pillows behind her, propping her up. She now wore gray sweats tied at her stomach and an oversized red sweatshirt with the Under Armour logo splashed across the front in silver. Her feet were bare and crossed at the ankle, and it wasn't until she held out her hand and wiggled her fingers that Katie remembered she was holding the wine.

"Shouldn't you be having tea or something?" Katie asked, before she could catch herself.

"Probably," was Addison's reply. She took the glass and sipped. "Aren't you having any?"

Katie blinked. "Me? Oh, no. No, I just…"

Addison made a pffft sound and waved a hand at her. "Please. We've got some work ahead of us, so it's not like you'll be driving any time soon. Besides, I don't want to drink alone." She moved her hand in a shooing motion, so Katie obeyed and returned to the kitchen to get herself some wine. Which was very, very good, she discovered upon the first sip. Her phone beeped then and she read a text from Meredith Fairchild asking Katie to remind Addison to take her meds.

"From one nanny job to the next," Katie muttered, typing a reply and heading back to the bedroom.

Addison had grabbed her laptop and now had it balanced on her thighs, black-rimmed glasses framing her eyes. The scene felt oddly intimate somehow, and Katie did a little stutter step in the doorway before continuing across the room. "Did you take your meds?" she asked, by way of distraction.

"No."

"Where are they?"

"Bathroom." Addison pointed to a door in the wall, eyes still focused on her laptop.

Katie went into the master bath and tried not to marvel at the sheer size of the bathtub, tried not to imagine herself soaking in it, completely submerged up to her neck because there was ample room to do just that. On the double-sink vanity, she found a pill bottle and brought it into the bedroom.

Without looking up, Addison patted the bed next to her. "Come here. I want to show you this."

Crawling across the bed of the person she worked for was a new and surreal experience for Katie, and she kept her jaw clamped shut to prevent a nervous laugh from escaping. Once settled next to Addison, she handed her the pill bottle.

With a half-frown, Addison took it, opened it, and shook a pill into her hand. She downed it with a mouthful of wine.

"I'm sitting here contemplating the wisdom of washing down drugs with alcohol," Katie said, unable to keep from looking amused.

Addison shrugged. "Gets the job done."

"True."

For the next hour, they sat together, Addison's laptop balanced on her right thigh and Katie's left, as she told Katie about some upcoming changes she wanted to make to the overall functioning of Fairchild Rentals. Katie listened to Addison's ideas, was drawn to her voice and the unexpected excitement in it. She wasn't sure if it was because Addison didn't feel well and her defenses were down or if it was the super-casual location, but for the first time since she'd started working for her the previous week, Katie saw what she felt was a little slice of "below the surface" Addison. The actual human part. It was nice. In addition, her cell rang several times, and Katie was shocked when she made a half-hearted swipe for it and Addison let her have it. Katie spoke to people, told them Addison was unavailable, and took messages. She piled the notes on her right side and laughed when Addison reached over her to try and grab them.

"No way. I've met you. You'll decide every one of them is urgent."

"Maybe they all are," Addison said, her voice uncharacteristically childlike.

"They're not. I promise."

Again, Addison surprised her by letting her win.

It was weirdly unexpected.

Addison started to slow down, Katie noticed, around four. Her voice got softer, her descriptions less enthusiastic, and Katie caught her wincing subtly as she rubbed her stomach.

"Are you okay?" Katie asked gently. "Maybe we should call it a day."

Addison tipped her head to one side, then the other, stretching her neck muscles. "I'm fine. I still need to answer email." She pulled off her glasses and pinched the bridge of her nose, then scratched her neck.

"Stop that," Katie said softly as she surprised them both by closing her own hand over Addison's and then pulling it away from the angry red marks she was leaving. "Nervous habit of yours." Katie took the laptop, slid it fully onto her own lap, and opened up Addison's email window. "Let's go through them, one at a time. You lay your head back and close your eyes and just recite to me what you want to reply. I'll type it and send it while you give your eyes and head a rest. Okay?"

There was a brief moment of hesitation and Katie did her best to leave it alone, not to poke at it, not try to convince her. She knew that, as simple as her suggestion was, it still involved Addison giving up some control, which Katie was learning was very difficult for her. So she waited, let Addison roll it around in her head. When she finally sighed, Katie gave herself a mental point.

"Okay."

"Excellent." Katie hit some keys. "All right. The first one is from Ed Hayes."

"He's my head of maintenance."

"He says he's got a lot of applicants for the opening Kyle left?"

Katie turned to Addison, whose head was back against the pillows, eyes closed, and watched as she nodded.

"Good. Tell him to set up interviews for next week and keep me posted on possible good fits."

Katie typed quickly, efficiently, and sent the email off. "Okay, next…"

They worked like this for the next ninety minutes, Katie a bit surprised by the amount of email Addison had received just in the short few hours they'd been at her loft. No wonder she always acted like she couldn't keep up. Maybe she actually couldn't.

Katie finished typing a response and turned to Addison. "Next is…" She let her voice trail off as she realized Addison had fallen asleep, her full lips slightly parted, her hands relaxed in her lap. Katie smiled, took some time and studied her face…the creamy complexion that was less gray by the day, the expertly applied makeup that made it look almost like she wasn't wearing any, the wisps of reddish-brown hair that curled in front of her ear. Addison really was a stunningly beautiful woman, and for a moment, Katie was awed by the idea of seeing her fully healthy. Soon, she hoped. For a moment, she thought it would be nice to just stay there, to sit and look at her for a while. Which was silly. Of course. With a smile, Katie quietly closed the laptop and carefully slid off the bed, not wanting to wake her. Being as silent as possible, she bent to gather her things together from the floor at the foot of the bed where she'd left them, aside from her jacket, and stood.

And stood.

And stood.

This was like looking at a different person. A person who was relaxed and unburdened. Addison looked peaceful, the corners of her mouth raised ever so slightly, making her appear softer and happier than Katie had seen before. And there was one other thing that Katie didn't really want to think about but couldn't seem to help.

Addison looked gorgeous. Strikingly so.

Katie swallowed hard as an almost irresistible urge to walk over to the side of the bed and brush some of Addison's hair off her forehead coursed hotly through her veins. Like liquid fire. She literally held herself in place, forced herself not to move until that urge passed. Then she blew out a long, slow breath and left the room, quickly and quietly and trying her best not to dwell on anything that had just occurred to her.

It wasn't until she was outside that she realized they'd driven Addison's car to the loft and that her own was still parked at the offices of Fairchild Rentals.

"Damn," she said quietly, standing on the street in front of Addison's building. She thought about calling Samantha but knew that could take a while. She didn't want to spend the money, but there was an Uber three minutes away, so she punched in her information and waited. The whole thing took less than ten minutes from pickup to drop-off, and soon Katie was in her own car, heading home.

It was later than usual, close to seven, before she arrived at the front door, and she had a quick flash of guilt for not letting her mother know she'd be late. That flash grew into a small trash fire when she walked in and saw the scene before her.

"I'm sorry, Mom," she said immediately, shedding her jacket, dropping her things inside the door, and hurrying into the kitchen where her mother was on her hands and knees, cleaning up what looked to be chili all over the floor. "What happened?"

Without looking up, Liz said, "Your father decided he doesn't like chili anymore."

"Where is he?"

"Upstairs. Will you go check on him, make sure he changed his shirt?"

"Would you rather I clean up?" Katie asked, uncertain but wanting to do what was best for her mother.

Liz stopped cleaning and looked up at her daughter. Her cheeks were blazing red and her eyes flashed with frustrated anger and unshed tears. It was an expression that showed up on her face more and more often lately, and it made Katie feel slightly nauseous while squeezing her heart at the same time. "No. I *really* need some time away from him right now."

Katie gave one nod and turned to head up the stairs, walking slowly enough to brace herself. It was something she often needed to do when about to deal with her ill father, as she rarely knew which one of his many moods she was about to get.

"Dad?" she called quietly as she pushed the door to his room open. Liz had decided to move him into his own room several months ago when it became clear that his middle-of-the-night wanderings were going to be a regular thing. That had been hard on her, Katie knew. She was sure her mother had never planned on being in a separate bedroom from her husband, but if she didn't now, she'd never get any sleep.

David Cooper was propped up on his bed, the TV remote in his hand, his gaze glued to a hockey game—a sport he'd never watched in his life but that now seemed to engross him. He'd taken to shaving his head years ago when it became clear he was destined to be one of those men with a donut of hair circling his skull. And Katie'd had to admit she liked the look on him, especially when he'd grown in a goatee. He'd looked younger somehow and extremely handsome. Sophisticated. Now his head was covered with stubble, as he wasn't always in the mood to let his wife shave his head, and she wasn't about to let him have free rein with a razor. His goatee was still there, but the rest of his beard was growing in around it, some dark, but most of it shockingly gray. Katie had never seen him look so old and small. His white T-shirt was stained with chili, and if she hadn't already known that, she might have panicked that he'd hurt himself—or somebody else.

Entering the room slowly and crossing to him, she said, "Hey there. How are you?" She sat gently on the edge of the bed.

He turned his gaze to her for a brief moment, and the few beats it took for him to register who she was tugged at her heart like it always did. While she'd initially done her best to prepare herself for not being recognized by her own father, Katie hadn't been at all ready when it had happened the first time; she'd spent hours afterward sobbing like a child. Now she cleared her throat and did her best to shake it off.

"Hey, how about we get you a clean shirt? This one's kind of messy. You didn't get burned, did you?"

He looked down at himself as if noticing for the first time that he was covered with food.

Katie went to the dresser and pulled out a clean white T-shirt. "Do you need me to help you take that off?"

David shook his head, sat forward, and pulled the dirty shirt over his head, leaving remnants of chili clinging to his stubbled chin.

Katie sighed quietly. "Okay, let me go grab a towel. I'll be right back." When she returned, she wiped the chili off her father's face while he kept his eyes glued to the television, barely acknowledging her presence. She helped him on with the clean shirt. "There. Better?"

CHAPTER SEVEN

Addison was in her office Wednesday morning by seven. A good ninety minutes before Janie was due at her desk and well before any other employee...except for Ed, her head of maintenance, who'd texted her at 6:15 that he'd be over before 9:00. Getting in that early was no easy feat that day, given that she felt like she'd been run over by a steamroller the night before. Katie had left her sleeping, and Addison was annoyed about that. There was so much to be done and she hadn't woken up until after ten, her bedroom dark, her neck stiff from the sitting position she'd been in.

The fact that her body had obviously needed the rest was deemed unimportant in her mind. Much less important than the fact that she'd lost several hours in which she could have gotten things done. She was also irritated when she went to listen to her voice mail and realized she had a dozen messages from yesterday afternoon. How had she missed them? She squinted into her quiet office and remembered that Katie'd taken her cell phone the previous afternoon. She must have turned it off when Addison wasn't paying attention.

Damn it. How did I not notice that?

Without her permission, her brain replayed bits and pieces of yesterday, of working together on Addison's bed, of Katie's warm and soothing voice reading emails to her and herself, eyes closed as she relaxed against the headboard, dictating responses. It felt like they'd gotten so much done; they made a good team. So how was there still so much to do today? Pursed lips, face wrinkled into a mask of annoyance, she grabbed a piece of paper and jotted a bunch of things down. Then she listened to every message, took down notes, and then began the arduous task of returning the calls that needed returning, sending emails to those people who didn't need an actual call, and then it was on to the sixty-seven emails in her inbox.

Addison was submerged, as if underwater. When the knock on her doorjamb came, she was startled to see it was minutes before nine. She'd killed nearly two hours without taking a breath.

She did so now, squeezed her eyes shut, then pulled off her glasses so she could focus on Ed Hayes standing uncertainly in her doorway. She gestured him in.

"How're you feeling?" he asked, as he settled his Santa Claus–like bulk into the chair in front of her desk. "Heard you were under the weather." Ed was a nice guy. A hard worker, a good boss to his maintenance crew, somebody who listened to what Addison wanted of him and got it done, whether or not he agreed with her decisions. His head was buzzed, leaving only a white fuzz, and his blue eyes were soft and kind. All his bulk was in his stomach, and she'd often wondered if it was simply a genetic trait he'd been forced to grapple with. Despite the extra weight and despite being in his sixties, he was strong and capable—Addison had seen him lift enormously heavy things without so much as a grunt—and he was invaluable to her.

"Fine," she said, waving off his concern. "No big deal." She could tell by the look on his face that he wasn't buying it and she wondered if he'd been talking to her mother. It was likely, as Ed had been hired long before Addison had taken over running Fairchild Rentals.

"Well, just make sure you listen to your body, you know? Stress is nothing to fuck around with." Despite the profanity, his tone was almost fatherly. He'd known her since she was a teenager, so it wasn't unexpected.

"I will," she promised, and they were on to other things. He left her with a stack of ten applicants for the spot left when Kyle Bannon had bailed; Ed had narrowed it down and wanted her to take a look, weed out anybody else she thought might not be able to cut it. She put the pile with the rest of the seven million things she needed to do, just as her phone rang and Ed silently waved his good-byes, then left.

The rest of the morning flew by. The pains in Addison's stomach were minimal, and for that she was thankful. Which didn't mean they'd gone away. They hadn't. But she found that if she kept busy with work, she could take her mind off them for chunks at a time. Though she'd done her best to ease up on the coffee intake, she was very tired and felt like she needed the caffeine boost. It didn't help her stomach.

If she hadn't glanced up at the clock at the very same moment Katie walked in, she'd never have noticed her personal assistant was late. Katie's pace was hurried, her expression slightly frazzled as she dumped her stuff on the round table and tilted her head at Addison.

"You were supposed to be at home," she said, as if this was the most obvious fact in the world. "I rang your doorbell and pounded on the door until your neighbor peeked out and scowled at me."

Addison blinked at her, a bit surprised by the slightly irked tone of her voice. Katie yanked her charger out of her bag, the white cord dangling like spaghetti as she bent to plug it in, then attached it to her phone. "I forgot to plug my phone in last night and it died at my last job. I couldn't find my charger, which was right in my bag the whole time, so I couldn't call you..." Her voice trailed off as she shook her head. Then, as if suddenly remembering she was talking to somebody she worked for, she stopped. Addison heard the audible swallow as Katie backpedaled. "I'm sorry. I didn't mean to sound snarky. That was out of line. I just...had a rough night and when I couldn't get ahold of you, I got worried, decided to try here before going home and making any panicked phone calls from there." She pulled three tiny bowls out of her bag and crossed the room, set them on the desk. "I read up on ulcers last night and I know you haven't been eating much." She pointed at the bowls. "One has almonds and one has some cheddar cheese cubes. The amino acids in them will help with healing. The third one is blackberries, which have high levels of antioxidants to help ease your symptoms." She paused, took a breath. "I'm sorry I'm late."

Addison nodded, hid her surprise at the kindness Katie had shown. "It's fine. No problem." Aside from the worried expression on her face that made her brown eyes slightly wider than usual and that put a horizontal divot at the top of her nose between her eyebrows, Katie looked terrific today. Her pants were black, her top a design in red and black. Her hair was down, but as soon as she'd plugged in her phone, she used the ever-present elastic on her wrist to pull it up into a messy bun. Addison was learning this was a habit Katie performed when feeling stressed. It left her neck exposed.

Which isn't a bad thing. Not a bad thing at all.

And then, before she had time to brace against it, Addison found herself entertaining the memory of Katie crawling across her bed, up next to her and making herself comfortable.

The vision was exciting. Enticing. And more arousing than she cared to admit.

With a clearing of her throat and a very literal shake of her head, Addison yanked herself back to reality. No, those types of thoughts would not do. At all. Enough of that. "I have some things here for you to do." She held up a piece of paper with the notes she'd written earlier.

Katie crossed the office and took the sheet, smiled a half-grin. "College-lined notebook paper. Old school, huh?"

Addison looked up at her. "Pardon?"

Katie's smile slid off her face and she wet her lips. "Just that…you usually send me an email. The handwritten notes were unexpected."

Addison nodded but said nothing, noting by the uncertain expression on Katie's face that she, Addison, was being rude and not at all forthcoming, but feeling in the moment that it was necessary.

Katie glanced at the list and Addison could actually see her deflate just a bit. Almost in the next second, a wave of guilt washed over Addison, and before she could second-guess herself, she was reaching for her keys, holding them out. "You can take the Benz. I know you like driving it."

Katie took the keys without making eye contact.

"And, Katie?" Addison waited until she had those brown eyes on her, then softened her voice. "Thank you for the snacks."

Katie's expression eased just the tiniest touch, but that was enough for Addison. "Sure."

Addison watched surreptitiously as Katie gathered her things back up and headed out again. The fact that she yearned for her to stay reminded her that sending Katie *away* was the right decision.

Even if she was a little sad and second-guessing herself about it now.

❖

"Okay, so driving this car doesn't suck," Katie muttered as she adjusted the seat. Addison's taller frame left the driver's seat so far back,

Katie could barely reach the gas pedal. She fiddled with the buttons and knobs until her five-foot-five body was in a much more driver-friendly position. Her bag was on the passenger seat, so she opened it and pulled out her phone and her charger. Addison's Mercedes was less than a year old and had a thousand more bells and whistles than Katie's old jalopy—including a USB for her phone charger.

The fall was slowly turning toward winter, the chill in the air much more noticeable of late. Katie started the car and let it run, taking special pleasure in the heated seats and heated steering wheel. She glanced at the list Addison had given her, disappointed that all her help yesterday had apparently meant nothing because she was back to doing mundane things and running silly errands. While she didn't want to complain, as it was a very easy job for the money, she wondered, not for the first time, why Fairchild Enterprises would hire Addison a personal assistant if she wasn't going to use it. Katie was smart. She was good with people and very organized. Addison was barely scratching the surface of the help Katie could offer her. What was apparent was that she didn't care. She didn't want the help. Which seemed woefully unfortunate to Katie, as Addison so obviously needed it. The woman was underwater.

That was too bad because, if Katie was being honest, Addison didn't seem to be healing as quickly as she could be if she'd share the burden. Oh, yes, she was always dressed nicely, professionally. Her hair was shiny. Bouncy. She smelled good. She smelled *really* good, actually, like lavender tinted with vanilla…the same scent Katie could sense in the car at that moment. But the slight shadow under her eyes hadn't lightened at all. Her energy was low and she looked like if she put her head down on her desk, she'd be asleep in seconds.

Katie sighed, willed herself to stop worrying about a woman who didn't care if Katie worried about her. She glanced at the list, was amused by the loopy, unexpectedly flowery quality to Addison's handwriting.

> *Pick up dry cleaning.*
> *Coffee and extras for break room. (We have an account.*
> *   Charge to that.)*
> *Drop off manila envelope to Ed Hayes at F.E.*

They were easy, mindless, unimportant tasks and Katie allowed herself another two minutes to be annoyed about them before shifting the car into gear and heading toward the dry cleaner, the first of her stops.

Not quite ninety minutes later, Katie slid the Benz into a parking spot in front of Fairchild Enterprises. When she'd come here to be interviewed by Jack Saunders, she'd been instantly intimidated not only by the size of the building, but by the class and elegance within. Katie wasn't a person who was ashamed of her own middle-class upbringing—far from it. But it was rare that she was surrounded by such…refined grandeur. The lobby was immense, with high ceilings and ornate light fixtures dangling from so far above her head, Katie wondered how they were cleaned. Which they obviously were, because they sparkled and shone beautifully, dust-free. The receptionist's desk was a giant horseshoe, a brass rail around the entire counter, wood underneath in a rich, dark hue. Waiting areas were set up on either side of the double front doors, the furniture leather and soft-looking, something you'd expect in a high-end living room rather than for visitors to a commercial real estate firm. The marble floors were burnished to an almost unrealistic shine and Katie's heels clicked as she approached the front desk to announce herself.

She didn't have to wait long before she was surprised by the appearance of Samantha.

"Hey, you," Sam said warmly and wrapped Katie in a hug.

"I didn't expect to see you," Katie said as she followed Sam down a hall and into the inner workings of F.E.

"I overheard the intercom when you were announced, so I said I'd come get you. I wasn't sure which office's intercom I heard, though. You here to see Jack?"

"Nope. Not today. Dropping some info off to Ed Hayes?"

"Oh, sure. I'll take you to his office." Sam's desk was to the right at the end of the hallway, but they turned left instead. "How's it going?"

Katie tipped her head from one side to the other and made a noncommittal sound, but before Sam could comment, they'd reached Ed's office.

"We'll revisit this later," Sam whispered, then rapped on the door.

"Come in."

With a turn of the brass knob, Sam pushed the door open. "Oh, I'm sorry. I didn't mean to interrupt. Mr. Hayes, Katie Cooper is here to see you. Ms. Fairchild sent her?"

"Oh, good. Send her in." That was not Ed's voice. Rather, it was the voice of a woman. One Katie recognized.

Sam stepped aside, squeezed Katie's arm, and said, "Catch you later." Then she disappeared back the way they'd come.

"Katie, come in." Meredith Fairchild waved Katie in, stood and grabbed a second chair. She was dressed beautifully, as always. Katie was used to seeing her photo in a lot of places around town. For Sale signs, newspaper ads, television commercials. But none of them did her justice. She was a strikingly beautiful woman, even in her sixties. Her blond hair had to be from a bottle, but it was gorgeous. Lustrous and shiny and nothing about it looked artificial. It fell in waves to her shoulders, resting gently on the navy-blue blazer she wore. It matched her skirt, the white shell underneath looking more elegant than simple. She wore understated yet expensive jewelry and just enough makeup to accent her natural beauty. It was obvious to Katie where Addison's good looks had come from. "Sit. Sit." Meredith gestured to the chair she'd moved. "Do you know Ed?"

"I don't believe we've met," Katie replied, reaching across his desk to shake a meaty hand. Ed Hayes had kind eyes. It was the first thing Katie noticed. She took a seat.

"So," Meredith said as she sat back in her chair and crossed her legs. "How are things going?"

"Good. Fine." Katie suddenly felt oddly nervous, so she reached into her bag and pulled out the manila envelope. Handing it across the desk to Ed, she explained, "This is from Ms. Fairchild."

Ed nodded, took the envelope. "Probably applicants," he said, looking at Meredith when he did so.

"For Kyle's job?"

Ed grunted.

"She did the right thing calling him and the girl in. One of them had to go." Meredith shifted, crossed her legs the other way. "She didn't really have a choice, given this political climate."

"Yeah, I know," Ed said, but his expression said otherwise.

"So," Meredith said and turned her attention back to Katie, who now understood that "so" was her opener to uncomfortable questions. "How is Addison feeling?"

"Oh, um…" Katie shrugged. "I didn't see her for very long today. Just popped into the office, she gave me a list of things to do and sent me on my way."

"She's in the office?" Meredith's body stiffened slightly, and that was the only giveaway that she was surprised.

Shit. Katie suddenly felt like she'd tattled. "Yes?" she answered with uncertainty.

Meredith's face hardened. "I specifically told her to stay home this week. *All* week. My God, that girl has the hardest head on the planet." She ran her tongue between her lips and teeth while she thought. Turning back to Katie, she asked, "What does she have you doing today?"

Shit, shit, shit. Yeah, this was definitely approaching tattletale territory, and Katie had no way out of it. Addison didn't sign her paycheck, but Katie still felt a weird loyalty to her. That being said, she really didn't have an option other than to tell Meredith what she wanted to know. Stifling a sigh, she pulled out the list and handed it over.

As Meredith scanned it, her lips tightened into a straight, bloodless line. "She has you picking up dry cleaning and going shopping?"

"Yes, ma'am." Katie felt awful. She couldn't explain it. She didn't owe Addison anything. The woman certainly hadn't been warm and inviting. *Well. That's not entirely true. She was completely different yesterday at her loft.* Katie gave her head a mental shake.

"Goddamn it." Meredith said it softly, but her ire was glaringly apparent as she looked up at Ed. "Why? Why does that girl insist on overdoing *everything*?"

Ed's ruddy face softened, and Katie got the impression he and Meredith had known each other a long time. "She's always done that, Mere. You know that. She's not acting any different than she ever has. What *is* different is that you can't take it anymore." He winked at her, which seemed to take any sting out of his words.

"Because she's going to work herself into an early grave." This time, Meredith's anger was replaced by parental anguish.

"Let's not get carried away," Ed said, and Katie felt like she shouldn't be there, like she shouldn't be privy to this conversation, like she was intruding. "Addison's a smart girl."

"Well, you'd never know it from the past couple of months," Meredith scoffed, but her body language relaxed. She turned to Katie and handed the list back. "Don't tell her we talked. And tomorrow? You go to her loft. She will have real work for you to do. Understood?"

"Yes, ma'am." Katie stood to go, but Meredith stopped her with a hand on her arm from her sitting position.

"I'm sorry. I don't mean for you to be in the middle. It's terribly unprofessional."

Katie nodded.

"Alas, that's the nature of a family business." She gave Katie's arm a squeeze and released her. "Thank you."

Katie could not get out of there fast enough, and once back in Addison's car, she let out a breath that made it sound like she'd been holding it for several minutes. Maybe this job was more trouble than it was worth. The last thing she wanted was to get caught up in some twisted family drama, some mother and daughter battle. She could find another part-time job easily. No big deal. She vowed to call Sam later that evening and see what she thought. Maybe Katie was overreacting. Maybe she'd just never seen this kind of family dynamic and that's why she felt so weirdly uncomfortable.

She shifted the car into gear. Whatever it was, she needed it to stop. Or she had to make it stop.

Katie was still thinking about possible other part-time jobs, which would inevitably mean less money, but also—hopefully—less awkwardness, when she got home that evening. Her father was in his La-Z-boy, apparently napping, while Judge Judy rolled her eyes at either a plaintiff or a defendant in her courtroom. Maybe both. Her mother was at the kitchen table, papers spread about, one hand in her hair. By the way some of it was sticking up on its own, Katie guessed she'd had her hand there a lot.

"Hey, Mom."

Liz looked up, startled for a split second before smiling at her. "Hey, sweetie. How was work?" She looked a little bit like a cartoon character as she extended her arms and quickly scraped all the papers into a messy pile in front of her, then shoved them into a folder as Katie came in and sat down.

"Eh. It was okay. How was Dad today?"

"It was a pretty good day," Liz told her. "Why eh?"

Katie shrugged. "Oh, no big deal. Just the usual."

"Running errands again?"

"Yep. I am the errand girl, apparently." She dropped her chin into her hand.

"You've never been good at coasting by. You like to be challenged. I learned that about you when you were in fourth grade."

"Really?" Katie smiled, knowing it was true. "Well, the pay is ridiculously good, so…"

Liz's expression grew serious as she closed her hand over Katie's forearm. "Honey. You do *not* have to stay in that job for the money."

"I want to help, Mom. That's why I moved back in."

"You moved back in to help me care for your father, not to pay our bills."

God, she was stubborn. And Katie knew if her dad was aware of the conversation, he'd feel the same way. They'd never had a lot of money, but Katie had never gone without as a kid. That being said, she knew she'd never win this argument, so she simply nodded. "Okay. Okay."

"Thank you." Her mother sat back, looking relieved. "There's some chicken in the fridge if you want. Your dad was hungry early today, so we already ate."

"That sounds good." Katie got up and headed for the fridge just as the phone rang. Liz answered it and it was soon obvious that she was talking to her sister, Katie's Aunt Beth. Katie listened to her talk, then lower her voice as she glanced into the living room. Then her volume would increase, and it would happen again. As she popped her plate into the microwave, she said, "Mom. Go talk upstairs. I'll watch him."

Liz grinned at her, mouthed a thank you, and was gone.

Once Katie could hear her directly above the kitchen, she immediately opened the folder her mother had been fretting over.

Medical bills. Utility bills. Etcetera.

Unsurprised, Katie shuffled through them, trying to make sense of the line items on the medical bills, of what was covered by insurance and what wasn't. Finally, when her brain hurt enough, she simply focused on any line that said, "currently due." Slipping three of them out of the pile, she stuck them in her bag to pay from her own checking account tomorrow. Her mother would have a conniption, but that was a risk Katie was willing to take, she decided, because her parents needed her help. Whether her mother would admit it or not, it was a fact. *If I have to steal bills to pay them, so be it,* she thought as she looked at her father. When he was sleeping like this, it was as if he was back to normal. It could be any regular day two or three years ago, him napping in his chair after dinner like he always did. There was no illness, no angry outbursts, no sudden sobbing, no lack of recognition. He was just her dad.

Eyes welled with unshed tears, Katie pulled herself together and made a decision.

She'd tough it out with the weird Fairchild family dynamics as long as she had to.

CHAPTER EIGHT

Katrina Fairchild had fallen in love with her big sister's loft the first time she'd set foot in it. It was trendy without being obnoxious, roomy without feeling like a warehouse, and surprisingly warm and inviting for such a wide-open space. You'd expect it to be cold with its high ceilings that were a maze of pipes and cylinders, all painted black, combined with the hardwood floors and enormous windows. But it wasn't. It was comfortable and almost cozy.

She finished brewing two cups of tea and carried them in to the living room where Addison was sitting on the couch. Her feet were on the coffee table, crossed at the ankle, and her laptop was perched on her thighs. Three folders were strewn nearby, one open with papers spilling out. Katrina set one cup of tea down on the table near the overstuffed chair and the other on the end table next to her sister's left arm.

"Where's the lap desk I gave you for Christmas last year?" she asked.

"Bedroom," Addison answered without looking up. Her cell rang and she scooped it up, barked a hello.

In the bedroom, the blinds were closed, and the bed was a rumpled mess. Katrina squinted at it, shook her head, and made the bed. Addison was a fairly neat person, and one of the things her siblings had always teased her about was the fact that she made her bed every morning without fail. Seeing it unmade in the middle of the day was slightly unnerving and a good sign that her sister was not herself. Bed made, Katrina opened the blinds to let in the daylight, scanned the room until she found the black lap desk with the hard top and bean bag bottom, and took it out to the living room.

"You're gonna kill your neck," she muttered while Addison talked on the phone. Lifting the laptop off her sister's thighs, she slid the lap desk underneath and adjusted it. Addison looked up at her, gratitude in her eyes, and gave a half-smile, already looking more comfortable.

Katrina took a seat in the overstuffed chair, which sat at an angle in the room so one corner of the coffee table pointed at it. She picked up her tea and sat back, relaxing while waiting for Addison to get off the phone.

She was worried about her big sister. She had been for a while now, just like her mom. Addison looked tired all the time. Her patience was near zero with everybody—employees, clients, and friends and family alike. She worked like a fiend and barely seemed to have time for anything or anybody that wasn't directly associated with her job. And now, with her ulcer and a couple of scares, she really needed to take a step back.

Which was something she'd never done in her entire life, Katrina knew, because she was pretty sure Addison had no idea how.

Ending the call, Addison tossed the phone onto the couch next to her.

"Drink your tea before it gets cold," Katrina told her, then sipped her own. "How are you feeling?"

"I'd feel better if people stopped asking me how I feel." Addison's eyes never left her computer screen.

"Quit being a bitch. People care about you. Though who knows why lately."

That got Addison's attention. Her gaze snapped up, met Katrina's, held. Addison broke first, blew out a breath. "You're right. I'm sorry. I'm feeling okay. I'd rather be in the office, but—"

"Mom insisted on you staying home?"

"Yes! What am I, twelve? And the personal assistant? Really?"

Katrina shrugged without mentioning that she thought the personal assistant had been a fabulous idea and took another sip of tea. Addison followed suit. "She's worried about you, Addie. We all are."

"Did she send you to check up on me?"

Katrina tilted her head to the right and just looked at her sister.

"Yeah, I just heard it. Sorry again."

"I don't know what's going on with you lately, but I wish you'd just take a breath. Lighten up a little bit. Work isn't the be-all and end-all, you know."

"Not for you," Addison muttered, but before Katrina could respond, Addison's phone rang and there was a knock on the door. Addison answered the phone, met Katrina's eyes, and jerked her head toward the door, eyebrows raised.

"Of course, Your Highness," Katrina said under her breath as she crossed the living room, shaking her head.

The woman on the other side of the door was, Katrina noted without even thinking about it, the polar opposite of Addison lately. She was smiling, open. Her stature was average—she couldn't be more than five foot five—but the energy she exuded was palpable. Katrina had heard about people like that, people whose energy and kindness were apparent from the second you met them, but she couldn't really think of one she knew. The woman's hair was dark, a little past her shoulders, her eyes brown and slightly almond-shaped. She wore black dress pants, a simple mint green sweater under a black pea coat that was too big for her, and minimal makeup.

"Oh, hi," she said, her smile faltering slightly. "I'm here for Addis—er—Ms. Fairchild?"

Katrina grinned. "Please. Call her Addison. Ms. Fairchild is our mom." She held out a hand. "Katrina Fairchild. Little sister."

"Katie Cooper. Personal assistant." They shook.

"Oh, right. Got it. Come on in." Katrina stepped aside and made room. Katie Cooper entered, shed her coat, and hung it on the coat tree. Then she took her briefcase and crossed the room to where Addison was just finishing up her phone call.

"Hi," Katie said.

Addison responded in what was little more than a grunt.

Katrina gave her a look that Addison pretended to ignore, then sat back down in her chair to finish her tea. "So, Katie, what do you think of working with my sister? Has she driven you to drink yet?"

"Ha ha," Addison said, typing.

"Not to excess," Katie replied. "Yet."

"So, like, a shot a night?"

"I'm up to three, actually."

Katrina laughed, and Katie chuckled quietly, not looking at

Addison. *Interesting.* Addison looked completely unamused by both of them.

Katrina stood, took her cup into the kitchen, and left it in the sink. As she walked back toward the living room, she slowed her steps, stopped and watched the two women on the couch, their backs to her. They were quiet, each typing away on her laptop, but there was an added element of a chill in the air coming from her sister; nobody could pick that up better than Addison's little sister, having been on the receiving end of it her entire life.

What's that about?

She stood for a few seconds more, but no words were spoken and Katrina needed to get back to work. With a clearing of her throat, she walked back into the room and grabbed her coat from the back of the overstuffed chair.

"All right. I need to get back to my office. Budget meeting at one." She put on her coat. "Addie, please take it easy. Okay?"

Addison barely acknowledged her.

Katrina slipped into the high-pitched, snarky voice she always used when doing an impression of Addison. "I will, Katrina. Thanks so much for coming by to check on me. It means so much to me. I'd get up and hug you, but I'm super busy here because I'm ultra-important."

A snort of a laugh burst from Katie, whose expression went immediately to *did I make that sound out loud?* Her dark eyes widened, and she rolled her lips in and bit down on them. That face alone made Katrina laugh.

"You two are hilarious," Addison said, shook her head, and went back to her laptop.

"I like you, Katie Cooper." Katrina pointed at Katie. "Maybe we'll see each other again."

"Maybe we will." Katie smiled, and Katrina felt an odd sense of being split. On the one hand, she loved the idea of somebody helping her sister out while she recovered. On the other hand, part of her felt bad leaving somebody as instantly likable as Katie with somebody who'd become as miserable as Addison.

Interesting, she thought again.

With a wave, she left the loft, and the strange certainty that Katie Cooper would be around for a long time, behind and headed back to the hospital.

❖

Well, that had been unexpected.

While Katrina Fairchild looked very much like Addison—physically, it wasn't hard to tell they were sisters—she was also remarkably different. First and foremost, Katie had found her friendly, something that seemed to come and go sporadically with Addison, and instantly likable. Second, she was much more relaxed than her big sister, something that was surprising given the fact that she oversaw the running of a very large research hospital.

"She seems really nice," Katie commented a few minutes after the door closed behind Katrina.

"Unlike me." Addison's voice was hard, her eyes fixed on her laptop.

Katie blinked at her in surprise. "I didn't say that."

"You didn't have to." Addison turned to look at her then, and Katie was taken aback by her eyes, by the very strange combination of flashes of anger and glimpses of sadness. "Did you have fun tattling on me to my mommy?"

Katie's eyes went wide. "I'm sorry?"

"I know you saw her yesterday. Was it necessary to give her a health report on me? Did you tell her I shouldn't be in the office?"

"I told her no such thing." Katie took a beat, swallowed, went on. "I can tell you this, though: Your mother is very worried about you. I didn't have to say anything to her to pick up on that."

Addison shifted her body slightly so she was facing Katie more directly. "She called me last night and she wasn't happy. She said I needed to stay home and recuperate. She said I wasn't letting you help. She said I was treating you like a gopher."

Katie's heart rate had kicked up and her stomach churned with nervous tension. She did not like confrontation, but she wasn't about to sit there and be accused of something she didn't do. "Look. All I did yesterday was follow your list. Your mother was in Ed Hayes's office when I got there, and she asked me what you had me doing that day."

"And you just had to tell her."

Her calmness being slowly eclipsed by her simmering anger, Katie's jaw tightened. "What should I have done?"

"Something else."

"Like?"

"Hey, if you're not smart enough to come up with something creative on your own..." Addison shrugged and went back to typing.

That was it.

"Excuse me?" Katie said, eyes still wide, but this time it was only anger. Anger at being insulted. Anger at this woman's audacity and at her condescending attitude. At her lack of enough respect to even offer up eye contact as she was slicing at Katie.

"You heard me."

Katie closed her laptop with a loud snap that got Addison's attention. Speaking through clenched teeth, she unloaded. "Let's get a few things straight here, *Ms. Fairchild.* Number one: I don't work for you. I work for your mother. So if you have an issue with how I do my job or how I answer questions posed by my boss, I suggest you take them up with her. Second, you don't know a goddamn thing about me—not that you've ever asked—so don't you dare presume that I'm not smart enough to go head-to-head with you. Just because I didn't have a company handed to me right out of college, that doesn't make you better, smarter, or more successful than me. And third..." She paused, the wind in her sails suddenly being shoved out of the way by emotion, as thoughts of her father with chili spilled all over his shirt and her mother with her hands in her hair trying to figure out how to take care of the bills assaulted her unexpectedly. "I need this job. And I'd be excellent at it if you'd just give me a chance. I need this job for the money and I need this job for my head so I can..." She cleared her throat, her face heating up with embarrassment. "So I can have five hours in my day when I don't have to think about how sick my father is or how exhausted my mother is or how nothing will ever be the same in my family again." Frustrated by the unshed tears in her eyes, Katie reached down deep, found the anger again, and hauled it to the surface. She looked directly into the startled eyes of Addison Fairchild and repeated quietly, "You don't know a *goddamn thing* about me, so I'd appreciate it if you'd keep your judgments to yourself. All right?"

Katie had the sudden, glaringly loud certainty that Addison didn't have people stand up to her very often. The expression on her face was priceless, an amalgamation of shock, shame, confusion. Overall, she just looked a bit...sheepish. Surprisingly, there didn't seem to be even a hint of anger, which confused Katie because she was pretty sure she was fired. Which would suck, but you know what? She didn't have to take this crap. From anybody.

Letting out a slow, quiet breath, she hefted her laptop and stood to gather her things.

"Where are you going?" Addison's question seemed genuine, her eyes surprised.

Katie blinked at her. They stayed like that for a long beat, Katie standing, looking down at Addison in surprise. Addison looking up at her from the couch, eyebrows raised expectantly.

"Um…I'm leaving?"

"Why?"

Katie felt the divot form between her eyebrows, like it always did when she was confused. "Because I'm…fired?"

"No."

"No?"

"No." Addison swallowed audibly and glanced down at her hands. "You were totally right. I was out of line. By, like, a lot. I'm very sorry." When Katie didn't sit back down, simply remained standing and blinking, Addison went on. "Please. Sit. I could use some help."

"Well." Katie's eyes darted around the room as she searched for some purchase, now that things had veered in an unexpected direction. "So much for my big, dramatic exit where I stomp out and slam the door behind me." She sat back down to a quiet chuckle from Addison. It was a sound she'd never heard before, and Katie liked it immediately. It was light. Higher-pitched than she'd expect. "All right. Should we start with email?"

And just like that, the heated conversation faded away. They worked steadily for the next hour, Addison answering phone call after phone call, putting out fires, listening to the issues of her employees, her tone not always brusque but rarely approaching friendly. Katie responded to Addison's emails, having gone through each one in the inbox. She clicked Send on the last one and glanced at Addison just in time to see her end a call, then grimace, a hand across her stomach.

"When was the last time you ate?" Katie asked gently, and touched Addison's arm.

"I don't know. Last night? I haven't been very hungry."

"I know. It's one of the symptoms of an ulcer, but you have to eat."

Katie set her laptop aside. "I'll be right back." In the ridiculous gourmet kitchen, Katie opened the fridge and was relieved to find a dozen eggs and some skim milk, along with two small yogurts, some mustard, a jar of pickles, and a bottle of Sauvignon Blanc that hadn't been opened yet.

Back in the living room, she looked down at Addison.

"What?" Addison asked, but her voice didn't carry its usual tone of impatience.

Katie took Addison's laptop and closed it. Setting it on the coffee table, she pointed to Addison's feet. "Take your shoes off. You're working from home, for God's sake, why are you wearing heels?" She kept her tone playful, and it worked. Addison's mouth turned up slightly at the corners and she kicked off her shoes. "Good." She turned to the enormous windows, where it was definitely looking like the end of fall. "Just sit here and look at how gorgeous it is outside. The colors of the leaves that are left, the crazy blue of the sky. No laptop. No phone." She reached down and snagged Addison's phone, slid it into her back pocket. "Just for a few minutes. Okay?" She waited for Addison's reluctant nod. "I'll be right back."

Fifteen minutes later, she carried a plate of scrambled eggs out to the living room and handed it to Addison, whose eyes widened.

"Wow. These look great."

Katie grinned. "They're just eggs. Eat them, please." She sat down on the overstuffed chair.

"Are you going to watch me eat them?"

"Yes, I am." Katie nodded, perched an elbow on the arm of the chair and her cheek against her fist.

Addison cocked her head slightly, as if she was going to argue, but decided against it. Instead, she picked up her fork and began to eat.

"So," Katie said, as Addison chewed, "I got an email from your mom that said to remind you about charity. No details. Care to fill me in?"

Addison groaned, gave an exaggerated eye roll. "Fairchild Enterprises is very big on giving to charity, as you know."

Katie nodded.

"My mom says that writing a check is nice, but making an appearance is better."

"Oh…so, like, it's great for Fairchild Enterprises to donate money, but it's even better if there is a visible member of the Fairchild family donating his or her time."

"Exactly." Addison scooped another forkful of eggs into her mouth and Katie did her best to hide her happiness, especially given that Addison "wasn't hungry."

"And do you have specific organizations you donate to?"

Addison searched the space above her. "We do, but Mom always lets me and my siblings choose an additional one if we want to."

"Do you have a favorite?"

With a shrug, Addison said, "Not really. I haven't really thought about it."

"Would you mind if I came up with some ideas?"

"Are you kidding? I'd love it. One less thing for me to worry about."

Katie feigned a gasp and sat forward.

"What?" Addison asked, confused worry on her face.

"I think you actually, *finally* just used your personal assistant. To personally assist you. There may be hope for you yet."

Their gazes held for a beat before a grin tugged up one corner of Addison's lips. "Ha ha. You're very funny."

But she did think it was funny. Katie could see that, not only by the half-smile but by the softening of Addison's gorgeous blue eyes.

Addison finished her eggs, and before she could set the plate down, Katie was up and holding out her hand for it.

"All right. Next, I want you to turn sideways and put your feet up on the couch."

"Katie. I have work to do." Interestingly, while protesting, Addison turned sideways and put her feet up on the couch.

"Yes, yes, I know. You're super important and can't take any time off, even if your stomach has a hole in it. I hear you. But guess what you have?"

Addison looked up at her then, a sparkle in her eyes. "A personal assistant?"

"Ding, ding, ding!"

"Again, very funny."

"Thank you, thank you. I'll be here all week. Tip your waitress. Now stay just like that. I'll be right back and we'll get to work."

By the time six o'clock rolled around, Katie and Addison had gotten a ton done. Two meetings set up for the following week, which Katie would be attending with Addison; nearly thirty emails responded to, twenty more sent; sixteen phone calls made. They'd gone through and organized Addison's calendar for the month—Addison's eyebrows had risen in surprise when Katie bluntly pointed out, "Wow, you really do need me. Your calendar is a *mess*. Double-book yourself much?"—and each of them now had a copy. The best part, as far as Katie was concerned? Addison was still reclined on the couch. Even better, she appeared more comfortable and relaxed than Katie had ever seen her.

With a glance at her watch, Addison turned to look at Katie, who was still on the overstuffed chair, but with her stocking feet crossed at the ankle on the coffee table and her laptop perched on her thighs. "You should get home. We got a lot done today."

"We did. See what happens when you let me do my job?"

"I do see."

Their gazes held and Katie realized that was, like, the third or fourth time. She liked this version of Addison. Very much, if she was being honest. But she also knew not to get attached because chances were, Crabby Addison would be back tomorrow.

As Katie gathered her things and slipped her shoes back on, Addison surprised her. "Hey, since we're working here all week, why don't you dress comfortably tomorrow? Nobody is going to see us." Addison wiggled her stocking feet to punctuate her point, then she shrugged as if to emphasize how nonchalant she was being, and Katie smiled at the obvious effort.

"That sounds great. But if I show up in sweats and you're wearing heels, we are going to have words. You get me?"

Addison chuckled that lovely chuckle. "Yes, ma'am."

"Good."

"Hey, Katie?"

"Mm-hmm?"

"Thanks for making me eat."

Katie stopped her gathering and looked at Addison. "You're welcome," she said softly. "Thanks for eating."

"I'll see you tomorrow."

"You will."

Once downstairs and in her car, Katie sat back in her seat and just absorbed the afternoon. It had been unexpected and weird and awesome—none of which had been on her plan for the day.

"Never a dull moment with that one," she said into the empty interior. She had one more day of this. Another day of being home rather than in the office. *I wonder how that'll go.* Shifting the car into Drive, she muttered, "I guess we'll find out."

CHAPTER NINE

"You're not in your pretty clothes today." Noah's observation was astute for a four-year-old, and Katie smiled down at him as they waited for the bus on Friday.

"You're right," she replied.

"Why?"

"Because I don't have to today."

"Cuz jeans are more cum-ter-bul?"

"That's exactly why." She touched his blond head as the bus pulled up.

"Ready, Noah? Come on!" Simon gave his brother a tug and Noah went willingly, but not before turning to wave at Katie. Their "byes" came in unison, which only made her heart swell as she waited for them to take seats, then waved to the bus driver as they pulled away.

Once she'd gathered her things and was in her car, Katie's phone rang. She hit the hands-free feature when she saw it was Samantha. "Hey, Sam."

"You can't answer my texts? Are you breaking up with me?" Sam's tone was playful enough, but Katie knew her well, recognized the slight hint of hurt in her words.

"I'm so sorry, Sammy. I worked a little late the past couple of days, and my mom's been having a hell of a time with my dad."

Sam's attitude sobered instantly. "Oh, man. I'm sorry, Kate. That was insensitive. Ignore me."

"No way. You're my BFF. I will never ignore you. Deal with it."

"How's the job? Still working for Miranda Priestley?"

Katie chuckled, then said, "You know what? For the first time since I started, I'm actually looking forward to seeing her today."

"Really. Explain."

Katie detailed the past couple of days as she drove, told Sam about Addison's insult and her response to it, how they'd actually worked as a team yesterday. "Not only that, I'm in jeans and a hoodie."

"Whaaa?" Sam gasped into the phone so dramatically, it made Katie laugh.

"Right?"

While Addison didn't dress *quite* as down as Katie did (and Katie wasn't really dressed as *down* as she could've been), she was definitely more casual than Katie had ever seen her. Her jeans were washed to a very light blue, the worn—though more likely "strategically placed for fashion purposes"—hole in the right knee somehow making them seem sexy. Addison was barefoot, her toenails polished a surprisingly fun shade of blue. Her top was a much-loved—judging by the frayed cuffs—black sweatshirt with the faded Adidas logo in white. Her hair was pulled back into a ponytail, a style that was simultaneously beautiful and fun, and Katie found herself standing in the entryway of the loft, simply staring.

Addison shifted from one foot to the other, her smile unsteady as she scratched at the side of her neck. "I know. I look like a slob," she said quickly. "I just—"

"No," Katie interrupted, probably more vehemently than she should have as she held up a hand to stop her. "No, not at all. You look gorgeously comfortable." At Addison's steady gaze, she thought it better to just push forward and not dwell on—or try to correct—what she'd just said, as that would only draw more attention to it. "Which is exactly what you should be. Perks of working from home, am I right?" She forced a laugh, hoping Addison hadn't heard the gorgeous part.

"You are." Addison visibly relaxed and they got to work.

For the next five hours, they worked steadily, just as they had yesterday, and it didn't escape Katie's notice that they'd really seemed to gel, that they worked smoothly and solidly as a team. What *had* escaped her notice—and apparently, Addison's, too—was how they'd shifted their bodies. They'd begun the afternoon on opposite ends of the couch, each with a laptop, tossing suggestions back and forth, asking each other questions about various things. But now, as Katie finished up a spreadsheet she'd been detailing, she looked up and realized the two of them were still at opposite ends of the couch, but now facing each other, their feet in the center and touching. Katie's gaze was captured by the sight, her own feet in black socks, Addison's still bare, all four moving slightly as they worked, touching, rubbing against the others, as if neither woman realized it.

Addison was typing, but when her typing abruptly stopped, Katie shifted her eyes up and saw Addison's gaze riveted on their feet. Surprisingly to Katie, Addison didn't look horrified or shocked or angry or embarrassed. She looked…amused. A ghost of a smile appeared on her face when she looked up and caught Katie's gaze, held it. Something passed between them in that moment, something Katie felt right down to her center. It was both exciting and alarming, and she wasn't sure what to do with it. After a beat, she cleared her throat and spoke.

"I have an idea for the Fairchild Rentals charity donation this quarter. Want to hear it?" Did her voice have a nervous tremble to it? She wasn't sure. She cleared her throat a second time.

"Absolutely." Addison closed her laptop and focused all her attention on Katie, and what was weird was that Katie could *feel* it. In her blood. Along her skin. Everything suddenly tingled, and a hard swallow forced itself down her throat.

"How do you feel about animals?"

Addison's brow furrowed. "Is that a serious question?"

"Um…yes?"

"I love them. Really, are there people who don't?"

Katie smiled. "Only idiots. So, have you heard of Junebug Farms?"

"The animal shelter? I have. I love that place."

"I know one of the volunteers, and her girlfriend is in charge of adoption there. I'm sure she could get us in to see the right person about donating, but I also thought maybe we could donate some time. Maybe walk some of the dogs or offer to help with the horses or goats."

A tiny gasp escaped Addison's lips and she covered her mouth with her fingers as if it startled her. "They have goats there?"

Katie grinned because, seriously, a week ago? She never would have described Addison Fairchild as cute. Or adorable. But she was both right then, with her wide, hopeful eyes. "They do."

"Then we must go there."

Katie's smile got wider; she could feel it stretch across her face.

"It'll be great for you to show your face there. I'll take some photos and we'll put them up on the website."

"And I'll get to play with goats."

"And you'll get to play with goats. Yes."

"I'm in."

"Good. I'll make the call."

Again, their gazes held for a beat or two extra before Katie's focus went back to her laptop and Addison's phone began to ring. Each woman returned her attention to work.

Neither of them moved her feet.

Growing up a Fairchild, family dinners were very uncommon. After all, Meredith Fairchild was the CEO of a multimillion-dollar real estate firm that she'd built from scratch. Where was she supposed to find the time to cook and eat dinner every night with her family? Her husband had done his best to be around for her and the kids, but once the kids had reached high school, he'd decided to spend most of his time in their Florida home. After that, dinner together was as rare an occurrence as the Buffalo Bills winning the Super Bowl.

Therefore, when there was a request for family dinner like there was that Sunday, everybody did their best to show up.

Meredith didn't cook. She'd never had the desire to learn, so simply didn't. Fairchild family dinners were always held in the same place: Scartelli's. It was a small but locally famous Italian restaurant that was on its third generation of Scartellis. Meredith had grown up with Peter Scartelli, and when she was forming her company, Peter was learning the ropes in the kitchen from his father, Joe Jr., who had learned the ropes in the kitchen from *his* father, Joe Sr. Eventually, Peter had decided to move the restaurant to a bigger location, and Meredith had helped him find the perfect building. Their fifty-plus-year friendship was solid as a rock, and they met often to discuss business, politics, and family.

Whenever Meredith scheduled a family dinner, Peter closed off one of his private rooms and took care of the Fairchilds and their people like they were royalty. When Addison arrived that Sunday evening, she was the last one. Meredith was seated at the head of the table with Jack

Saunders and his wife to her right—Jack wasn't technically family, but as family dinner discussions often turned to Fairchild Enterprises business, it was handy for him to be present. Plus, the Fairchild kids had known him almost all their lives—and Ed Hayes and his wife to her left, Ed falling into the same category as Jack. Katrina and her husband, Evan, sat to Ed's left, and across the table from them was Jared Fairchild, the youngest and the only boy. Addison hadn't seen him in several weeks, so she went to him first as he caught her eye and stood with a smile.

"Addie," he said tenderly, as he wrapped her in a hug. "I feel like I haven't seen you in months." He was taller than Addison, younger, and boyishly handsome. His light reddish-brown hair was always a bit too long, swooping across his forehead just enough to be charming but not enough to make him look sloppy. The freckles that dotted his face made him look even younger than his twenty-eight years.

"Same," Addison said, as she let go and looked past at the small blonde next to him. "Hi, Laura," she said to her brother's wife, and held out her arms for a second hug.

Laura Fairchild was quiet and reserved, which meant she was also underestimated. The youngest partner in her advertising firm, her soft-spoken manner and calm demeanor often took people by surprise. Jared had been a handful as a college student, but when he'd met Laura, it was as if every bit of the reliable, strong, intelligent man he could be came screeching to the forefront. Addison had never met a couple who complemented each other the way her brother and his wife did.

Moving around the table, Addison greeted both Jack and his wife, then moved on to her mother, kissing her on the cheek. Meredith grabbed Addison's hand and squeezed it before letting her pass by so she could greet Ed and his wife.

Grabbing the chair next to her brother, Addison sat. The din of conversation went on for a few more moments as a waiter came in to take Addison's drink order. She asked for a glass of Malbec and was rewarded with one what seemed like mere seconds later. She took a sip as her mother spoke up.

"I'm so glad to see you all. It's been too long since we've had dinner together, so I'm glad everybody could make it."

Two waiters came in with large bowls of pasta and salad and a platter piled high with meatballs. Scartelli's served its food family style, in large bowls for passing along and sharing with the others at the table. A plate in the center of the table was piled high with slices of warm Italian bread, and Addison grinned when Evan reached for it first. He smiled sheepishly when he made eye contact with her.

"No worries, Evan. I am well acquainted with your love affair with bread."

"Don't tell my wife," he stage-whispered, and Katrina rolled her eyes.

"Please. I've met you," she said, and bumped against her husband.

Conversation picked up and leveled off and shifted, as it always did when they were all together, and it was always a mix of personal and business discussion.

"Jared, how are the Brits doing?" Meredith asked, twirling her spaghetti on a fork.

Jared nodded as he finished chewing, then said, "Great. All five stores are on schedule to open next week."

"Great. They'll catch the tail end of the Christmas rush," Meredith said, with a nod.

Jared ran the arm of Fairchild Enterprises that oversaw four shopping malls in two counties. "Have you seen any of the ads?"

"I saw one on a local channel yesterday," Katrina commented.

"And I heard one on the radio on my way in last week," Jack added.

"Good. Perfect." Jared went back to his salad.

"Katrina?" Meredith didn't need to elaborate. Her daughter knew what she was asking.

Katrina gave an elaborate update regarding the hospital and research center, including current construction, donations, an upcoming Christmas fund-raising gala—"You're all coming, yes?"—and some ideas she had for the upcoming new year.

Meredith gave a nod of approval. While she was not one to be overtly congratulatory, the expression on her face said she was impressed with all Katrina's accomplishments. "And yes, I do expect each of you to make an appearance at the gala," she said, pointing with her fork. Nods went around the table. "And have you taken care of the issue with that doctor and his subordinate?" Her voice hardened.

Katrina had a moment of looking a bit deer-in-the-headlights, but she recovered quickly, and Addison didn't think their mother had noticed. "Oh, yeah. All set."

Meredith Fairchild was a stickler for rules, especially rules that she'd made and especially around situations that could tarnish the sterling Fairchild Enterprises reputation. "Good. We can't have fraternizing of any kind. It's too easy to push it into the realm of sexual harassment, and given the way things are going in this country right now..." She let her voice trail off, most likely knowing she'd said this exact thing to her people a dozen times now.

"Addison? How are you feeling, sweetheart?"

"I'm fine, Mom," Addison said, then opened her mouth to give her own update. Meredith's voice stopped her.

"And how is the assistant working out? Are you letting her help?"

Addison pressed her lips together and counted to five, then spoke slowly, deliberately. "Yes, I'm letting her help. Thank you."

"And when is your next appointment with Dr. Garber?"

"Next week."

"Good. Don't miss it."

"I won't." Addison tried to keep the frustration out of her voice, and something in her mother's tone kept her from pushing, kept her from pointing out that she wasn't a child and that she actually had some progress to report as well. She stayed quiet instead. Her eyes met Katrina's, and her sister's sympathy was apparent as she sent a slight grimace across the table.

Later, as they all sipped after-dinner coffee and the talk had become individual conversations, Katrina scooted her chair around the table so she was next to Addison.

"She's just worried about you," she said quietly, making sure nobody else heard.

"I know," Addison said, on a sigh. "But I'm not twelve."

"No, you're not. But you've been running yourself ragged for months now, and she's really concerned you're going to give yourself a heart attack."

Addison cocked her head to the side and gave Katrina a look. "I'm thirty-one."

Katrina shrugged. "I'm just telling you what I know."

"I was hoping she'd talk a bit about retiring."

"Yeah, me, too. I mean, the first of the year isn't very far away."

Addison nodded. What she wanted to say was, "When is she going to decide who takes over?" But she knew that Katrina and Jared both hoped it would be them. Addison wanted it so badly she could taste it. It was the elephant in the room, and none of them wanted to point to it.

"Should you be drinking that?" Katrina asked with a glance at the coffee, her question pulling Addison back to the present.

"Probably not," Addison said, then picked up her cup and took a sip.

Not long after, they all stood and began saying their good-byes. Evan and Jack were talking football while Katrina, Laura, and Jared discussed a new client Laura had been dealing with for several months now. Addison took the opportunity to snag her mother's attention.

"Hey, Mom, I was wondering how things were looking for the first of the year." Doing her best to fix her face so her expression was unassuming, she raised her eyebrows innocently.

Meredith, of course, saw right through her, as most mothers do. The simple arching of one eyebrow was enough to say, "I know what you're asking and why you're asking it and when I'm ready to tell you, I will," without using any words.

Addison sighed, needing to let Meredith know she wasn't happy with this response.

"You haven't gotten any pushback from Kyle Bannon, have you?" Meredith asked instead, smoothly changing the subject.

"No, Mom. He's the one who chose to leave. He has no grounds for pushback."

"He knew better. You can't be sleeping with your subordinate at work."

"It wasn't harassment, though, Mom. They're a couple." Addison was surprised to hear herself defending Kyle, given how easy it had been for her to let him go. What was that about?

"I don't care. She was his subordinate. I can't stand for that kind of impropriety. I won't. Not when it's my name at stake."

As Meredith turned her attention to Jack's wife, a flash of Katie Cooper suddenly hit Addison so hard, she found herself taking a subtle step back with one foot to steady herself. Katie at the opposite end of the couch in Addison's loft. Katie, in her jeans and hoodie, hair in a messy bun, bottom lip caught between her teeth as she worked. Katie, focused on her laptop, completely unaware of Addison's eyes on her, her feet moving subtly against Addison's.

What the hell?

Addison squeezed her eyes shut, feeling not only surprised by the image but a bit battered, and she willed it away as best she could. A hand on her back pulled her attention around and she looked into the blue eyes of her sister, so much like her own.

"Hey, you okay?" Katrina asked as she handed Addison her coat.

"Yeah. Totally." She answered too quickly, could hear it in her own voice.

"You sure?"

Addison took her coat, slid an arm in. "I am. Promise." Her stomach had begun to make its dissatisfaction known about a half hour earlier, and she was anxious to get home. Good-byes were tossed around the room, and a few moments later, she was in her car and pulling away from Scartelli's.

Thank God.

But instead of feeling better once she got home, Addison found herself bombarded by frustration. She was frustrated at her mother for not making a decision about who would take her seat at the head of Fairchild Enterprises. Addison was the eldest, so it made sense it would be her. But Meredith Fairchild liked to surprise people and often did so by bucking tradition. So while it really was anybody's guess, Addison had been working her ass off for the past year. Longer, even. She'd forgone vacations, long weekends, relationships. Everything had taken a back seat to her job. Even her health was taking a beating. She told herself that once she took over for her mother, she'd take a breath. Relax the smallest bit and do more delegating—none of which would end up actually happening, of course, and she knew it. She was frustrated with her health for limiting her abilities and her energy and causing her near-constant pain.

What surprised her most, though, was her frustration with Katie. Which made no sense. What in the world did she have to be frustrated about? Katie was there to help her. That was her only purpose. And when Addison could get out of her own way long enough to actually let Katie help, it was worth it. So this odd wave of annoyance, of irritation she suddenly felt around her assistant was confusing.

"Seriously," she whispered aloud in the empty bathroom, having decided a hot shower might feel good right then. "Why in the world should I be frustrated with her?" she asked her reflection in the mirror as she pulled her hair up. Weirdly, her reflection wouldn't look her in the eye.

CHAPTER TEN

Katie was so tired.

No. Not just tired. Tired was too simple a word. Too general. Too vague. No, Katie was body-numbing, bone-deep, could barely move her limbs *exhausted*. Her eyelids were surely lined with sandpaper. The kind with the large grit. Her brain was running at less than half speed, or so it felt. Yawns cranked her mouth open at alarmingly regular intervals.

As she pulled into a parking spot at Fairchild Rentals, she squinted, racking her brain to recall if she'd changed Simon out of the sweatshirt he'd dribbled strawberry jam on before she put him on the bus. She knew she'd meant to but could find no memory in her head of actually having done it. "Damn it," she muttered, as she slid the gearshift into Park.

It had been a very bad night that had led into a very bad morning, which Katie was now expecting to turn into a very bad day. It was only logical. And it was how her luck seemed to be running lately.

Even the weather agreed, the sky a weird combination of silver, gray, and almost-black that might have looked classy as part of an outfit of some kind but was just ominous as a ceiling to her world. She had to make two attempts at hauling herself out of her car before she succeeded. Thunder rumbled through the clouds as she grabbed her computer bag and her purse, and the sky opened up just as she slammed the door closed. The drops of rain—which would most likely freeze in short order—were so big they felt like pellets falling on her head as she jogged toward the front door and let herself in with an exhalation of sheer relief.

Janie had a candle burning on her desk, and though Katie couldn't see the label, she could smell the cinnamon/apple combination and it made her stomach growl loudly. Janie looked up with a grin.

"Miss lunch?" she asked pointedly.

Katie grimaced. "Now that you mention it, I did." The truth was, her stomach had been churning sourly since last night when her father's irrational anger had gotten so out of control, he'd tipped the kitchen table over, breaking dishes and scattering food all over the floor.

"I have half a turkey sandwich left over from mine," Janie offered helpfully. "You're welcome to it."

Katie was touched, truly. "You're very sweet. Thank you, but I'm going to pass. Stomach's a little off today."

Janie gave a nod. "Let me know if you change your mind."

"I will." Katie smiled her thanks and headed in the direction of Addison's office. She felt oddly different today as she made her approach. After last week's time of dressing casually and working on the couch together, Katie felt like they'd finally settled into a comfortable rapport. Addison seemed more relaxed, like she'd let go of some of her usual...uptightness, for lack of a better word. She talked more, she listened more, and she smiled more.

This was becoming a thing, Katie finding herself actually looking forward to spending the next few hours with Addison Fairchild. A nice thing. A thing she liked. The other thing she liked? Addison was healing. She looked much less tired. She actually smiled every now and then, which made her so much more fun to look at that Katie found herself having to be careful of staring.

Katie slowed her walk when she found herself within earshot of the office. She couldn't see in, as the blinds were closed, but Addison was on the phone and Katie enjoyed the sound of her voice. It had a lower timbre than one would expect from looking at her feminine appearance. Not husky. Not gravelly. Just...low. And rather sexy, if Katie was being honest with herself.

Yeah, enough of that. No lusting after your sort-of boss, Cooper. Not cool.

Katie's excitement to see Addison was short-lived, though. The second she walked into the office, she could tell things had shifted. Addison barely glanced up at her, and when she did, there was no smile, not even in her eyes. She lifted her chin in acknowledgment, but that was about it.

Stifling a sigh of disappointment, Katie took up her station at the small round table and unloaded her things. Why was she surprised? Why didn't she allow for the disappointment? She'd known this morning that the day would simply be a continuation of last night and early this morning when her father refused to get out of bed. She hated leaving her mother to deal with the stress all by herself, but she'd insisted Katie go to work. The boys needed her.

More disappointed than she cared to admit, she resigned herself to just getting through the day as best she could. Katie shed her coat...and groaned. There on her light blue shirt, right around her rib cage, was a bright red stain of strawberry jam. Right. She was supposed to change Simon's shirt *and* her own.

"Son of a bitch," she muttered, pulling the fabric away from her body to assess the damage. She should at least try some cold water, see if she could dilute the jam a bit. Otherwise, that stain was never coming out.

When she looked up, Addison was watching her with a hooded expression on her face that made Katie's stomach flip. Then she was yanked back into her phone call, blinking rapidly and verbally sparring with whoever was on the other end of the line. The spell broken, Katie headed for the ladies' room.

Yeah, what a great fucking day.

❖

Monday was not Addison's favorite day of the week—really, was it anybody's?—but that Monday in particular felt...so many things. Annoying. Tiring. Stressful. And a little cruel.

She watched Katie leave the office, shaking her head in obvious irritation over the stain on her shirt, watched the gentle sway of her hips, the way her dark hair fell forward as she bent to get a closer look at the mess. Absently, she listened to the office manager at one of her complexes, but mostly, her attention was on Katie.

There was a part of Addison that wished they were back in her loft. Things had been different there. Felt different. More relaxed and comfortable. Less tense and stressful. And she knew why, she'd known why for several days now.

She liked Katie.

She *liked* her.

And that could be a problem. For so many reasons, it could end up a very big problem.

Addison hadn't been with a woman in a long time. She couldn't remember exactly how long, mostly because she'd stopped keeping track—way too depressing. Throwing herself into her work had seemed to be the best solution, the best way to keep her focused on other things. And it had worked. She'd accomplished so much in the past couple of years and she was proud of it. All her hard work would hopefully pay off in a matter of weeks when her mother announced that she would take over as CEO of Fairchild Enterprises.

Yep. It would all be worth it.

Thinking of her mother, of course, was just another reminder of why Addison needed to get any improper thoughts of Katie Cooper out of her head. Meredith would never stand for something like that. And frankly, after her vehemence in firing Kyle Bannon's girlfriend, Addison had zero legs to stand on when it came to fraternizing with an employee.

This entire train of thought was silly anyway, because who said Katie even felt the same way? What made Addison think that, in different circumstances, different lives, different worlds, Katie would even give her the time of day? This whole thing was based on assumption and, honestly, physical attraction. Addison couldn't let herself get derailed by such trivial things.

As if on cue, Katie returned, the stain lighter, but still there and now accentuated by a wet circle of darker blue around the red. Her dark brows met in a V at the top of her nose, and when she sat down at the round table, she let out an exhalation of subtle exasperation. It was kind of cute.

No! No, it's not cute! Nothing about Katie Cooper is cute! Or pretty. Or sexy. Or appealing in any way! Just no.

Addison closed her eyes and scratched at the side of her neck as her office manager continued to blather away on the phone. She'd moved on from snow removal preparation to the need to find a new company to contract the repair of appliances. Addison listened, said, "uh-huh," when it was appropriate, and studied her fingernails, the surface of her desk, her keyboard—when had that gotten so dirty?—anything to keep her focus from the woman across the office.

It took nearly another ten minutes before Addison was able to extricate herself from the phone call, and she'd noticed thirteen emails had come in while she'd been on it. With a loud sigh, she opened the first one, read, and began typing. She got through an entire sentence before she could feel eyes on her.

When she looked up, Katie was staring at her. Their gazes held for a beat before Katie finally said, "Hi." Somehow, she was able to fit irritation, a little anger, and even some hurt into that one tiny word. Addison felt the guilt surge up and heat her cheeks.

With a clear of her throat, she said, "Hello, Katie. How are you?"

"Just dandy," Katie responded, and her sarcasm hung in the office like a layer of gray fog.

Addison gave a nod, torn between asking Katie if she was okay—which, of course, could lead to a big, in-depth, personal conversation that would totally defeat the purpose of staying distant and aloof—and simply going on with her work. The ringing of the phone saved her from having to choose, and she picked it up. "Addison Fairchild."

Katie continued to stare at her. Addison could feel it, and it took every ounce of energy she had not to look up and be snagged by those rich brown eyes. She knew if she did, there was a very good chance of her becoming lost, saying something she shouldn't. Worse, *doing* something she couldn't. It was a weird feeling, that moment, and Addison wasn't sure what to do with it. She swallowed hard, and when the phone call ended, she pretended it hadn't for an extra minute or two so she could gather her thoughts and calm the blood in her veins that felt suddenly hot. Too hot. Racing through her body at warp speed.

She cleared her throat a second time, and that got under her skin. Clearing your throat told people you were nervous, uncertain, weak, and Addison hated that. She let the annoyance of it take over, and that came through in her tone of voice. She was sure of it.

"I've emailed you details on a couple calls you can make for me. I also need some things from Office Max. You can take my—" She didn't get a chance to finish her sentence because Katie stood up, crossed the office, and shut the door. She moved so she was standing in front of Addison's desk, determination in the few steps she'd taken. Hands parked on her hips, she tilted her head to one side and those brown eyes flashed with…something Addison couldn't put a finger on. Anger? Yes, absolutely. Confusion? Maybe some. And…no. Addison mentally shook her head. Not going on to the other thing. Not going there.

"What are you doing?" Katie asked. Her voice was quiet, but the tone was serious, sharply focused.

Addison swallowed. "I'm sorry?"

"What are you doing?" Katie repeated, one hand out, palm up. "I thought we'd ironed things out last week. I thought we'd put the stoically professional, bitch-on-wheels persona to rest, at least with me. What the hell happened?"

"I don't—"

But Katie wasn't done. "Last week? You were a person. An actual, warm-blooded human who talked to me and listened to my suggestions and smiled at me and looked at me. Today? It takes me three minutes to realize you're back to being a robot."

A robot? Ouch. Addison opened her mouth, but Katie pushed on.

"One day, you're amazing. The next, you can't even look at me. One day, you're not only my boss, but you feel like my friend. The next, you treat me like an unwanted intern. Sometimes, I wonder if we could maybe have something beyond our jobs. Others, I wonder how I ever could've even thought that. It's like you have a fucking split personality around me. What is the deal with you, Addison? Because I don't get it."

Addison went still as Katie's words sank in. She wanted to be angry. She wanted to bite back, which she knew from experience she could do quickly, before Katie even realized it. She wanted to remind her personal assistant who ran this company, who wasn't about to stand for a subordinate speaking to her like that.

But she couldn't do any of those things because right then, right in that very moment, Katie was more beautiful than anybody Addison had ever laid eyes on. She was poised. Her confusion had caused dots of pink to form on her cheeks, making her look flushed, as if she'd just run a race. She hadn't raised her voice at all, and aside from dropping the one F-bomb, her anger had remained almost…cool.

It was her eyes, though. Her eyes, the color of melted chocolate chips, weren't angry. They weren't flashing any longer and they didn't match her posture or her tone of voice. Her eyes were pleading, but they were also something else. Her eyes carried pain, but they also carried something else.

Addison had no choice.

No choice. No control.

She pushed her chair back and stood, her eyes riveted to Katie's. In six quick steps, she was around the desk, and when she reached Katie, she didn't stop to think. She didn't even stop walking. There was no hesitation, no tentative internal discussion. She simply took Katie's face in both hands as she walked her backward until the small of Katie's back hit the round table and forced them to remain where they were. Katie's hands grasped Addison's forearms as they stood that way, barely two inches between their bodies.

Addison searched Katie's eyes, found surprise, but no fear. No hesitation. But desire? Oh, she found that. She found piles and piles of that, and it was all she needed to see.

Addison's gaze dropped to Katie's mouth. Her lips were parted in surprise, the bottom one full, both shining with gloss and temptation and promise.

No choice. No control.

"God, Katie." It escaped Addison's lips on a whisper just before she brought her mouth down to Katie's and kissed her.

The world around them dissolved. The office, the ringing phone, the pinging email announcements, the soft hum of conversation outside the closed door…all of it faded from existence. There was only now, this moment, this kiss, and Addison let herself melt into it; she could do nothing else. The softness of Katie's lips beneath hers, the taste of watermelon lip gloss, the tiniest touch of Katie's tongue, it all kept Addison rooted to her spot, kept her hands holding Katie's face— gently, but unwilling to let go just yet. It was as if their mouths were made for exactly this activity, for kissing only each other. Addison's knees felt rubbery and her heart hammered in her chest as a surge of pleasure hit her low in her body. God, had she ever had a kiss this good? This exciting? This much of a turn-on? The warm wet of it, the softness, the arousal. She shifted her head, moved to the left now, and doubled down, deepening the kiss more when she felt Katie's mouth open underneath hers, and she pushed her tongue inside. She reveled in the small whimper that came from Katie's throat, in the feeling of Katie's hands—one tightened its grip on Addison's forearm, the other let go and moved to Addison's waist, pulling her in closer.

I could get lost in this kiss.

The thought echoed through Addison's head and she almost laughed because the reality was, she *was* lost in that kiss. Already. Totally, utterly, completely lost, and she was okay with that. Better than okay. She never wanted to come up for air. She wanted to stay right there, just like that, with her body pressed against Katie's, her hands in Katie's hair, her tongue in Katie's mouth, for all eternity.

The jarring knock on the door was like a plot device from a '90s rom com, and both Addison and Katie jumped apart, literally.

Katie's eyes were wide, her lips were swollen, and her cheeks were flushed as she brought her hand up to her mouth. Addison suspected their expressions mirrored each other's. She took another step backward, brought her own fingers to her lips as the full weight of what they'd just done settled on her, and she swallowed hard.

Another knock.

"Yes?" Addison stuttered, then cleared her throat so the word was more than a croak, tried again. "Yes?"

The door opened and Janie stood there, a tentative smile on her face. "Hi there. Sorry to interrupt. This just came for you." She held out a FedEx envelope, which Addison blinked at for a beat before reaching out to take it.

"Oh. Yes. Thanks."

Janie looked from her to Katie, who was now staring at her shoes, and back again, a slightly puzzled expression on her face. Then she smiled weakly and left, pulling the door shut behind her.

Silence reigned for several moments before either of them spoke. Katie opened her mouth three times as if she was about to say something. Then she closed it again and just stood there with that wide-eyed stare, eyebrows raised expectantly, eyes almost black.

"Yeah," Addison said, nodding. "I know. I know. I'm sorry. That probably shouldn't have happened."

Something crossed Katie's face. Was it disappointment? Addison didn't give herself time to look or analyze. She turned quickly and moved back around behind her desk. "I'm sorry," she repeated. "That won't...that can't...that won't happen again." She sat, so many emotions racing through her right then, she thought she might faint. Her stomach cramped painfully, and she clenched her jaw to keep from showing it.

Several more beats of silence went by before Katie spoke. "So, um, do you have a list for the store?"

Addison squinted at her, not following, her brain still a haze of panic, embarrassment, and Katie's mouth.

"You said you needed some things from Office Max." When Addison still didn't seem to follow, Katie's voice dropped to a whisper. "I have to get out of here. Please." The pained confusion of her expression squeezed at Addison.

"Oh. Right. Okay. Sure." Addison picked up her cell, grimaced at the missed call from her mother, and pulled up her list app. "There. I texted it to you."

Katie gave one nod and turned to gather her things. She stayed turned away from Addison.

"Katie," Addison said, not at all sure what to say next, but Katie held up a hand, forestalling any further words.

"No. It's fine. It's totally okay. I just…I need to get out of here."

And just like that, she left the office and was gone.

The office felt empty. Not only of Katie's presence, but of light. Of color. Of air. Addison tried to focus on work. She turned to her computer, looked at the sheer volume of email that had come in within the past fifteen minutes, and she wanted badly to concentrate on it. That proved to be next to impossible because of the one question that kept running through her head.

What the hell do I do now?

CHAPTER ELEVEN

*W*hat the hell do I do now? The question plagued Katie as she sat in the parking lot of Office Max.

Kissing her boss had been a bad idea. No, she hadn't made the move, but she'd thought about it. Oh, how she'd thought about it. Played it out in her head. Over and over. Which didn't mean it still wasn't a very bad idea. "A really, really terrible idea, Cooper," she whispered into the emptiness of the car. Shifting her gaze to her reflection in the rearview mirror, she pointed angrily at it as she said, "You're a smart girl. Smarter than most. You know better."

She'd also tipped her hand when she was giving her little speech to Addison. Saying she thought they might have something had been as much a surprise to Katie as it had to Addison. She'd had no idea those words were going to slip out, and when they did, she felt inexplicable relief. Had she been holding that in and hadn't even realized it? Regardless, it seemed like saying the words had unleashed something in Addison as well.

God, the look on her face, in her eyes when she crossed the office toward me? That want? That crystal-clear desire? It doesn't get any sexier than that.

Katie swallowed hard as her blood seemed to speed up in her body and a slight throbbing began—or rather, started up again—between her legs.

And let's talk about that kiss.

No. She shouldn't dwell on it. She knew that. Addison had said as much. It shouldn't have happened. They couldn't do it again. What if people found out? Samantha had regaled Katie with many stories of what a stickler Meredith Fairchild was about her employees fraternizing with a subordinate.

"God, it was one kiss," Katie said to her reflection. "Doesn't have to mean anything. Relax about it."

But what a kiss it was.

For somebody who was so good at projecting herself as cool, aloof, untouchable, Addison Fairchild knew *exactly* what to do when it came to kissing. Holy good God, Katie had never been kissed like that. Never in her life. She could have stayed there forever, Addison's hands cradling her face, Addison's tongue doing indescribably sexy things to her mouth. Katie hadn't wanted it to end.

But it had.

That knock on the door was like a slap, and the panicked look on Addison's face washed away any sensuality in an instant, like a bucket of ice water thrown on them, the regret clearer than if it had been written across her forehead. All eye contact disappeared.

Katie blew out a breath of disappointment as she pulled into the parking lot of Office Max. What a fucking mess. She wanted to talk to Sam about it, but since she worked for Fairchild, Katie didn't want to put her in the position of knowing something damning. Not that she'd blab. She absolutely wouldn't; Katie trusted her with her life. But this was something she had to deal with on her own. She'd opened this door. It was her responsibility to close it again. And lock the damn thing.

The ringing of the phone on her desk startled Samantha out of a daydream, and her body flinched at the sound. She picked up the handset but continued to gaze out the window. The gray and rain of earlier had traveled on to its next stop, and now there were cute, puffy clouds moving along an electric-blue sky at a fairly good clip, aided by the gentle wind she could see rustling what few leaves remained on the trees.

As she told the caller that Jack was out of the office for a meeting, her eyes caught the clock in the corner of her computer screen and she marveled at how it could possibly only be 3:00. God, the day was dragging.

She jotted a message for Jack—he was old school and preferred handwritten messages on those little pink slips over voice mail—and then glanced toward the hallway coming from the lobby. Walking toward her at a rather quick pace was none other than Addison Fairchild.

God, she was gorgeous. Sam was a devout heterosexual, loved everything about the male form, but she was not blind. She could absolutely appreciate the beauty of a woman, and Addison Fairchild was nothing less than beautiful. She wore a black pantsuit—she was always dressed like she was headed to a job interview any time Sam had seen her—and it was as if it had been tailored for her. Maybe it had, Sam had no way of knowing. All she was sure of was that it fit her like a glove. Her long coat was thrown over one arm, her purse over the other shoulder. Her heels were of modest height. Sam wondered if that was because Addison was already fairly tall or if she had trouble walking in anything higher. Sam loved super-high heels, but only if she was sitting or standing. Walking in them could be such a challenge...

Expecting her to pass on by, Sam was surprised when Addison stopped at her desk. Up close, she was even more stunning, and Sam absently wondered what her skin regimen was, Addison's face was so smooth, like she was made of porcelain.

"Hi, Samantha," Addison said, her voice low, but her eye contact steady. "Do you have a minute?"

Sam furrowed her brow, as this was a very unusual request—and also, she was surprised Addison even knew her name—but nodded anyway. "Of course." She folded her hands on her desk and waited.

Addison's eyes darted around the room as if looking for something, and she pointed toward an empty conference room. "Can we go in there?"

Sam followed her gaze, puzzled. "Um, sure."

They walked in silence until they arrived at Conference Room C, which was about half the size of A and B. It was used for client meetings or small committee gatherings. Sam flipped on the lights and Addison closed the door behind them, looking a bit...out of her element. Uncertain. But she seemed to shake it off and pulled out a chair, then took a seat at the small rectangular table.

"Tell me about your friend Katie."

Well, that was a surprise. A weird one. Samantha sat down as well. "What do you mean?" The trepidation in her voice must have been clear because Addison held up a placating hand.

"No, no. Don't worry. She's doing great. She just..." Addison raised her blue eyes toward the ceiling and seemed to search it for a beat or two. "She seems kind of stressed out and I don't want to pry. Is she okay?"

Relief washed through Sam. Okay, Addison was concerned about Katie. That, she could deal with. "She's okay, yeah. She's got some stuff going on at home and she nannies in the morning for two little twin boys. She adores them, but they can take some energy. She's got a lot on her plate."

Addison pressed her lips together, her forehead creased with what looked like worry as she nodded subtly. Sam didn't know her well enough to make that call, but that was how it appeared; she seemed... worried.

Addison said, "She mentioned something about her father being sick."

Sam sighed. "Yeah. He's got dementia. Early onset. It's moving really quickly and it's been tough for her mom, emotionally and financially. We used to share an apartment, but Katie moved back home to help out."

"Does she have siblings?"

"No. Only child."

"I see." Addison seemed to take it all in. Sam could almost picture the wheels and cogs in her head churning. She wondered why, what this information was for. Addison shifted then, seemed almost to come back to life somehow. She rapped her knuckles on the table, the worried expression gone. "Okay. That helps. Thank you."

That was it? "Oh. All right. You're welcome."

They stood together. Addison opened the conference room door and waved for Sam to leave ahead of her.

"Do you know if my mother is in?"

"I believe she's in her office," Sam said and gestured with her chin.

"Thanks."

Sam watched as Addison walked away, all tall and gorgeous and commanding. Seeing her worried, if that's what it was, was an odd experience, and she wondered what exactly that was all about.

She'd have to call Katie tonight.

❖

Well. That was enlightening.

Addison walked toward her mother's office, knowing she probably shouldn't have asked Katie's friend to spill details about her personal life, but also understanding that Katie was a private person. Addison had flashed back to Katie telling her how much she needed her job, and at the time, that hadn't seemed like anything Addison needed to delve into.

Things were different now, though.

They'd kissed.

No. They hadn't kissed. They'd *made out.*

In a very big, very sexy, very memorable way.

And now she found herself wanting to know more about Katie, little details, things that made her tick.

Which was bad. Very bad. Addison knew that. It was a path she shouldn't even *glance* at, let alone venture toward or walk along. Nothing could happen. Nothing. Not one single thing. The kiss was a mistake. End of story.

And yet.

Thank God she reached her mother's office and put the brakes on this unproductive train of thought. She rapped on the doorframe, and Meredith looked up from her computer and over the rim of the glasses perched on the end of her nose.

"Addison. Hello, sweetie. Come in."

Meredith's office was about three times the size of Addison's and appointed with expensive furniture and knickknacks that she'd acquired throughout her three decades of business. Her desk was huge and deep cherry, the chair she sat in burgundy leather that looked buttery soft. The wall behind her was all shelves and covered with books, framed photos of Addison and her siblings, and various awards Meredith had received from the city and its organizations over the years. Curtains hung from the windows in a cream and pink pattern, giving the room a splash of femininity. A wet bar had been built into the corner within the past couple of years, and it always amused Addison, as she'd only seen such a thing on television. She'd grinned as she'd asked Meredith, "What, are you on *Mad Men* now?"

Meredith's glasses were on a sparkling chain around her neck, and she took them off, let them dangle. "This is a nice surprise," she said as Addison took a seat. With a gesture toward her computer, Meredith told her, "I'm dealing with another of those sexual harassment cases, this time at Riverview." She was referring to one of the malls owned by Fairchild Enterprises.

Addison's stomach rolled. "Staff trying to date?"

"No, no. This one's an *actual* sexual harassment case. One of Jared's senior security guards has been accused by his female new hire of making unwanted advances." She blew out a breath, as if this happened all the time and she was feeling overwhelmed by it. Which wasn't exactly untrue. "It's his word against hers, and Jared's having some trouble figuring out how to handle it."

"I can imagine." Addison knew her brother well, knew he could handle conflict when he had to, but it stressed him out. He'd been a tenderhearted boy growing up and he was a tenderhearted man now.

"Maybe you can talk to him."

Addison's eyebrows went up. "Me?"

"Yes, you. You handled your issue so well a few weeks back. Jared doesn't know how to be firm when it comes to people he knows personally. I've told him a hundred times not to become friends with his employees, but he doesn't seem to hear me."

"He likes everybody, Mom. That's how he is. He's a nice guy."

"Still. You're great at maintaining distance. Maybe you can give him some pointers."

"Sure." Addison smothered a scowl, not liking the description but knowing it was true. She'd made it a rule not to socialize with her staff. She kept herself apart from them. Above them, if she was being honest. She threw holiday parties for them but didn't attend. She rewarded them with company dinners when they'd earned it, but made a quick appearance, then left them to it. No, she didn't socialize with her staff because doing so would inevitably cause problems. And just like that, her brain tossed her an image of her standing in her office, kissing Katie Cooper senseless—Katie Cooper, her personal assistant—and she suddenly felt overheated. Uncomfortable. And very much like a fraud.

"How are you feeling?" Meredith asked, thank freaking God, and Addison was able to refocus her attention on something that wasn't cranking her body temperature to dangerously hot levels.

"I'm okay."

"Standard answer from my oldest daughter." Meredith's half-grin took any sting out of the words. "Are you taking care of yourself? Have you lightened your load? Given some of it to your assistant?"

Addison flashed first to the dozens of emails she needed to deal with, as well as the three meetings she had tomorrow. Then she thought about Katie, wandering the aisles at Office Max, doing meaningless errands Addison could easily give to an intern or an admin. She kept her sigh internal as she nodded and lied to her mother. "I am."

"Good." That seemed to appease Meredith, as she moved on to a new subject. "Your sister's Christmas gala is in three weeks. You're going, yes?"

It wasn't really a question and Addison knew it. "Yes, of course."

"You should bring a date."

Addison blinked at her, taken aback by the odd suggestion. "I should bring a date?"

"Absolutely. I think it would be good for people to see you with someone on your arm. Or you on someone's arm. There will be investors and such there, you know. Important people."

Addison's mind began to race. What was her mother saying? Was this a subtle hint to prepare her for taking over F.E.? Was her mother telling her without telling her that appearances would matter at the gala? And also, a date? She did her best not to groan out loud. Maybe she could talk Sophie into accompanying her.

"And not Sophie," her mother said as if reading her mind. "A real date, not a pal. You must have dozens of women who'd jump at the chance." She smiled warmly.

Sweet Jesus, how was she going to manage to find a date to a ritzy gala event in less than three weeks? The ideas of an online ad or maybe an escort service popped into her head and her eyes went wide for a split second when she realized it. She stood up quickly, the sudden need to get the hell out of there almost too much to bear.

"Going already?" Her mother's voice held a tinge of disappointment.

"Yeah, I still have some things to do." Not a lie. Not a lie at all. There were always a million things to do when it came to her job.

"Well, it was nice to see you anyway."

"You, too. Talk to you later." And with that, Addison was free. She hurried through the open area, past Samantha's desk without looking at her, down the hall and out the front doors. She reached for the handle of her car door when a stabbing pain ripped through her abdomen and nearly doubled her over. She clenched her jaw molar-crackingly hard, squeezed her eyes shut, and braced herself against the car with one hand, willing her breaths to continue. In and out. In and out. She breathed through the pain until it eased up enough for her to actually drop into the driver's seat of her Mercedes with a groan of relief.

Okay, that was bad.

She remembered that she'd forgotten to take her antibiotics that morning. She'd also forgotten to eat today. Probably not helping the situation at all, but she was rarely hungry. She vaguely recalled the doctor telling her that a loss of appetite was a symptom of an ulcer and that she still needed to get some food into her system.

Once she'd started the car, she leaned her head back against the headrest for a moment to let it warm up on this cold November day. Out of nowhere, she thought about Katie making her eggs last week and how nice it was to have somebody take care of her like that. Without warning, her eyes welled up and a lump formed in her throat.

Addison allotted herself five minutes to sit and…do whatever it was she was doing. Wallowing? Being sad? Feeling self-pity? She didn't know and she didn't like it but allowed it to run its course. To combat it, she mentally cataloged everything she had left to get done today and calculated that she'd be in the office until at least 8:00. Fairly typical.

And then a laugh bubbled up from deep inside her as she recalled the conversation only minutes ago. How the hell was she supposed to find a date in less than three weeks when she worked well past dinner most nights of the week and often on weekends? It would be impossible. Not to mention, she hadn't had an actual date in, what was it now? Over a year? Closer to two?

I think it would be good for people to see you with someone on your arm.

Her mother's words echoed through her head. That *had* to mean something. Didn't it? People were more trusting of somebody with a spouse or partner. That was a fact. It was a big part of why her mother and father had stayed married even though their relationship had dwindled down to just being friends and her father lived in their Florida home year-round, flying back to make appearances when necessary.

"Goddamnit," Addison muttered as she put the car in gear and headed back to the office, doing her best to shove all of this out of her head for at least a little while.

Inside the front door to Fairchild Rentals, three Office Max bags sat in front of Janie's desk. Janie had her coat on and was gathering her things, and she smiled at Addison.

"Katie dropped that off. She wasn't sure where it all went, and I told her I'd take care of it in the morning. I hope that's okay."

"Sure," Addison said, and forced a smile she didn't feel. Her disappointment at not seeing Katie again today was something she almost tangibly felt, like little unpleasant pinpricks to her skin.

"Have a good night," Janie called after her.

Addison made a conscious effort to smile and actually give a response as she moved past Janie's desk, recalling her mother's comment about her being distant. She waved over her shoulder as she walked by and called, "You, too," but what she really wanted to do was sprint to her office, slam the door shut, and hole up in it for the foreseeable future. Once there, she shed her coat, dropped her purse on the floor, and tried to ignore the fact that she could somehow smell Katie lingering in the air, a mix of citrus—lime?—and something else mouthwatering yet subtle. She flopped into her chair like her body was suddenly boneless as all the air left her lungs. She felt deflated.

She missed Katie.

What the hell was she supposed to do about that? Because one thing was clear: she had to do *something*.

CHAPTER TWELVE

H i, Katie-cat. How was your day?"

Her father's words almost brought Katie to tears as she walked through the front door, he sounded so...*normal*. His blue eyes were clear, he'd been shaved so he looked less unkempt than she was getting used to, and he was smiling at her. *Smiling*. Like his old self.

She simply stood in the entryway and blinked at him.

Thank God her mother was on the ball and breezed into the room to save them from awkward silence. "Hi, honey. How are you?" She took Katie's coat and kissed her on the cheek. "We've had a really good day today."

That would have been obvious even without Liz saying so, because even she looked relaxed. She was showered, dressed in jeans and a tank with a flannel shirt over it, hanging open. Her eyes were sparkling, and she looked exceptionally less tense than usual.

"I see that," Katie said, then crossed to her father and kissed him on the cheek. "I'm glad one of us did." She squeezed his shoulder. "Hi, Daddy."

Liz made a sound of sympathy with her tongue and hung Katie's coat up in the closet. "You're home earlier than usual."

It was true. She'd bailed at 4:30. She shouldn't have, but she couldn't handle facing Addison again with her brain as muddled as it was. She needed to time to sit. To absorb. To marinate. Because seriously? That kiss?

God. That kiss...

"Did something happen?"

Katie was yanked back to the present by the concern in her

mother's voice, and she forced a small smile. "It's fine, Mom. I just needed to come home." When it looked like her mother might press for more, she smoothly changed the subject by sniffing the air. "What smells so good?"

"Pot roast," her father said, still with the smile.

Katie looked at her mother, who shrugged and said softly, "I know."

"Do I have time to change?" Katie asked, looking down at her shirt. "I've had strawberry jam on me all day long."

"I hope that was one of the twins and not just you." Her mother winked.

"Ha ha. I have no trouble finding my mouth, thank you very much."

"Oh, I know. I've been watching you eat for twenty-nine years." Liz tugged on a hunk of Katie's hair. "Go change. Dinner's in about an hour." She went to sit by her husband, reached out, and took his hand as they watched some show about log cabins. Katie watched them for a beat, her heart warm.

Allowing herself a few minutes to just bask in her family was something Katie had to do on days like this. She wasn't fooled, though. She wasn't delusional. She knew this wouldn't last, especially now that it was evening. That's when her dad always went downhill. Sundowning, they called it. He was more lucid in the mornings, and much less so in the evening and at night, so his clarity right now was kind of amazing. She wanted to stay there, to sit in his lap and talk to him, but the image of her parents sitting like they used to before he got sick was too precious. She couldn't take that from her mother—she saw so much of the bad and so little of the good. Katie smiled at them, then headed upstairs to change into her My Day Was Crap sweats and take off her godforsaken bra.

Her phone pinged a notification of an incoming text as she pulled her sweats on. It was Sam.

Hey, you. Home yet?

Katie typed back. *Yep.*

Good day?

Katie stood topless in her room as her fingers poked out a response. *Meh.*

Crap sweats?

Katie sent back a smiley and a thumbs up. *You know me so well. Time to chat?*

She loved talking to Sam. She really did. But right then, she didn't want to miss any more time with her dad while he was actually…there. *Not at the moment. Dad time.* She knew Sam would get it. *Maybe later or in the a.m.?*

Sam agreed, and Katie tossed her phone onto her nightstand to charge, then headed back downstairs.

The almost-normal lasted for a good forty-five minutes longer before her father began to show signs of fading. They weren't drastic, which Katie thanked God for. They were just that—a fading, like he was slowly disappearing. He got quieter. His eyes seemed less sharply focused. He blinked a lot. Still, Katie and her mother were able to enjoy dinner with him just like old times. He ate and smiled and tossed a roll at Katie like he always used to.

And they laughed.

God, how long had it been since they'd laughed?

Katie cleaned up the kitchen when it was time to take her father upstairs to wash up and get him settled into his room. Forcing herself to embrace the positive aspects of the evening rather than rail against the unfairness of the disease, she let herself bask. And remember. And smile. And…breathe. She was going to lose her father completely. But not tonight.

It was almost an hour later when her mother came down and blew out a breath of relief. Katie had brewed a pot of coffee and was pouring two mugs as Liz pulled out a kitchen chair and dropped into it.

"Thanks for cleaning up," she said.

"Of course. How is he?"

"Watching some fishing show on TV. He never watched that kind of thing before."

"Fishing shows?" Katie set the mugs on the table and took a seat opposite her mom.

"Fishing shows. Hunting shows. Poker tournaments. Old kung-fu movies."

"And hockey." Katie chuckled.

"Right. Can't forget the hockey."

"He's a man's man."

"He is now." They laughed and then Liz took a sip of her coffee, her eyes never leaving Katie's face. She set her mug down, propped her chin in her hand, and studied her. Katie shifted under the gaze, unable to stop herself. "What's up?" Liz asked softly.

"What do you mean?"

Tipping her head to one side, Liz raised an eyebrow.

Katie sighed. "I hate it when you do that."

"Do what?" Feigned innocence and a smothered grin.

"See right through me like I'm made of Plexiglas."

"I'm your mother. It's my job."

"Yeah, yeah."

"So? You gonna tell me what's wrong? Or just sigh some more?"

Katie sighed again.

"Funny. You've been a little off since you got home, and I don't think it's because of your father."

Katie didn't hide things from her mother. Never in her life. Not even her sexuality. Her mom had always made a safe, loving space for her to be honest and open, and just the thought of not telling her something important made Katie's insides churn unpleasantly, like she'd had too much lemonade on an empty stomach. "It was a weird day," she finally said.

"How so? The twins?"

"No. No, the twins were the twins, strawberry jam aside."

"Your afternoon job, then?"

Katie nodded.

"With the boss lady?" When Katie gave her a wide-eyed look of surprise, Liz said, "Allow me to point out once again that I am your mother and I know you like nobody ever will. Also, I can read you like a book and I've always known when you've found a woman attractive." She began to tick off on her fingers. "Your freshman English teacher. Your volleyball coach. That camp counselor. Your RA in college..."

Katie groaned and dropped her head down onto the table with a thud.

Liz chuckled quietly and reached across to tousle Katie's hair. "Listen. I'm stuck here all day with a man who sometimes knows me and other times is a nine-year-old. Let me live vicariously. Tell me the story."

Turning her head slightly so she could squint up at her mother from the surface of the kitchen table, Katie wrinkled her nose. "Fine." She stood up and went to the cupboard above the refrigerator. "I'm gonna need something more than cream in my coffee." Pulling down a bottle of Baileys, she opened it and poured some into her mug. Eyebrows raised in question, she held it up.

"Gimme."

Katie sat back down and they both sipped their much stronger coffees, Katie looking at hers as fortification. Then she met her mother's gaze and held it for a beat. Two beats. Three, before she simply blurted it out. Said the words out loud for the first time. "Addison kissed me. Addison kissed me today."

Liz stopped with her mug halfway to her lips. She blinked. Stared. Stayed perfectly still for several long seconds before saying very softly, "Oh, my."

"Right?"

"Well. That is...unexpected."

"Tell me about it."

Liz cleared her throat and looked at Katie. "Like...a quick peck? On the cheek? Or the lips?"

"Oh, it was on the lips and there was nothing quick peckish about it."

"I see." Liz sipped again. "And? How did this transpire?"

Katie wet her lips and then told her mother about the shift in Addison's demeanor from last week to this, how she seemed to go back and forth in the mood department, friendly and almost warm one day, cold and distant the next. Smiling as she recalled working on the couch at Addison's loft, she told her mother how much they'd gotten done those few days, how easy they'd been with each other. The smile slid off her face as she talked about the first few moments with Addison that afternoon. "And...I blew up at her." Katie wrinkled her nose.

Liz made that face she'd always made when Katie did something she'd known better than to do. "Katie."

"I know, I know. But I couldn't help it." With a grimace, Katie shifted her gaze to the back door, gazed out the window even though the darkness had settled in and she could only see the kitchen reflected back at her. "We had such a bad night with Dad, and I got very little sleep and the twins were fine, but they can still be exhausting, and then I got to Addison's office and she could barely look at me and then rattled off all these mundane chores for me and I couldn't take it. I just couldn't. I let her have it."

"What did you say?"

"I told her I didn't understand her."

"And then?"

"And then she marched across the room, grabbed my face, and kissed me." Katie was completely comfortable talking about intimate things with her mother; they'd always had a great, very open relationship. But this felt…different somehow. The way Addison's kiss had made her feel, the longing it had stirred in her, the way she'd wanted it to go on and on, how it had felt to put her own hands on Addison and pull her closer. It all felt so…intimate. So private. Something Katie wanted to hold close for a while, guard, keep possession of, so she didn't go into more detail.

"Wow." Liz sipped her coffee, and Katie could tell she was sifting through all the things she wanted to say. She'd always been one to think carefully before she spoke. Unlike her daughter. "Rather… inappropriate."

Katie tipped her head to one side, then the other. She hadn't really thought about that aspect of it. But she quickly dismissed it. "Yeah, I guess it would've been if I hadn't kissed her back."

"Ah." Another sip. Another moment of silence. "What are you going to do now?"

Katie sighed loudly and shook her head, remembering how badly she'd needed to get out of Addison's office, away from her before it was impossible. But she also remembered how much she'd wanted to stay, to explore that warm, soft mouth some more, to let her hands wander the peaks and valleys of what lay beneath those very expensive, very professional business clothes. "I don't know. I don't want to lose this job. The pay is ridiculous and we need it."

"Yeah, about that." Liz set her mug down and looked pointedly at Katie. "I noticed a couple of bills missing."

Katie lifted her mug to her lips and said, "I don't know what you're talking about," before taking a sip.

Liz's expression softened. "Honey. I don't need you to do that."

"Mom. I love you. I do. But yes, you *do* need me to do that. I want to help where I can. Let me. That's why I took this job. Okay?"

Liz didn't look happy about the situation and she didn't nod or say anything in the affirmative. Instead she inhaled slowly, then exhaled at the same speed before she spoke again. "I think I'm going to hire a home health aide." She said it quietly, her gaze fixed on her coffee. Then she grabbed the bottle of Baileys and splashed more into her mug.

Liz's face made it very clear it wasn't a decision she liked. She was fiercely independent and liked to think of herself as able to handle a lot more than she actually could. Or should. So Katie knew she had to step carefully, even if she thought this was a fabulous idea. Which she did.

"I think that's a good idea, Mom." Katie kept her voice low, kept most of the enthusiasm out of it, as she reached across the table and covered her mother's hand with her own. "His insurance should cover at least some of that, right?"

"A good chunk of it, yes."

"Good. Good." As if on cue, they could suddenly hear footsteps clomping around above them, then a slamming door. When their tandem gazes shifted from the ceiling back down to each other, Katie said, "I think it will be good for you to get a break every now and then. You can't do this twenty-four hours a day, Mom. It'll wreck you." They were hard words to say, as Katie realized she was basically telling her mother to let go of the love of her life a little bit. And they both knew that a little bit of letting go could very well lead to a little bit more. And a little bit more. And a little bit more, especially as David became less and less himself and more and more of a stranger.

A crash sounded from above. Liz sat up straight as if bolstering herself.

"I got it," Katie said.

"No, honey—" Liz held out a hand, but Katie stood.

"Mom. You've been here all day. Just sit here and drink your Baileys." She winked to try to lighten the mood. "I got this."

Upstairs, Katie could feel herself mentally bracing, her usual routine and automatic preparation for dealing with her father. "Dad?" she called quietly. His room was empty, the television still on and showing a ball-capped man pulling a swordfish out of the ocean with his fishing rod. Down the hall a bit more, the bathroom door was closed, and a sliver of light shone under it. "Dad?" She knocked lightly on the door, then pressed her ear against it to listen.

The door opened so quickly that it startled a little yelp out of Katie. Her father shoved past her, literally, and her back hit the wall of the hallway with a thud. With determined steps, he marched down the hall and back into his room.

Katie caught her breath, swallowed the surprise, and followed him. When she reached the doorway to his room, he was back in bed and seemingly riveted to the TV "Everything okay?" she asked him.

He turned to look at her, his blue eyes utterly blank. Katie felt the lump form in her throat.

"It's Katie-cat, Dad."

He smiled a smile that didn't quite reach his eyes, but she'd take it. "Katie-cat."

"You okay?"

He nodded once, then turned back to the fisherman.

Katie watched him for another moment before turning away and heading to her own room. She needed a minute. She also needed this day to be over. She'd had so much more than enough.

CHAPTER THIRTEEN

The next several days were different. There had been a shift. Katie didn't know exactly why, what had prompted it, if it had been the kiss—it must have been, right?—but they didn't talk about it.

Probably not the best course of action, the not talking, and Katie knew it. So many times, it was on the tip of her tongue to say something, to ask about it, to see if Addison had any feelings on the subject whatsoever, but every time, she chickened out, and she knew exactly why.

Because she *liked* this version of Addison Fairchild. She liked her a lot.

While she hadn't gone all the way over to the relaxed and friendly nature she'd had those two days last week in her loft, Addison had still moved much closer to that end of what Katie now referred to—only in her head—as the Addison Fairchild Attitude Spectrum. The only errands she sent Katie on were to pick up food, be it a late lunch or an early dinner, and it was almost always suggested by Katie. Whenever she agreed, Addison always ordered enough for Katie to share. Katie did her best to remain gentle and unobtrusive, but she also did her best to make sure Addison actually ate. It didn't always happen, but Katie kept track. Other than those occasional food runs, Katie stayed in the office. She helped answer and make phone calls, and in a surprising stroke of trust, Addison gave Katie access to both her email account and her personal calendar. So not only did they construct email responses together, with Addison dictating her thoughts and Katie putting them into words and then sending them, but Katie completely revamped Addison's calendar and then kept it neat and organized. She sent her an email at the end of each day to give her a rundown of what she had scheduled for the next day. It seemed to work fantastically well. Addison had a lot of meetings in a typical week and she'd started letting Katie tag along to them, asked her to take notes. More than once, they'd come back to the office to discuss what had transpired and Katie had picked something up that Addison had missed.

Turned out, they made kind of an amazing team.

Try as she might to forget it, to set it aside and chalk it up as a one-time thing, their kiss was never far from Katie's mind. She wondered if Addison ever thought about it. Had she enjoyed it? Was it something she'd rather forget? Was it in a box on a high, high shelf in Addison's mind? Because much as she'd tried to put it there in her own head, it kept working its way back down to front and center for Katie. It stayed in her thoughts. It even invaded her dreams, and she knew she needed to share it with somebody.

She'd texted with Samantha on and off all week, but they'd both been so crazy busy that the messages felt like quick little drive-bys, little "hey, how're you doing, I'm crazed but wanted to say hi, catch you later" type blurbs. It wasn't until Friday night they actually connected by phone.

"I can't believe I'm actually talking to you," Katie said, after having confirmed by text that Samantha was home. "Why are you in on a Friday night?"

"I could ask you the same thing."

"That's easy. I'm a loser and have no life. What's your excuse?"

"Well, I'm certainly not as pathetic as you are," Sam said with a laugh. "I have worked my butt off all week and I'm exhausted. I think I might be coming down with something."

"Uh-oh." Katie flopped back on her bed. She could hear her father's TV broadcasting some sporting event through the wall. The day hadn't been a bad one, but it also hadn't been easy, her mother had reported. That seemed to be par for the course now.

"How's your dad?" Sam asked, as if privy to Katie's thoughts.

Katie sighed.

"That bad, huh?"

Katie gave Sam a quick rundown of how it had been going, the ups and downs—mostly downs—and that a home health aide would be coming for the first time tomorrow.

"That'll be good for your mom, right?"

"It will. But…" Katie recalled the expression on her mother's face as she spoke on the phone with the organization that would send help. It was a combination of relief, hope, and utter sadness. "I think it's just a reminder for her that he'll never get better. A reminder for both of us, really. But I'm at work and she's here all day, so more so for her." And as had become a seemingly regular occurrence lately, Katie was pretty sure she could feel her own heart crack a little bit in her chest.

Like she sensed that a subject change would be a good thing, Sam said, "Speaking of work, I got a little visit earlier in the week from your boss. Which was…odd."

"My boss has an office in your building. Why would that be odd?"

Sam gave a small groan. "I keep forgetting you were hired by Mrs. Fairchild. I meant Addison."

Katie furrowed her brow. "Addison came to see you? That does seem odd. How come?"

"To pump me for information about you. That's why I texted you Monday, but then we both got busy and I forgot until tonight."

"What does that mean, to pump you for information?" Katie sat up on her bed, feeling a mix of curiosity, happiness, and irritation.

"It wasn't anything devious," Sam said with a scoff. "In fact, she seemed kind of worried about you. Said you seemed stressed and asked me if you were okay. I told her about your dad. I'm sorry, maybe I shouldn't have, but she really did seem concerned."

What the hell? "She could've just asked me."

"Agreed."

Katie didn't mention that she'd unloaded on Addison more than once and that maybe she was *afraid* to ask Katie directly if she was okay. She had to give her the benefit of the doubt.

"I actually thought, after I got past the weirdness of it, that it was kind of sweet."

"What else did she ask?" Katie found herself softening because she felt like she was slowly getting to know Addison better, and if she was genuinely worried—so worried that she sought out Katie's best friend—well, that *was* kind of sweet. Still odd that she wouldn't just ask Katie what she wanted to know, but kind of sweet just the same.

"Not a lot. If you had siblings." Sam paused, and Katie could picture her looking up at the ceiling the way she always did when she tried to recall something. "Actually, I think that was it." Another pause. "Her worry seemed pretty real, Kate, like she cares about you."

Katie took a deep, full breath and let it out slowly.

"What?" Sam asked, as if she could read that exhalation. "Tell me."

And Katie spilled it. All of it. Everything. The attitude shifts of Addison's that gave Katie whiplash. Working at her loft. The unexpected kiss in the office. The current pleasantness. All of it. When she finished, Sam was quiet for so long, Katie wondered if the call had dropped.

"Wow," Sam said finally, and Katie could almost hear the gears whirring in her BFF's brain. "She actually kissed you? Right there in her office?"

"Yeah, that was a surprise," Kate said with a chuckle.

"A good surprise?"

A happy little moan escaped Katie's lips before she could catch it. "Oh, God, yes."

"Well, she's fucking hot for an ice queen. Which makes no sense, I just realized." She laughed, then added, "I didn't know she played on your team."

"Me neither."

"That must've been a happy little discovery."

"Mm."

They were quiet for a moment before Sam asked softly, "What now?"

Katie half shrugged even though Sam couldn't see it. "No idea. I mean, we haven't talked about it. Haven't even mentioned it. I think she might just want to forget about it. I don't know."

"Maybe you should bring it up."

Katie made a noncommittal sound. "I don't want to jeopardize my job. We really need the money right now, and until something full-time comes along for me, I'd like to hold on to this paycheck."

"You know, I just thought of something. Mrs. Fairchild would have a meltdown if she knew her daughter was making out with her personal assistant. She's nuts about that fraternizing rule. Remember when that guy in sales asked me out?"

"Oh, right! A couple years ago."

"Yep. She hauled him into her office so fast…"

"No wonder Addison wants to forget it." How could Katie have not remembered that? It certainly put a bit of a new spin on things for her. No, she didn't want to lose her job. And she didn't want to put Addison's in danger either. Was that even a worry when you worked for your mom? She gave her head a good shake. "I think...I'm just going to leave it."

Sam seemed to agree. "I think that's probably the way to go. Sadly."

"Yeah."

They talked a bit more, and when they finally hung up, Katie lay on her bed, staring at the ceiling and absorbing the new information she had.

Addison had been worried about her.

That didn't seem to fit very well with the woman she'd first met when she began this job. It fit better with the woman she was working with *now*—and the reality of it made her wrinkle her nose and give her head a slight shake. Addison Fairchild almost did seem to be two different people: Cool Businesswoman Addison and Addison the Person. And while it was true that Cool Businesswoman Addison had her place and was definitely interesting to observe, she was not the version that was taking up space in Katie's head. No, Addison the Person was far more intriguing.

How do I get her *to come out and play?*

❖

The past two weeks had gone so well, Addison often found herself smiling for no reason. It was early December. Thanksgiving had come and gone, and there was a light, fresh dusting of snow on the ground that gave the world a clean-slate look. Three of her five rental complexes were filled to capacity with renters—the first time that had ever happened. And her schedule felt somehow...smoother. Easier. More streamlined. She gave the credit for that to Katie. Her calendar girl, as Sophie had labeled her.

It was almost noon on Friday when her phone rang, and she snatched it up just as Katie walked through the doorway looking like she hadn't slept in days. Addison furrowed her brow as she put the phone to her ear and said her name.

The entire time she talked to the office manager of one of her complexes, she followed Katie's movements with her eyes. She was wearing black dress pants and a gray sweater today, her hair up, and she looked neat and put together, as always, but there were occasions when Addison realized how much she missed casual, jean-clad Katie, the one in her loft, the one in sock feet and a messy bun. Half listening to the caller, she continued to watch Katie set up for her afternoon. Watched as she pulled her laptop from her bag, set it down, opened it. Watched as she draped her coat over one of the other chairs at the table, like she did every day. Watched as she took a deep breath and then stared at her workstation, like she wondered if something was missing. That was unlike Katie. She was generally sure, determined, confident in her day. Today, she looked a little bit…lost.

Katie glanced up and met Addison's eyes, and Addison gave her a little wave hello. Katie tossed back a small smile that didn't quite reach her eyes, then pointed to the door and held up a finger. Addison took it to mean she'd be right back, so she nodded her assent as she half listened to the caller. She watched Katie leave and tried not to think about how much it bothered her to see her so off her game.

Just as Addison was wrapping up the call, Katie returned, two cups of steaming coffee in her hand. She set one down on Addison's desk and returned to her own space.

Addison finished her call. "My God, that woman can talk," she said. "I've had to fake reasons to hang up."

Katie smiled and sat in front of her laptop as Addison squinted at the coffee she'd brought. As if reading her mind, Katie said, "Yes, I know you prefer your coffee black unless you order a latte, and yes, I know I put cream in that one."

"A lot of cream."

"If you're going to continue to drink too much coffee—which we both know is hard on your stomach—then maybe the extra cream will take some of the edge off it once it's in there and poking at your stomach lining."

Addison looked up at her and their gazes met warmly.

"I mean…" Katie lifted one shoulder in a half shrug. "Based on my abundance of medical expertise and all."

Addison grinned, relieved by the attempted humor, which was much more like Katie. Still, she seemed off, but before Addison could open her mouth to ask about it, her phone rang again. "Damn it," she muttered and snatched it up.

"Are you ready for the gala next weekend?" It was her mother. No greeting, no preamble usually meant she was buried in work and had no time for trivial discussions. "I need you to be ready, Addison. This is important."

"Yes, Mother, I know." Katie shot a glance her way and Addison made a show of rolling her eyes. "You've called me three times this week."

"Well, you have a habit of waiting until the last minute."

"Have I ever not shown up for something like this?"

"No, you haven't." There was reluctance in her mother's voice, and that gave Addison the tiniest bit of satisfaction.

"Then stop worrying. I'll be there."

"Do you have a date yet?"

Addison's irritated sigh was apparently all Meredith needed to use her "I give up" tone.

"Fine. Bring Sophie, then. I don't care."

That quality in her voice, the one that said this was exactly what she'd expected of Addison, even though Addison didn't quite understand why her having or not having a date was an issue at all, got under Addison's skin like a tiny burr inside her collar, pricking at her, poking, niggling, and Addison was suddenly hit with a little shot of rebellion. Which happened from time to time when it came to her hard-ass of a mother.

They finished the call, Addison's snark evidently obvious, as Katie looked up with a look of surprise. Addison groaned.

"Moms, huh?" Katie asked.

"Moms." Addison shook her head, kept her eyes on Katie. "Are you okay today?" Addison fought the urge to cross the room and put a hand on Katie's shoulder, on the back of her head, to pull her into a hug. It was a strong urge, but she managed to stay in her seat.

Katie nodded. "I am. Long night is all."

"And twin four-year-olds this morning."

"Exactly."

They stayed that way for a beat or two, Katie smiling at Addison from across the room, Addison smiling back, and Addison marveled at how dorky they must have looked in that moment.

"Hey, are you busy next Saturday night?" The words were out and floating in the room between them before Addison even realized she was about to say them.

Katie's eyebrows went up. "Me?" At Addison's nod, she wrinkled her nose. "I don't think so. Why?"

Can't really back out now. Addison threw caution to the wind and tried hard not to think about what she was doing. "How would you feel about coming to the Christmas gala my sister is throwing to benefit the hospital?"

Addison scratched at her neck as she waited for Katie's response. She didn't stop to think about the blowback, the consequences of bringing a subordinate as her date. In that moment, she didn't give a crap what her mother thought. What anybody thought. Katie's face had lit up a bit at the question, and that was enough for Addison.

"A gala, huh? Sounds fancy."

"It's pretty fancy," Addison agreed. "Katrina goes all out. Lots of big names there, investors, important people." She could see that her words were not making Katie feel any more comfortable, and she snapped her mouth shut.

"Why me?" The question was just above a whisper, and it didn't surprise Addison. They'd never talked about the kiss from a couple weeks ago, and that was on her. She was pretty sure if she'd brought it up, Katie would have a conversation with her about it. But Addison had chosen the "if we don't talk about it, we can pretend it never happened" route and that hadn't really helped her at all. She took a deep breath and decided to be as truthful as she could.

"Because I'd like to, for once in my life, attend one of those things and feel like I can be myself. Like I don't have to put on a show. Like I don't have to play a role. Like I can just be me." She paused, cleared her throat. "I feel like I can do that with you."

Her words surprised Katie. It was glaringly apparent from her widened eyes and the slight parting of her lips.

"It's okay," Addison said, waving a dismissive hand when a moment went by without a response. "It was silly of me to ask. No big deal." Hiding her disappointment was something she'd become pretty good at, so she put that skill into practice right then.

"No," Katie said, her voice quiet. Gentle. "No, I'd love to go."

"Yeah?" They shared a look across the room, one that was charged with…something Addison didn't want to analyze. No, that was a lie. She wanted to analyze it in a very big way. She *shouldn't* analyze it. So she didn't.

Katie nodded and her expression softened. "Yeah."

"Good."

They smiled like a couple of idiots for another moment before Addison shifted the subject back to work. Katie seemed relieved by the move and, just like that, they fell into what had become their easy, daily routine, and their remaining hours together consisted of work.

As Katie was packing up to go home, she said, "Don't forget the shelter next week. Friday at two."

"You're coming, too." As soon as she heard the words, Addison grimaced and scratched at the side of her neck. "Sorry. I mean, I'd like you to come, too."

Katie narrowed her eyes at her, but her expression was light. Soft. "Spend a couple hours playing with dogs and cats and goats and horses? Yes, please."

Addison's relief surprised her. "Good."

"And stop scratching your neck. You're going to leave ruts."

Addison grinned. "Yes, ma'am." She watched as Katie slid into her coat, a black pea coat that seemed a bit on the large side. It was super cute, though, especially once she donned a red knit hat and matching mittens and scarf. "I like that coat."

"Thanks. It's my dad's. A little big for me, but…" Katie let the sentence dangle and that told Addison all she needed to know. Katie wanted to be close to her father, and the coat helped her with that.

"It looks great."

Katie's wide grin was everything. "See you on Monday. Have a great weekend."

"You, too." Addison watched as Katie left and felt conflicting emotions as she did so. A warmth and comfort she hadn't felt in longer than she could remember, and a sense of abject terror, of dread.

With a hard swallow, she pushed it all down and refused to deal with it. Any of it.

After all, that's what Addison Fairchild did best.

And she knew it.

CHAPTER FOURTEEN

W hat are you doing, Addie?" Sophie's voice was soft. Softer than Addison thought she'd ever heard it before, and that gave her pause. Sophie didn't speak softly. As a petite woman in a male-dominated field, she couldn't afford to. She was a pro at making sure she was heard.

Now, though, she sat quietly on a barstool in Vineyard, the wine bar they frequented. She sipped her Rosso, and her blue-eyed gaze was intense as she waited for a response. Addison had never been able to lie to Sophie and she wasn't about to give it a shot now. She'd already told her everything, including that ill-advised, but still toe-curling, kiss. Sophie's first reaction had been insulted anger at having just learned about it *now*, when it had happened more than two weeks ago. She'd pushed that aside, though, and let Addison continue until she finished with today...and the invitation she'd extended to Katie.

"What are you doing?" Sophie asked again.

Vineyard was packed on that Friday night, and Addison was grateful for that. She felt less exposed somehow than if she'd been sitting alone with Sophie. With a deep sigh, she took a sip of her own wine, a Cab, and shook her head. "I'm not sure." It was as honest as she could get.

"Listen." Sophie shifted in her seat, tucked some blond hair behind her ear, and leaned in a bit closer. Pressing a hand to her chest, she said, "*I* have no issues with you banging your assistant."

Addison glared at her. "I'm not banging her. What are you, a fourteen-year-old boy?"

"You know what I mean. It's been a long time since you've developed an interest in anybody, so there's a part of me that's thrilled."

"But?"

"But I worry." There was so much crammed into those three little words. Addison knew Sophie well enough—and Sophie knew *her* well enough—that no elaborations were needed.

"My mother."

"Your mother."

"I get that. I do. And I love you for it." Addison sipped her wine. "But it's not a big deal. Mom wants me to bring a date. Katie knows the business, and I thought it'd be good for her to meet some of the bigwigs…and that it might be nice for her to have a night out."

It was all very unlike Addison, rather atypical behavior, and Sophie knew it. Addison could tell by the slight squint she gave her over the rim of her glass.

"You made out with her."

"A couple weeks ago. And nothing since. That was just…" Addison hated to downplay that amazing kiss, but she felt like she had to, both for Sophie's sake and for her own in general. She shook her head. "It was nothing."

Sophie stared at her some more. Because Sophie knew her. Addison did her best to maintain eye contact, to not waver, and finally, Sophie exhaled.

"Fine." Sophie set down her glass. "You could've taken me, you know. I make a great date."

Addison grinned, knowing that Sophie's feigned hurt wasn't all feigned. "I know. There will be more galas, don't you worry."

"Just…" Sophie's voice trailed off as she took a sip of her wine and seemed to fight to grasp her thought. "I hope you know what you're doing."

"Yeah, me, too."

Later that night, Addison lay in bed, staring at the ceiling. It was late—she didn't want to look at the clock and see just how late—and she'd been awake in the dark for a very long time, her brain whirring like a blender, way too much information as the ingredients in a very stressful smoothie.

Addison was not a wimp. She was not a weak woman by any stretch of the imagination. Not at all. Not even close. Nobody would describe her that way and she wouldn't describe herself that way. Yes, she'd been handed a pretty cushy job, but she'd excelled at it all on her own. She was a smart businesswoman and a savvy entrepreneur. She'd studied and she'd learned, and when there was an issue or a problem, she faced it head-on and dealt with it.

Like, 99 percent of the time, at least.

That other 1 percent...

Turning onto her side, she let a small groan escape her lips. They should have talked about the kiss, she and Katie. They should have addressed it, talked about it, and moved on. She wished they had because now it was too late to do so without making it weird. She couldn't walk up to Kate and be all, "Hey, remember that time we kissed, like, sometime last month-ish? Good times, huh?"

Addison pulled a pillow over her head and screamed into it. After doing so a second time, she felt the tiniest bit better.

Rolling onto her back again, she blew out a breath and let her lips raspberry with it. "Okay," she said aloud, quietly. "That's it. Done. Gonna let it go now."

Katie's job was only temporary. They both knew that. Once Addison's health had improved and she was ready to move into her new job and take over her mother's position in the company, everything would be right in the world again.

Until then, no more dwelling.

"No more dwelling. Enough."

This was actually something Addison was good at: mentally directing herself into some kind of action. If she decided to do something—or not do something—that was that. So if she chose not to dwell, not to think about the kiss or about Katie in any capacity other than *personal assistant*, that's how it was going to be.

She could do this.

She could.

Couldn't she?

❖

"Wow, it's cold," Addison commented as they left the warmth of her car and stepped out into the brisk December air. A visible shudder ran through her body as she pulled on a pair of navy-blue mittens.

"Part of me was worried you'd be wearing a suit, heels, and a businesslike-but-not-very-warm coat," Katie teased her as she made a show of taking in the ivory down jacket and blue scarf, hat, and mittens. "But you surprised me. You even have mittens."

Addison grinned. "I am full of surprises."

"Apparently." Katie adjusted her own hat, painfully aware of not looking nearly as put together as Addison—but knowing she'd be warm—and said, "Shall we?"

With a nod, they headed across the parking lot of Junebug Farms, a no-kill animal shelter. It was a sprawling, one-story building that sat on a large plot of land. To their right was a huge barn that housed horses, donkeys, and other rescued livestock. When the sound of what could only have been bleating goats carried across the property to their ears, Addison stopped in her tracks, her attention piqued like a dog that had just smelled meat.

"Did you hear that?" she whispered and Katie couldn't help but laugh at the almost childlike widening of her eyes.

"I did hear that." Katie took her arm and gave a gentle tug, still smiling. "Let's go inside first, and then I'm sure we can talk to them about letting you see the goats."

That weird shift that had happened between them? Yeah, it had stuck, which was beyond shocking to Katie. After the two blow-ups she'd leveled at Addison, and after the kiss—God, the kiss—Katie had felt like the ground beneath her feet was unsteady, like she stood on a fault line and any second, her world would just split open and swallow her. Instead, the opposite had happened: Things had steadied. Addison treated her like an assistant rather than an intern right out of college, and they'd fallen into an easy rhythm in the office.

They hadn't talked about the kiss. At all. Like, hadn't even mentioned it. That was weird, right? Because it hadn't been a peck. They hadn't been drunk and exercising poor judgment. No, it had been one hell of a kiss, yet neither one of them had even hinted at it. At all. Katie almost had. After she'd found out from Samantha that Addison was now privy to her situation at home, she had to wonder if that wasn't the reason: pity. Before the kiss, Addison hadn't had any insight into Katie's life other than knowing her father was ill. After the kiss, she knew the details of his dementia and how hard it was on Katie and her mother, both emotionally and financially. Maybe Addison felt sorry for her and didn't want to add any more complications to her life. Or maybe Addison was scared off by the thought of somebody with the baggage of an ill parent and a mountain of bills.

While Katie didn't like either of those possibilities, she finally *did* like her job. She was taking on more responsibility. Addison had given her access to almost everything. And most of all, it seemed like Addison was healing. Her stomach pains seemed fewer and farther between, and whenever Katie gave her something healthy to eat, she ate it with minimal complaint—she had to complain a *little*, she said, for principle's sake, which made Katie grin.

So, maybe the not talking was the right thing?

With a mental shrug, Katie hauled herself back to the present as Addison pulled the door to Junebug Farms open and held it for her.

They were immediately hit by the noise.

Much sporadic barking. Happily squealing children (the two school buses in the parking lot were probably indicators of a field trip). Ringing phones and the hum of voices of the people who answered them. Katie and Addison stood side by side just inside the door, not moving, taking it all in.

"Wow," Addison said, for the second time in five minutes.

"Yeah," Katie agreed.

As they stood there, a woman came out from a hallway straight across from them. She was very pretty, dressed in a navy skirt, matching blazer, and heels. Even from several yards away, she gave off an air of authority and sophistication as she crossed to the horseshoe-shaped desk on the right side of the room, said something Katie couldn't hear to the woman behind it, then looked over at them. With a nod, she headed their way.

"Look," Katie whispered to Addison. "A business suit. She's your people."

"You're hilarious."

"Are you Ms. Fairchild?" the woman asked as she approached. She was even prettier up close, with chestnut brown hair and a smooth, porcelain complexion. Black-rimmed glasses framed very blue eyes.

"I am," Addison replied and held out a hand. "Please. Call me Addison. And this is my assistant, Katie Cooper."

"Catherine Gardner, CFO," the woman said as she shook Addison's hand and then Katie's. "We're so grateful for your donation, and we're thrilled you decided to pay us a visit."

It was interesting and oddly exciting and a strange sort of turn-on to watch Addison slip into business mode right before Katie's eyes. Not that she was ever not in it, but there were some slight shifts that Katie was sure she wouldn't notice if she didn't work with Addison every day. She stood a bit taller, her chin just a smidge higher, her shoulders back slightly. Katie wondered if this was a thing she'd perfected when dealing with men and it had just carried over. She made a mental note to ask her sometime.

"First things first," Addison said, and pulled an envelope from her purse. "Here's our annual donation from Fairchild Enterprises. Thank you for all you do for the animals in our community."

Catherine Gardner took the envelope and, tastefully, did not open it to look. She nodded her thanks, and then her smile widened. "So, you're going to hang around for a bit, yes?"

"We thought we'd volunteer for a few hours today, get a feel for the place, then maybe talk to our staff back at home base about doing the same."

"That's wonderful to hear," Catherine said, and her smile seemed to morph from businesslike to genuine. "We can never have too many volunteers. Where would you like to start? Any preference?"

"Addison's got an almost unhealthy love for goats," Katie said, knowing Addison wouldn't. "Any chance she could play with them today?" She looked up at Addison, who looked only slightly mortified, judging by the blossoms of pink on each cheek.

Catherine Gardner leaned in close. "No worries. Everybody loves the goats." With a wink, she said, "Let me get somebody to take you to them."

Addison stayed stoic and professional until Catherine had clicked away and was out of earshot. Then she leaned toward Katie and gave a nearly inaudible high-pitched squeal of delight. "Goats!"

Seeing her like that—less stoic and unemotional and more, well, *human*—had a strange effect on Katie. Still. Even after many weeks. It was terrific, of course. That was a no-brainer. But it was also... Katie mentally searched for the words as Addison apparently tried to channel her excitement by very subtly bouncing up and down on the balls of her feet. It was intriguing. It was a draw. It was goddamn sexy was what it was.

And if she thought Addison's anticipation of the goats was cute, she was not at all ready for the adorableness that took over when they actually got to the goats. Addison climbed right into the penned area behind the young man who led them to the warm barn. As he explained that there was a goat house where they were in the summer but lived in the barn in the winter because it was heated, Addison nodded and made sounds that said she was listening and was absolutely in her glory. Katie watched in delighted awe as Addison held a baby goat in her arms, crooning to it softly and cuddling it. Katie made sure to take photos with her cell phone, many for the Fairchild website and a couple just for herself. Addison gave attention to each one of the seven goats on-site, two of which were tiny little ones. She looked in their eyes, spoke to them like they understood her, helped feed them, and just loved them in general. Katie did all of that as well, but it wasn't nearly as satisfying as watching Addison do it. It was like she was a completely different person, and Katie was reminded of the split personality assessment she'd hurled at Addison a few weeks ago.

They stayed for nearly three hours, until the sun had set and darkness began to close in.

"God, I hate that it gets dark so early in winter," Katie muttered as they trudged across the property toward the parking lot.

"Me, too."

Addison had remote-started the car, so it had at least begun to warm up a bit when they finally reached it and settled inside. They were quiet for a moment before Addison turned to Katie and said, "I smell like goats."

"You absolutely do." Katie chuckled, taking note of the scent combination of hay, dirt, manure, and fresh air. "I'm sure I do, too."

"Little bit," Addison said with a wink as she pulled off her mittens so she could grip the steering wheel. "I think we should write up a memo to send out to employees about volunteering here."

"That's a great idea." Katie furrowed her brow as another thought came to her. "What about mentioning it to all the renters? Could we do that?"

"I never thought of that," Addison said. "I like it."

"We might need to offer some incentive."

Addison squinted at her. "What do you mean?"

"Well, I think people tend to have good hearts and want to help. But I also think they're generally lazy and if there isn't something in it for them, they may not be as inclined. You know?"

"That's a good point." Addison nodded slowly. "Let me think about that, see what I can come up with."

They drove in silence for a short while before Addison asked, "You ready for tomorrow night?"

"Oh, you mean for the super-fancy Christmas gala that will be filled with dozens of high-society, very important people, in front of whom I am terrified of doing something stupid? Like spilling a drink? Or worse, tripping on my heels and spilling a drink *on* somebody? That part of tomorrow night?"

Addison's eyes stayed on the road, but Katie could see the corner of her mouth tug up. "Yes."

"Totally ready. Absolutely ready. Never been readier. No worries."

"I mean, maybe we should be worried. We know how well you and glasses filled with liquid get along…"

Katie slapped her hand against her chest where her heart was. "Oh! She strikes a deadly blow!"

They laughed together, then a beat went by before Addison turned to give her a quick look. "Seriously. You're not freaking out, are you?"

Katie felt the grimace distort her lips. "A little, yeah."

"Would you rather skip it?"

Trying to read Addison's expression in the dark interior of the car was difficult, but Katie was pretty sure she saw enough: concern, a little bit of worry, and something else…something that said she hoped Katie would say no. So Katie was honest. "Of course not. I want to go. Very much. Honestly, I think it makes sense that I'm nervous." She gave a one-shouldered shrug. "You do this kind of thing all the time. The last fancy gathering I went to was my senior prom."

"So…three years ago?" A teasing lilt.

"You're funny," Katie said. "More like ten."

"I see. Well, a few nerves are healthy, I suppose, but really, Katie, you have nothing to be nervous about. I've seen you interact with strangers, people you've just met. You're great. And people like to talk to you. You make them feel comfortable."

Well, that was an interesting compliment. Katie decided not to question it, just to take it. "Thanks."

"Listen…I usually need to chill out and unwind a bit before these things. Are you busy tomorrow, early afternoon? Like, one? Want to come with me?"

Now that the home health aide was visiting regularly, Katie had less guilt about doing things because her mother was starting to have less guilt about doing things. Katie was scheduled to watch her father in the morning, but the aide was coming at noon and staying through dinner. Katie's mother had agreed to cover the evening so Katie could go to the gala.

"I'm free. Where are you taking me?"

```
                    AQUI
        REAL FOOD, EVERY DAY
        F-0672  PAGER    87  #Party 1
        ANDY A     SvrCk: 88 18:19 06/01/19
        RESTAURANT
        AQUI2

    SPEC MAHI MAHI              13.89
    LIME CHX SALAD              10.99
    +16 OZ.HORNITOS ROCKS -R,
      rocks margarita no salt    9.50

                    Sub Total:    34.38
                         Tax:     3.18
                    Sub Total:    37.56
    06/01 18:19 TOTAL:        37.56


            "LOCALLY OWNED
              AND OPERATED
            SINCE DAY ONE"

    201 E. Campbell Ave, CA, Campbell 95008
               (408) 374-2784
             WWW.AQUICALMEX.COM

    Pager #:      87
```

CHAPTER FIFTEEN

"How is it possible that you've never done this before?" Addison asked in disbelief as they waited for their appointment.

"It's just never been something I thought about," Katie said, and Addison wondered if she'd taken offense. "I am perfectly capable of polishing my own toes, thank you very much." Her tone was light, but there was an undercurrent.

"I'm sure you are. But having somebody else take care of your feet for an hour or two is so much more than polishing your toes." She glanced up to see the manager waving her toward them and she stood, held out a hand. "I think you'll enjoy this. My treat."

"Oh, no. I can pay for—" Katie started to speak as she put her hand in Addison's, but Addison squeezed it tightly.

"No. No arguments. I asked you to this gala tonight and I know you're nervous. The least I can do is help you relax beforehand." It took a split second before she realized exactly what she'd said, the double entendre of it, and she felt her eyes blink several times.

"There are other ways to get me to relax, you know," Katie said with a wink, obviously following Addison's train of thought, but then her face immediately shifted to mortification, as if she couldn't believe what she'd just said.

They stood completely still in the waiting area of the salon, looking at each other with wide, weirded-out eyes before they both started laughing at the same time. Neither of them addressed the remark. They simply headed toward the back where the pedicure chairs were.

Yup. That's what we do. We address nothing. Addison mentally shook her head, marveling at how consistent they were, and let go of Katie's hand when it occurred to her how nicely it fit in hers and how much she was enjoying the feel of that.

"How often do you come here?" Katie asked, as they settled into the big, soft, comfy chairs next to each other and submerged their feet into the warm, bubbly water. She picked up the remote control and immediately began pressing various buttons, making different faces at Addison depending on which button she pushed.

"Maybe once every month or two? More often in the summer."

"Yeah, nobody sees your feet in the winter but you."

"True." She laughed as Katie's eyes went wide, then rolled back in her head. "Massager?"

Katie nodded as her chair hummed. "Oh, my God, I need one of these chairs." She leaned her head back, let it loll from side to side. "Of course, I'd never get any work done because I'd be doing this all day."

"Exactly the reason I haven't had them installed in the office. Yet."

When the pedicurists arrived and took seats on their little rolling stools, Katie turned to Addison, her face beaming like a child at Disney for the first time. An unfamiliar warmth spread through her body as Addison smiled back.

"Girls' day out?" Katie's pedicurist—whose name tag read Patti—asked them.

"We're going to a *gala* tonight," Katie said, emphasizing the word just a bit.

"Ooh, I have never been to a gala." Patti went to work on Katie's cuticles and toenails.

"That makes two of us," Katie said as she watched carefully, like she was studying each step in the process.

"You're both going?" Addison's pedicurist was named Jodi, and she glanced up as she asked the question.

"We are," Addison replied. "It's a Christmas gala. A fund-raiser."

"Well, it sounds glamorous," Patti said.

"Right?" Katie's grin was contagious and Addison was suddenly very glad she'd dragged her here.

After a few minutes, the conversation split so Patti and Jodi were chatting amongst themselves.

"What will it be like there tonight?" Katie asked her, voice low like the question embarrassed her a bit. "Like, how many people?"

Addison pursed her lips as she thought. "I don't know, a couple hundred? It's a pretty big gathering each year. Katrina does it up."

"Wow." Katie's eyes went wide and her eyebrows rose up and Addison sensed a bit of dread coming off her. That V that formed at the top of her nose when she was thinking too hard appeared with a vengeance.

"Hey. No big deal," Addison said, and reached across to grasp Katie's forearm. Meeting her eyes, she searched for the right words, wanting—no, *needing*—to make Katie feel better. "Just…think of it as a show. That's what I do. Everybody is dressed to the nines, and I like to see if I can figure out things like who's going to get drunk first and which couple will get in an argument."

"Okay, that does sound fun." Katie's demeanor relaxed immediately. "We could make a game out of it."

Inexplicably happy that she'd wiped away the "stress V," as she'd started calling it in her head, Addison let herself relax a bit more into the buttery softness of her chair.

"So, he loses a sock," Patti was saying. She looked up and made eye contact with Addison. "My new husband, I'm talking about," she clarified.

"They've been married for six months," Jodi informed them as she picked up Addison's foot and went to town on her heel with a giant file like she was grating Parmesan.

"He gets down on his hands and knees to look for it, and he finds…" Patti let the sentence dangle, obviously waiting for anybody to fill in the blank.

Jodi gasped dramatically. "No!"

With an exaggerated nod, Patti said, "Oh, yes."

Jodi sank her head down between her shoulders as she stage-whispered to Addison and Katie, "Her vibrator!"

Katie snorted a laugh, which made Addison join her.

"No big deal, right?" Patti asked.

"Right," Katie said.

"Wrong!" Patti countered. "A huge deal, as far as he's concerned. Huge."

"Ugh." Jodi shook her head. "Such a guy."

"I don't get it," Katie said, looking from one woman to the other and back, then over at Addison, who shrugged.

"If I have a vibrator, then something must be missing," Patti explained.

"Well, that's just silly," Katie said.

"Which is exactly what I said to him. I asked him, do you jerk off?"

"Of course he does," Jodi scoffed.

"Of course he does," Patti repeated.

"What did he say?" Katie asked.

"He got all stuttery and weird, stumbling over his words, like he wanted to say no but knew there was no way he could. So I explained that it's the same thing."

"And?" Katie asked, leaning slightly forward. Addison watched her, thoroughly amused by how enthralled she was with the whole discussion.

Patti just smiled and shook her head. "He's having trouble. Just can't wrap his brain around it. It's completely undone him, poor guy."

"Men," Jodi said, joining Patti in more head shaking. They both chuckled good-naturedly, and it was clear they weren't bashing the male of the species. They were just slightly mystified by them.

The next hour went on like that, individual conversations combined with discussions that all four women took part in. Addison wasn't one to chitchat with her pedicurist—or her hair stylist or her bartender or her letter carrier—but she found herself loving the fact that Katie apparently was. And when Katie was part of the conversation, Addison wanted to be as well. A new experience for her that she wasn't quite sure what to do with.

After giving them instructions to sit and let their polish dry for a bit, Patti and Jodi moved on to their next clients.

Katie wiggled her deep-plum-tinted toes. "I love this color."

"It looks great on you," Addison said, and it did. Went perfectly with her olive skin tone.

"And yours," Katie said, shifting her focus to Addison's red. "Very snazzy. Glamorous."

"That's me. Snazzy *and* glamorous."

Katie held her gaze, that infectious smile playing across her face. "This was fun, Addison. Thank you."

"You're welcome. I'm glad you could come."

"You know, I thought for a minute this might be a fun thing to do, just me and my mom. Something to give her a break and help her relax. But then I remembered that she hates people touching her feet."

"Mine, too."

"Your mom?"

"You touch her feet and she will kick you in the face. No questions asked."

Katie's laugh appeared again, and Addison loved how much she'd heard it today. "Same."

"They don't know what they're missing."

They were quiet as they gathered their things and headed toward the front of the salon where Addison paid the bill. While she hated to let Katie go—it had been such a fun time just hanging with her for reasons other than work—she knew she'd see her later.

"I'm glad it isn't snowing," Katie commented, looking down at her feet—in flip-flops—then out at the parking lot, which was wet but would allow them to get to their cars without ruining their pedicures. Or freezing their feet off. But just barely.

"Oh, I almost forgot," Addison said, as she turned to Katie. "I'm sending a car for you tonight."

Katie blinked at her, those big brown eyes filled with surprise. "I'm sorry?"

Addison cleared her throat, her worry about overstepping suddenly very prominent in her head. "I know things at home have been hard. I want you to be able to drink at will tonight and not worry about driving. So I'm sending a car to pick you up. I have to be there a bit early, but the driver will let me know when he arrives, so I can meet you."

"I…" Katie looked down at her pretty toes. "I don't know what to say."

Addison knew uncertainty when she saw it. She knew what pride looked like. She understood that Katie wasn't one to take charity. She would also bet that when it came to asking for help, Katie had trouble. "You don't have to say anything." She smiled, hoping that would show Katie she wasn't being patronizing or trying to offer charity. "I'll see you tonight."

With that, she pushed through the door and into the chilly winter air. She'd never been nervous about these gatherings. Galas, fund-raisers, dinner meetings. They were all par for the course when you were involved in a large corporation like Fairchild Enterprises. Addison considered them her duty. Plus, they allowed her to mingle with the higher-ups, the wealthy, the people whose ears she might need at some point down the line. So she always dressed up and went and mingled and smiled and listened. But she was never nervous.

Tonight, though?

Yeah.

It was barely three in the afternoon and she already had butterflies.

As she shifted her car into gear and pulled away without looking back at Katie, she promised herself not to overanalyze those nerves. Because they weren't the nerves you got when you were about to enter a room full of strangers. Or the rolling stomach feeling that often came with giving a speech.

No.

These nerves? There was only one definition that fit, and she knew it.

These were date nerves.

❖

"Don't just stand there, Mom. Tell me what you think?"

Katie was nervous. She was a giant bundle of tension as she stood in front of the full-length mirror in her mother's bedroom. Liz stood behind her, having just zipped up the "little black dress," as Sam had called it when she lent it to Katie, and simply blinked. As Katie watched her mother's reflection, Liz's eyes welled up.

"Oh, no," Katie said, holding up a hand. "Don't you cry, Mom. If you cry, I'll cry and it'll ruin my makeup."

Dutifully, Liz bit her bottom lip until her tears eased back but brought her fingers to her lips. "You look..." She shook her head slowly as she seemed to search for the right description. "Stunning. You're gorgeous and you're stunning and you are going to stop people in their tracks tonight. Addison Fairchild won't know what hit her."

While Katie had been sure to inform her mother that nothing further had happened since the kiss a couple weeks ago, not even a mention, Liz was undeterred. "Mom. I told you. This is a work function."

She'd said the same thing to Samantha, who'd come over to bring the outfit and to help Katie with her hair, before she'd left. Sam's reaction was almost identical to Liz's. "*I've* never been invited to such a 'work function,'" she said, making air quotes even as she arched an eyebrow and grinned.

"Trust me, she won't be thinking of work when you walk in," Liz said. "Just look at you." Hands on Katie's shoulders, she turned her back to face the mirror.

The woman staring back at her looked damn good. Katie could admit that. Samantha had said she had the perfect dress for Katie to borrow, as Katie's wardrobe was very low on items that fell into the cocktail dress category, and she had been right. It was black, not tight, but rather…form-fitting, as Liz had described it. Long, sleeveless, and sparkling, and it hugged every curve Katie had in the most flattering of ways. Her hips, her shoulders, her breasts. Speaking of breasts, it showed much more cleavage than Katie was used to, the fabric dipping into a deep V, but both Sam and Liz had insisted it was the perfect amount. Sam had also lent her a small black clutch that sparkled like the dress, and a diamond teardrop necklace to fill some of that expanse of skin left by the dress's neckline. The strappy black heels were the perfect complement, though Katie hoped she didn't have to do too much walking in them. "Beauty is pain," Sam reminded her when she complained. "Walking in heels? It's a muscle. You'll pick it up."

Katie had simply rolled her eyes and stepped into the shoes.

"I love these," Katie's mother said, interrupting her thoughts as she wound a corkscrew curl that hung in front of Katie's ear around a finger. "You had these when you were little. Your grandma called them ringlets."

Katie's hair was in an updo, but several little pieces had been left hanging and Sam had curled each of them into corkscrews, which now hung near her ears and along the back of her neck. She could feel them brush the sensitive skin there when she moved. "Samantha did a good job."

They stood quietly for a moment, mother behind daughter, both gazing into the mirror. Finally, Liz kissed Katie's temple. "You ready?"

Katie took in a deep breath and held it before slowly releasing it. "As ready as I'm going to get, I think." A glance at the clock told her she had no choice. "The car should be here any minute." She grabbed the clutch, filled it with her phone, lip gloss, and a small container of mints, then snapped it shut. With a nervous chuckle, she said, "I feel like I'm heading off to the prom again."

"Me, too. Did I mention that Addison gets points for sending you a ride?" Liz asked as she ushered Katie out of the room.

"Yes, Mom. Like, nine times."

"Well, she does."

"I'll be sure to tell her."

In the living room, Katie's father sat watching television, the home health aide they had most often sitting nearby with a magazine. She was a large African American woman named Rhonda who was incredibly gentle with David and seemed to always be smiling. Katie could always tell when she was on duty because the energy in the house felt...calm, warm and loving.

"Good Lord, David, look at your gorgeous daughter," Rhonda said, touching David's arm to get his attention. He turned his head to regard Katie and Liz as they came into the room. "You ever seen anything so beautiful?" Rhonda asked him.

"I never have," David said, and though there was a hint of uncertainty in his eyes, Katie felt like there was some part of him that not only saw her but recognized her. She'd take that.

"Thanks, Dad."

The doorbell rang before any further conversation could be had, and Liz pulled the front door open.

"Ms. Cooper?" The man was dressed head-to-toe in black and tipped the black cap on his head. He looked like he'd just stepped out of a movie about business tycoons.

Liz stood aside and waved an arm toward Katie. "Honey, your ride is here."

Katie blinked at him as she moved toward the door so she could see past him. Then she stood still and blinked some more at the black stretch limo parked out front.

Addison had sent her a limo.

"Wow," she breathed quietly as her mother handed her a long, elegant coat, also borrowed from Samantha.

"I'm Ty," the driver said with a smile as he held out his hand.

Katie shook it, forced herself to stop gawking like somebody who'd never seen a nice car before. "Hi, Ty. I'm Katie."

"No new snow, Ms. Cooper, and the walkways all seem to be pretty clear, but..." Ty crooked his elbow and Katie dutifully held on.

With a quick glance back at her mother, she let the giddy child inside her that was jumping up and down with utter glee send a big smile. Then she collected herself and walked next to Ty until they got to the limo and he opened the door for her.

Addison had sent her a limo.

Chapter Sixteen

S o?" Robert Kehoe had an arm around Addison's shoulders and he pulled her in tight, close to him so he could speak in her ear. His grip kept her from shifting away. He was in his eighties and she'd known him since she was a child, but it was still uncomfortable and Addison had to make a conscious effort not to squirm. "Are you ready?"

"Ready for what?" she asked him, keeping a smile plastered on her face. Robert Kehoe was one of the richest men in the city, and he'd invested in many aspects of Fairchild Enterprises.

"Ready to take over for your mother," he said, an unspoken "duh" lacing his tone.

"Robert," she said, purposely speaking to him teasingly. "She hasn't made that decision yet. You know that."

Kehoe made a sound that fell between a snort and a scoff. "Please. We all know it'll be you. Only makes sense." He squeezed her to him again and she tried not to stiffen noticeably. "You're the oldest child."

"That I am," Addison said, and absently wondered what her stickler-about-sexual-harassment-issues mother would say if asked whether she still wanted Kehoe's copious investment dollars even though he enjoyed putting his hands all over her daughter as if she were property. She didn't have a chance to continue that train of thought, though, because anything coherent in her mind simply faded away right then, like morning fog being burned away by the sun. From where she stood with Kehoe, she was almost dead center of the largest room in the convention center, and she could see in every direction. The only direction that caught her eye, however, was the one that led to the open double entrance to the room. Walking through it was, without a doubt, the most beautiful woman she'd ever seen.

The dress was black. Sleek. Showed enough skin to warrant a second glance. A third. Maybe a fourth.

The hair was up. Elegant. Classy. Addison wanted to touch it, play with it, then mess it up.

Katie was nervous. Addison could tell by the expression on her face: eyes slightly wider than usual. Smile there, but not quite genuine as she stood a few steps in and searched.

Addison knew exactly who she was searching for.

"Thanks for the vote of confidence," she said to Robert Kehoe, as she gently disentangled herself from his grasp. "Excuse me." And she made her way across the room.

She could tell exactly when Katie saw her because her face shifted from uncertain to relieved to...something else entirely. Katie's brown eyes darkened as they ran over Addison's form, seemingly on their own, something Addison decidedly did *not* hate. Katie's throat moved as she swallowed, and she wet her lips.

Addison stopped in front of her. "My God, you look gorgeous," she said quietly, and meant every word.

Katie flushed a pretty pink as she said, "I was going to say exactly the same thing about you. Wow. Red is definitely your color."

"You like it?"

"Like it?" Katie glanced up at her and opened her mouth as if to say more, but then thought better of it. "Yes. I like it. Very much." She made a show of looking around the room, then cleanly changed the subject. "There are so many people here. People I don't know."

Addison found herself both relieved and disappointed by that. "Yes."

Katie moved closer to Addison and said, "Don't leave me," with a wink and a grin as she gripped Addison's wrist.

"Not a chance."

❖

Walking through that crowd of wealthy, successful people while at Addison's side was...it was almost surreal to Katie. Like walking in a dream when your feet don't feel like they're actually touching the ground. Like you're floating. She was out of her depth here, that was undisputed, but at the same time, being next to Addison made her feel strong somehow. Safe. Not something she'd felt with Addison before. In fact, she'd felt the opposite of safe with Addison since the moment they'd met, for the most part. But tonight? Tonight she felt safe, like there was no place she'd rather be. Like there was no place else she *should* be.

Fact of the matter was, she had the most beautiful date in the place, hands down. God, could Addison turn heads—and she did. Her dress was fire engine red, with cap sleeves and a plunging V neckline. If Katie was worried about her own cleavage, then Addison must be scandalized by hers. Katie was. The V plunged almost to Addison's belly button, and Katie absently wondered how she was keeping her breasts in place. Double-sided tape? Had to be. And all that skin was distracting, to say the least, but somehow, Addison looked nothing less than classy. Elegant. Her hair was partially pulled back, the rest hanging in gorgeous, soft-looking waves around her face and shoulders that made Katie's fingers flex with a nearly uncontrollable urge to touch it, tug gently on it.

As they strolled through the room, Addison stopped to greet various people. Many were sixty or older. Most were male and white, though there was an occasional woman who made it obvious by her confidence, her carriage, the way she commanded the attention of those around her that *she* was the one with the checkbook.

"Addison!" one of those women said, as they approached. "It's so good to see you. How are you?" She was tall and sophisticated, in a royal blue cocktail dress that made her blue eyes stand out, her silvery hair in an updo.

"I'm terrific, Mia," Addison said, as she leaned forward. They air-kissed like women on television. "How are you? And Frank? The kids?"

"Everybody is just fine. Couldn't be better." Mia's gaze moved to Katie.

"This is my personal assistant, Katie Cooper. Katie, this is Mia Carver. She's the founder of—"

"Carver Financial," Katie finished with a nod, as she held out her hand. She'd done her research just in case this exact situation cropped up. "So nice to meet you, Mrs. Carver."

"Please. Call me Mia. Mrs. Carver is my mother-in-law."

Mia and Addison exchanged a few more pleasantries and then Addison gently took hold of Katie's elbow and they moved along. In the distance, Katie could see both Addison's mother and sister. Meredith was deep in conversation with two couples, so Katie turned her attention to Addison's little sister.

Katrina looked beautiful, her dress black, her hair swept up like a wave of sunset. She turned to see them approach, and her smile grew wide. She held out a hand as they got closer and pulled Katie into a hug. "I'm so glad you came. I didn't know Addison was bringing you. Are you having fun?"

"I am," Katie said honestly. "It's…a lot." She pursed her lips and scrunched them to the side, which made Katrina chuckle.

"It definitely is." She turned her attention to Addison as she asked, "Do you remember the first gala we came to with Mom?"

"God, yes." Addison's blue eyes widened at the recollection. "We were so cocky." They both laughed and Addison fixed her gaze on Katie, told her the story. "The three of us had all been put in our positions with F.E. and, frankly, we all kind of thought we were hot shit."

"We so did," Katrina said with an eye roll.

"And Mom had prepared us, told us that things would be formal, that there would be very important people here, and above all else, we were"—Katrina joined her as they said in tandem—"not to embarrass her."

"And?" Katie asked, thoroughly enjoying the banter between the sisters.

"I spilled champagne on the CEO of a tech company," Addison said, matter-of-factly.

"I walked right into the dean of a prominent university while holding a plate of Swedish meatballs," Katrina added.

"And Jared hit on the daughter—and VP—of the head of the city's largest bank." That line came from Meredith as she joined them.

"Truth," Addison said. A server carrying a tray of champagne walked near them and Addison grabbed two flutes, handed one to Katie. "Hi, Mom."

"Addison," Meredith said. Katie was struck by how very regal she always looked. Any time they'd met, even casually in Meredith's office, Katie thought of her as incredibly polished and dignified and not a little bit intimidating. Tonight was no different. Her dress was a shimmering silver and draped off one shoulder. Her blond hair was styled simply but still looked elegant, and her entire body sparkled with diamond jewelry—chunky earrings, two huge rings, and a heavy-looking bracelet that somehow still came off as feminine. "I see you brought your assistant." Her eyes landed on Katie, and while her smile seemed friendly, Katie bristled slightly at the tone she used on "assistant."

"I brought Katie," Addison said, stressing her name. "Yes. Katie, you remember my mother?"

"Of course." Katie reached a hand out. "Always good to see you, Mrs. Fairchild."

"There's James Lang over there," Meredith said to Addison as she let go of Katie's hand. "He's been asking to speak with you."

Addison leaned toward Katie's ear. "James Lang owns three complexes in another county and he's been thinking about selling for a while now."

"Then go," Katie told her, waving her away with a hand. "Go talk to him. I'll be fine."

"I've got her," Katrina said.

Katie tried not to stare as Addison walked away from them. Not to stare at the triangle of bare back her dress left visible. Not to stare at the way the lights seemed to make her hair glimmer. Not to stare at that gentle sway of her hips as she moved. After a moment, she caught herself, blinked rapidly, and took too large a swallow of her champagne. When she glanced at Katrina, there was a smile on her face, and she knew she'd been caught.

"So, Katie," Katrina said, mercifully not mentioning the ogling. "Tell me what you've been doing for Addison. What tasks?"

Meredith Fairchild standing so close made Katie nervous. She wasn't sure why, as she'd spoken with her more than once. But there was something about her *tonight* that felt...different. Less friendly. When Meredith seemed to recognize somebody she wanted to talk to and excused herself, the wave of relief that washed through Katie surprised her in its intensity.

"Don't worry about her," Katrina said quietly, near Katie's ear. "Her bark is usually much worse than her bite."

"Usually?"

Katrina grinned. "Usually. So, back to you. Do you enjoy working for Fairchild Rentals?"

Again, as she had been the first time they'd met in Addison's loft, Katie was struck by the differences between Katrina and Addison. They looked enough alike to be sisters, but Katrina was softer. She didn't have the intimidation factor that Addison did...maybe she'd worked on that, since she ran a hospital. Katie imagined empathy was a necessary trait for such a job. Katrina had kind eyes and you immediately felt comfortable around her. Katie had no qualms whatsoever about talking to her.

"I enjoy it now," Katie said with a chuckle. "Not at first."

"She was giving you stupid stuff to do."

Katie nodded, surprised. "Did she tell you that?"

"No. I just know my sister. She's a bit of a control freak." Katrina held her thumb and forefinger mere millimeters apart. "She doesn't like to give up anything to anybody, even when it's for her own good. She's always been that way."

"How come?" It occurred to Katie that maybe her question was out of line. That maybe it was too personal, none of her business, and Katrina would tell her so. But she had the weirdest, strongest urge to know. To understand. Addison worked like a fiend, and from what Katie had seen over the past month or two, she didn't have to. She had lots of help at her disposal. Lots of options.

"I have theories," Katrina said, her voice almost wistful. "Jared and I have talked about it a lot over the years."

"Jared's your brother?"

Katrina nodded. "He's the youngest. I'm in the middle. Addie's the oldest."

"Right."

"I think our mother was hardest on her, trained her early on that she had to be the best, no matter what. After all, my mother started her own company in a male-dominated field. She'd met just about every obstacle possible by then, and I think she wanted to prepare Addison early, so she'd be ready. Then, after Jared and I came along, she eased up, relaxed a bit in general, but Addison really didn't. I think she equates her level of success with her worth to our mother." She wrinkled her nose and looked at Katie.

"That makes me sad," Katie said, and she meant it. The idea of

Addison basing her worth as a human on how successful she was at work was kind of heartbreaking.

"Me, too. I've tried to talk to her about it, but she won't listen."

"She's definitely stubborn."

Katrina snorted. "You think? And once my mom retires and passes the torch along to Addie, she'll never have a chance to slow down. She won't let herself."

"I worry about her." Katie said it quietly, actually didn't mean to say it aloud at all, but Katrina heard.

"You've been good for her." At Katie's furrowed brow, Katrina went on. "I've seen a bit of a change. Not huge, but a little bit of a softening. A little bit of a drop in her shoulders, a very subtle relaxation. For Addie? That *is* huge." She studied Katie for a moment before adding, "I think you put her at ease." They both noticed a man gesture to Katrina from several people away. "I need to go talk to this man," she told Katie.

And then she was alone.

Meredith wasn't far, but she was absorbed in conversation, and honestly, Katie found herself slightly uncomfortable around her for the first time. Rather than inch her way closer to that small group, Katie lifted her chin and did her best to project confidence and surety. She finished her champagne and set the empty flute on a table behind her, where it was almost immediately picked up by a member of the waitstaff. His cohort drifted by and offered her another, which she took. She sipped and scanned the room over the rim of her glass.

People watching was something Katie had always enjoyed, even as a kid. She loved to come up with stories for other people in restaurants or stores or the library. Now her eyes traveled over all the sparkling, gorgeous colors, and for the first time since she'd arrived, she noticed the holiday decorations. An enormously beautiful Christmas tree decorated in twinkling white lights stood sentry in a corner. All the tables were lined with white lights and pine boughs. Wreaths hung on the walls, and when she cocked her head to listen, she picked up Christmas music being piped in at a very low volume. Her head began to bob, as if on its own, to "Rockin' Around the Christmas Tree."

She took another sip of her champagne as she continued her people watching, but her gaze was snagged just like a fish on a hook. There was Addison, directly across from her, talking with a very handsome man. He apparently said something funny and she laughed, tossed her head back and exposed her long, elegant throat for all to see. For Katie to see. The sound of that laughter carried across the room and Katie was reminded how wonderful it was, how rarely she heard it. From where she stood, the man's dark hair looked thick and lustrous—and also like a gale force wind wouldn't move it. His teeth were very white and every time he leaned closer to Addison, he put a hand on her upper arm.

Katie felt her nostrils flare the second time he did it, but she immediately recognized the feeling as jealousy and shockingly inappropriate and did her best to tamp it down. Which didn't work because, of course, she was jealous. *Of course* she was. They'd only had the one kiss, but God, the chemistry? They had it in crazy amounts. Nobody could make Katie feel *literally* weak in the knees with just a look from across the room the way Addison could. For about the millionth time, Katie wondered why Addison had never mentioned that kiss, but—also for the millionth time—she remembered that she had never mentioned it either and was just as much to blame for any feelings of incompleteness that resulted.

Maybe it was time to talk about it.

Was it? Or was it too late? She remembered thinking a while ago that she would just make it weird if she brought it up. That was still a valid concern, but…

Was this the champagne talking?

Maybe she should just casually touch on it… *Oh, hey, Addison. Remember that time we made out in your office? Yeah, what was that anyway? And could we do it again? Because the sight of you in this red dress is…doing things to me. Naughty, naughty things…*

Yes. This was definitely the champagne talking.

Katie looked at the glass she held, studied the golden liquid, watched the bubbles form and surface. *Champagne is beautiful. It really is. So pretty.*

"God," she muttered to herself. "I need to eat."

She set the champagne down right where she'd set the last one, and it was scooped up just as quickly, which made Katie stifle a giggle as she looked for some food.

Which, it turned out, was everywhere. How had she not seen it? There was a huge table against one wall covered with hors d'oeuvres, and she got herself a plate and began filling it. A crab cake, many crackers topped with cheese, and three stuffed mushroom caps made up her first course. She popped a cracker into her mouth and instantly felt better. As she reached for a napkin, she felt her. It was so weird, how she knew Addison was behind her before she even spoke.

"I'm sorry," she said, her voice low, a little husky, and insanely sexy.

Katie finished chewing, swallowed, gave herself a beat before responding. "For?"

"I promised I wouldn't leave you alone, and that's exactly what I did not twenty minutes into this gathering."

Katie turned to face her and was once again unexpectedly hit by Addison's beauty. *God, it should be illegal for somebody to look like this.* And her proximity; she was standing very much in Katie's space. Which Katie didn't mind even a tiny bit. Her stomach fluttered in the most pleasant of ways.

Addison smiled hesitantly, obviously worried Katie was upset with her.

Without thinking about it, Katie reached up with one hand and touched the side of Addison's face, stroked it just once, tried not to notice how dark Addison's eyes went. "No worries. I'm a big girl, and you have to mingle." Removing her hand, she forced a chuckle. "I realized I hadn't eaten when the champagne started to go right to my head." *And other places...*

And in that exact moment, Katie realized that she wasn't the only one fighting against the current here. Current? No. Riptide was more accurate. They stood like that, face-to-face, their bodies mere inches apart, eyes locked on one another, for what felt like a very long time. Katie swallowed hard, the food on her plate suddenly forgotten as she sank into those blue eyes, into that gaze that contained so much more than what anybody looking at the two of them from afar could see.

"Come with me," Addison said, and just the sound of those three words—the slight tremor, the low register, the commanding tone—had Katie's breath hitching in her throat. She set her plate down and allowed Addison to take her by the hand.

There was nobody else in that party room. No party guests. No waitstaff. All Katie could see was the enticing vision of red in front of her, and there was no way in the world she wasn't going to follow it.

Addison led her out the door of the enormous room that housed the party and down a hall to their left. The music faded, as did the din of conversation and the clinking of plates and glassware. Soon the only sound was that of their heels clicking down the deserted hallway. They passed several closed doors until they came to one that Addison stopped at and pushed open.

No lights were on and Addison left it that way as she closed the door behind them, but there was a window with no blinds, the moonlight giving what looked to be a small, unused office a bluish tint. It was quiet, and it was sexy being in there alone with Addison. It was so incredibly sexy.

Katie let her gaze roam from the window back to Addison, who took a step toward her so their bodies almost touched, but not quite. Addison's shoes made her three inches taller than normal, but Katie's strappy ones lifted her as well. Her nose at Addison's chin, she looked up into those eyes.

God, those eyes.

There was so much in them when you took the time to look.

Right now? Excitement. A little fear. And hunger. Sweet Jesus, the hunger.

Katie tipped her head up, thinking she couldn't wait one more second for that mouth to be on hers, but Addison pulled back subtly. Katie tried again. Addison repeated the gesture and the slight lift in the corner of her mouth clued Katie in.

"You're teasing me," she whispered.

Addison's hand came up, slid along Katie's cheek, warm fingers curled around the back of her neck and she leaned in so very slowly, her lips a hair's breadth from Katie's. Their noses touched as Addison shifted, tipped her head the other way and then back.

Katie whimpered.

Actually whimpered.

"Please, Addison." Another whisper, words she had no control over. They just tumbled from her, laced with want. With need.

"Please what?" Addison's whisper was just as sexy as her low, husky voice. Maybe more so in that moment.

Katie brought her hand up, touched her fingertips to Addison's full bottom lip, pretty sure her entire body was about to burst into flame. "Please kiss me. Please. Kiss me."

She barely got the last word out before Addison's mouth was on hers, and Katie heard herself whimper again at the blessed contact. Everything fell away until nothing existed in Katie's world but Addison's mouth, her tongue pressing into Katie's. In an unexpected blast of clarity, she realized she could no longer tell where she ended and Addison began; they were one. Addison's hands were everywhere... gripping the back of her head, at the small of her back, pressing them impossibly closer to each other, cupping her ass. Katie tried to focus, tried to concentrate on the glorious body under *her* hands, let them slide and stroke and skim along it. When she felt one of Addison's full breasts, she gently squeezed, her thumb brushing against the bare skin left exposed by fabric. She wrenched their mouths apart long enough to speak.

"This dress, by the way?" she said quietly, sliding both hands up to that open V. She looked into Addison's shockingly dark eyes. "Fucking killing me."

"Yeah?"

"You have no idea."

"Oh, I think I might, because I've wanted to rip yours off since the second you walked through the door."

A laugh bubbled up from deep within Katie and escaped before she could catch it.

Addison's brow furrowed. "What's funny?"

Katie's gaze fell on Addison's mouth, on her kiss-swollen lips, and the smile grew more serious. "I was thinking earlier how strange it was that we never talked about that kiss in your office, and I was wondering if I should bring it up or if I'd just make it weird." Her voice dropped to a whisper as she pulled Addison's mouth down to hers. "I guess I don't have to now, huh?"

There was no time. No clock. They kissed for what might have been hours or might have been minutes. Maybe years. Katie couldn't tell. And she didn't care. She wanted to make out with Addison Fairchild forever; that was the only clear thought in her head.

"Come home with me," Addison said then, and had to clear her throat, repeat herself.

Katie nodded. "Yes." There was no question. No hesitation. She wanted this more than she remembered ever wanting anything in her life. "Yes."

If they could've snuck out a back door, they would have, but it was

December and thirty-seven degrees and they were in evening wear and their coats were near the front entrance. They walked side by side back down the hall, sound and light growing as they approached the coat check. Katie smiled at a man who walked past them, and she wondered if he could tell simply by looking at her that she'd had Addison's tongue in her mouth less than five minutes ago. She swallowed hard as a fresh surge of arousal poked at her lower body, and she brought her fingers to her lips.

"Stop that," Addison whispered, and when Katie looked up at her, she was grinning. "God, you're beautiful."

Katie blushed; she could feel the heat in her face, her ears.

The coat check person handed over their coats to Addison and she thanked him. Turning to Katie, she asked, "Shall we?"

With a nod, Katie followed Addison toward the front entrance of the convention hall where many drivers seemed to be hanging out. Ty caught her eye and immediately sprang into action.

"Ready to go already, Ms. Fairchild?"

He held the door for them, then offered both elbows as they crossed the walkway to the limo that was parked in the horseshoe driveway, along with several others. Katie was surprised to see it was running, which she hoped meant it was warm inside. As if on cue, a shiver ran through her body.

"Almost there, Ms. Cooper," Ty reassured her.

The car was warm. Blissfully so. Once they were settled in the back seat and facing each other, Ty took his place behind the steering wheel. Watching them in the rearview mirror, he asked Addison their destination.

"My place, Ty. And could you close the privacy screen, please?"

Ty gave a nod and then a black partition slid up into place, effectively ensconcing them in the back seat, alone in the dark. Before Katie even registered what was happening, Addison switched seats so she sat next to Katie, their thighs pressed together. Katie looked up at her, at the raw desire on her face, and wondered if it mirrored her own.

Addison laid a hand on Katie's thigh, rubbed her thumb in a circle on her knee, watched her own movements. "For the record, I really want to kiss you right now, but I'm afraid if I start, I won't be able to stop."

Katie completely understood that, especially given the fact that she couldn't make herself form actual words because the nerves in her leg seemed to be connected directly to her center, and it felt like tiny little explosions were being detonated there. She forced down a swallow, then covered Addison's hand with hers, halting the movement. When Addison looked up at her, Katie tilted her head slightly and arched one eyebrow in what she hoped came off as a sexy expression.

Judging by Addison's heavy-lidded gaze and the way she wet her lips, Katie was pretty sure she'd succeeded. Addison gave her a small nod of understanding and said simply, "Okay."

❖

If she was asked in a court of law—on the witness stand, her hand on a Bible, as she swore to tell the truth, the whole truth, and nothing but the truth, so help her God—to recall aloud the path from the limo to inside her loft, Addison would sit in unhelpful, blinking silence. She honestly had no memory of that. It was as if they were in the limo, Addison's hand on Katie's warm thigh, Katie's warm hand on Addison's, holding it in place, and then suddenly, they were in the loft and then kicking off their heels and then Addison was leading Katie by the hand down the hall to her bedroom. For the first time in her life, Addison understood what it felt like when somebody said they "lost time."

But none of that mattered. Not the limo ride. Not the fact that Addison had left the gala much earlier than expected and that she hadn't exactly been subtle about leading Katie out of the party. Not that she would certainly hear about it later. No, she tucked that all away, refusing to worry about any of it right now.

None of it mattered.

The only thing of any importance was this moment. Right here. They stood in Addison's bedroom, the dim light from the hall spilling in just enough for them to see each other. Katie was breathtaking. Literally. When she'd walked into the party, all the air seemed to leave Addison's lungs, and all she could do was stare. She still felt a little light-headed, even now, standing in front of Katie, torn between wanting to simply stare at the beauty of her in her evening attire and wanting to see what was underneath that evening attire. *Everything* that was underneath.

Katie took a step toward her, which left very little space between them. She lifted a hand and wrapped her finger in a chunk of Addison's hair, gave it a gentle tug. Addison heard her swallow, and when Katie looked up, her dark eyes had gone impossibly darker, almost black.

Addison was all about the buildup. The anticipation. She ran the backs of her fingers along Katie's cheek, felt the heated skin, heard the slight increase in her breathing. Katie's hands moved, gripped Addison's waist, pulled her in, closer, so their hips pressed together.

Addison's gaze fell to Katie's mouth. Those full, delicious lips that were now parted, glistening, and any plans she had of drawing out this foreplay flew right out the window.

She couldn't wait any longer.

This kiss was slower, not nearly as frantic as the one earlier, but it was no less heated. In fact, it was more so. Addison felt it, that red-hot wave of arousal, of desire. It seemed to start at her toes and work its way up, aiming right for her center where it set up a subtle throbbing as she kissed Katie Cooper with everything she had.

Addison was lost, with no idea about anything but the mouth beneath hers. When Katie pulled hers away, Addison felt like part of her world had been taken, and a tiny sound of protest pushed from her lips.

"God, Addison," Katie said, her breathing ragged. She ran her fingertips across Addison's bottom lip, and when Addison leaned in for another kiss, Katie pulled back and one corner of her mouth tugged up. "Wait," she whispered, then took a step back. Reaching up, she unfastened whatever was holding her hair in place, and it tumbled down around her shoulders, the curls still present, making her look sexily tousled. She waved one finger up and down in front of Addison. "I want that dress off." Her voice was quiet, but firm. Commanding. Addison arched a brow, deciding to play a little bit.

"Aren't I the boss around here?" she asked.

"Not tonight," Katie replied simply and in the same tone. "I'd do it myself, but I'm afraid I'd get impatient and just rip it." She paused, looked pointedly at Addison. "Off."

Yeah, okay, that was hot. Addison could admit it. So much for playing. Reaching behind her, she pulled the zipper at the small of her back down slowly, then ran her fingers along the V in the front to loosen the adhesive she'd had to use to prevent any wardrobe malfunctions.

After that, she was able to grip the front and simply pull each side down, over her arms. Her eyes never left Katie's face as she pushed the dress over her hips and let it drop into a red pool of fabric at her feet. Katie's gaze on her felt tangible, as if she could actually feel her eyes as they roamed over her nearly naked body.

"My God," Katie said, her voice an awed whisper. "You were wearing a thong all night?"

"I was."

"I wish I'd known—" Katie barely finished the words before holding up a halting hand. "No. It's probably better that I didn't." She stepped closer to Addison and, with that same halting hand, made a move to touch her.

Addison caught that hand in mid-reach, and when Katie looked up in surprise, she shook her head. "Your turn," she said. "Much as I hate to see that gorgeously sparkly dress go, I'm much more interested in what's under it."

Katie stared at her for a moment, and Addison almost wondered if she was going to refuse. But then she turned her back to Addison, lifted her hair off her shoulders, and waited. Understanding, Addison held her breath as she slowly pulled the zipper down, exposing Katie's back and her black bra, and Katie stepped away before Addison could touch.

Facing her again, Katie peeled the dress off and, like Addison, let it puddle on the floor around her feet. She stood there in a black lace bra and matching string bikinis, and Addison had a hard time catching her breath. Or forming a thought. Or speaking. At all. Instead, she simply brought her fingers to her lips and slowly shook her head in complete and total awe of the beauty on display in front of her.

Apparently, Katie wasn't about to wait any longer. Addison saw the shift, saw it on her face just as readily as if Katie had said it out loud. Her eyes narrowed under heavy lids. Her nostrils flared slightly. She wet her lips with her tongue. And then she moved. She quickly stepped out of the dress, took the two steps needed to put her directly in front of Addison, grabbed her head in both hands, and crushed their mouths together in such a flurry of action that Addison had no time to do anything but yip out a little cry of surprise and then let herself sink. She couldn't help it. If she had to sink with somebody, she could think of nobody she'd rather go under with than Katie Cooper.

Making out took on a whole new level of eroticism when both women were almost naked. Addison flinched in surprise when Katie found her breast, kneaded it gently before quickly zeroing in on a nipple, pulling a gasp from her throat. Addison held her tightly, pulled her in closer, and felt the expanse of Katie's back under her palms, the skin warm, silky. She felt like she couldn't get Katie close enough, tried to pull her more tightly against her own body.

One thing she was sure of: She'd had enough of standing. Slowly, she backed them toward the bed until Katie's thighs hit the mattress. She sat, then slid herself backward, her eyes never leaving Addison's, until she was sitting in the middle. Addison crawled after her, on top of her, forcing Katie to lie back.

"It's so hard to go slow," Addison whispered, her lips millimeters from Katie's. "I want to. I really do."

Katie's responding smile was filled with understanding. "I know. I want to go slow, too." She stroked Addison's cheek as her eyes became hooded. "Maybe we can do that later." With a quick move, she flipped their bodies and Addison found herself on her back without even realizing it had happened. Katie's mouth was on hers before she could protest. And then she didn't want to.

Addison had never been with any woman like Katie. In the past, her sexual partners—and there hadn't been many—expected Addison to take the lead. And she had; she didn't mind that. But Katie taking the lead was new. Refreshing. And fucking sexy as hell.

Using her knees, Katie pushed Addison's legs apart, braced over her on all fours, and just…looked. Her eyes roamed Addison's body, slowly scanning over her neck, her shoulders, stopping for several long seconds at her breasts. She brought one hand up, laid it on Addison's throat, stroked the skin there. Trailed it down to cup a breast, and she looked directly into Addison's eyes as she kneaded it, stroked it, finally focusing on the nipple, gently squeezing it, seemingly gauging Addison's reaction. Which was to suck in a breath and to have no control over the gentle rocking of her hips.

Katie looked down and saw the movement, and a sensual smile spread across her face. "Did you want something, Addison?" she whispered.

"Yes. I want you."

"You're gonna have to wait your turn, I'm afraid." Then Katie took the other nipple into her mouth and sucked. Hard. Addison felt the gentle pain of teeth and hissed in a breath. "Sorry. Too hard?"

Addison grinned and shook her head.

"Good." Katie shifted her position, moving her knees up, which forced Addison's legs farther apart. Again, she stared into Addison's eyes as she trailed her fingers down Addison's stomach, along the outside of her thigh, then up the inside. When she brushed against Addison's center, the touch was so subtle, Addison wondered if she'd imagined it. Then Katie did it again, and this time, there was no imagining. Again and again, Katie skimmed her finger over Addison, feather-light, until Addison was tossing her head back and forth, lifting her hips in a plea for more contact, one hand gripping Katie's forearm, the other crushing the corner of the pillow under her head.

"Damn it, Katie," she said through clenched teeth. She couldn't take any more. "Please. *Please.*"

"Well, since you asked nicely."

Katie's fingers plunged into Addison's wetness and Addison was pretty sure she was going to simply explode, leave a pile of ash on her very expensive sheets. But that didn't happen right away. Katie pushed in, circled, pulled out. Slowly, over and over, until Addison couldn't pinpoint exactly what she was doing at all. Was she inside? Was she touching her center? It all blurred into one mind-blowing wave of pleasure...and that's when the explosion happened.

Katie stayed with her, kept her hand pressed between Addison's legs as the orgasm ripped through her, forcing sounds from her throat she'd never made in her entire life. Every muscle in her body tightened like it might snap, and she lifted her hips off the bed as she grasped blindly for the headboard, something, anything to hold on to. If asked her own name in that moment, she'd have had no idea. Nothing mattered but the unfathomable pleasure that blasted through her body and the woman that had caused it. Nothing.

With no idea how long it took her to come down, for her heartbeat to return somewhat to normal, for her lungs to work again, Addison finally opened her eyes. Katie was on her side, braced on an elbow, head in her hand, her other hand stroking Addison's stomach.

"Hi," she said, a very satisfied smile on her face.

"Oh, my God," Addison said, surprised to find herself still a little breathless.

"I will take that as a compliment."

"Please do. That was…that was…" Addison shook her head. No words.

"I will take that as a compliment as well."

Addison nodded and turned her head slightly to look into those rich brown eyes. Eyes that were sparkling. Eyes filled with kindness and caring. Eyes of a woman she… Before she realized it was happening, Addison felt her own eyes well up. *What is happening?* screamed through her head as she clenched her jaw tightly and willed away the emotion.

Katie's entire expression softened as she used her thumb to wipe away the one tear that must have escaped. "It's okay," she whispered.

There was only one way to eclipse the embarrassment that threatened to swamp Addison, and she grabbed onto it. In one quick move, she had Katie on her back, Addison's entire body stretched out above her. "It will be," she said, just before she kissed Katie with every ounce of energy and feeling she had. And when she finally pulled back, Katie's eyes were wide, her breathing ragged, and she made a sound that was a sexy cross between a whimper and a moan that had Addison instantly wet all over again.

Yeah, this was going to take a while.

CHAPTER SEVENTEEN

*T*hank *God for Uber*, Katie thought, as she never seemed to have her own car anymore. She sat in the back of a Toyota Camry driven by "Karl" and wondered if he could tell by looking at her what her night had been like. Did she look like she'd spent hours making love with the most beautiful woman she'd ever seen? Did she smell like it? And that thought made her grin. And blush a little. And sink down into her seat...which brought to her attention the pleasant soreness that she'd woken up with. A little stiff here, a little tender there...

God, what a night.

Katie hated to leave this morning, but she knew she should get home to help her mother with her father. While it was true that having the home health aide helped immensely, she still felt like she should be there more often than she was. Her mom was still exhausted and her father wasn't going to get anything but worse. When Katie had texted last night to tell her mom she would be staying at Addison's, Liz was nothing but excitedly supportive. Still, Katie wanted to get home. She needed to.

She probably should've woken Addison up, but she looked so gorgeous, so beautifully peaceful when she was sound asleep. So different than her tense alertness in the office. Her breathing was deep and even, her lips slightly parted, the comforter covering most of her but leaving one leg enticingly visible. Katie knew if she did wake Addison up, she wouldn't be leaving any time soon. So she'd hunted for paper and left a note. Then, not wanting to get back into her dress and heels from last night, she snagged a pair of yoga pants, a bright blue sweatshirt, and some Nikes that were only about half a size too big for her.

What could only be described as a dreamy sigh escaped her lips as Karl pulled up in front of her house. She thanked him and headed inside.

"Well, there she is." Her father's cheerful voice surprised Katie, made her stand in the foyer and blink for a beat before reminding herself to take every moment she could and savor it. David sat in his chair watching what looked to be *Deadliest Catch* on the television. "Hi, Katie-cat. Have a fun night?" he asked her.

With a nod, Katie crossed over to kiss him on the cheek as she said, "I did. Very much so," and tried to hide the tears that welled in her eyes, just as they did every time her father actually seemed like *himself.* Her mother came from the kitchen, wiping her hands on a dish towel, a knowing grin on her face. When Liz raised her eyebrows, Katie chuckled and held up a finger. "Let me go shower first."

As she undressed, she held the sweatshirt to her face and inhaled deeply, taking in the unique scent of Addison. She couldn't describe its combination accurately—a blend of something spicy, something woodsy, something edible—but knew beyond a shadow of a doubt that it was her. If she were blindfolded and given three different shirts to smell, she'd easily be able to pick out which one belonged to Addison. She felt surrounded by that scent and she loved that, was almost reluctant to get in the shower and scrub it all away. She actually lingered on the bath mat for a long moment before sighing and stepping inside.

The hot water of the shower reminded her how sore she was as it beat on her shoulders, her thighs. Even her nipples ached, and the sudden flash she got of Addison's mouth on them, her hands, her fingers, sent a surge of wetness between her legs that had nothing at all to do with the shower. She stood under the water for a long time, her hands folded near her chin—she could still smell Addison on them—while her brain played her a sexy little montage of the previous night. Naked bodies, sweat-slicked skin, whimpers and moans and cries. The feel of Addison's astonishingly sexy body under her hands, her mouth. The feel of Addison's hands and mouth on Katie's own body. How they'd hurried and slowed, then hurried, then slowed. Addison's beautiful blue eyes filling with tears after that first time, and how sweetly embarrassed she'd been by them. Katie let the water beat down on her until she was pink from head to toe and the heat began to taper, which was a good thing because her memories had her overheating in a major way.

She got out, dried herself off, and put on her own leggings, but opted for Addison's sweatshirt again. There was something about wearing Addison's clothes that made Katie feel closer to her somehow, kept the memories of last night alive, fresh. She left her hair wet, her face devoid of makeup, and headed downstairs to face all the questions her mother surely had.

Liz sat at the kitchen table with a cup of coffee. Voices from the living room told Katie that the home health aide had arrived.

"You look much more relaxed than you have," Katie said to her mom, as she got herself a mug and filled it with coffee from the fresh pot on the counter. It was true. She still looked very tired and a little sad—always a little sad—but the stress that usually veiled her features was a bit less obvious.

Liz sipped her coffee as Katie took a seat across from her. "Speaking of relaxed, tell me about your night."

It was interesting to look at her mother then. Interesting because, as an adult, Katie could now see different aspects of facial expressions that she never noticed as a kid. For example, right then, Liz's face held a combination of emotions, and Katie knew her so well that she could see each of them clearly. There was curiosity, of course. There was an edge of excited "tell me all the dirty details," as if they were college roommates. There was also a sheen of worry, of concern, and Katie understood that just as well as the other feelings because she had her own worry and concern. She'd slept with her boss. On top of that, she had developed feelings for her boss.

In the grand scheme of things, neither was good, but she honestly wasn't sure which was worse.

❖

When Addison opened her eyes on Sunday morning, she noticed a couple of things right away. First of all, she'd slept like a baby and now felt more rested and energized than she could remember feeling in…well, she couldn't remember when. Ever? It was possible. Second, she was alone in the bed. She lay there listening for several moments but finally came to the conclusion that, yes, she was by herself. The disappointment she felt about that was a little bit stronger than she wanted to acknowledge, but when she turned her head to her right—the side of the bed Katie'd fallen asleep on last night—and saw the note propped up against the bedside lamp, that disappointment faded. Addison rolled onto her stomach and reached for the piece of paper.

I had to get home to help with my dad and I couldn't bear to wake you, you looked so peaceful. Had an amazing time last night. Text later.

Katie had drawn a swirly little heart and signed her name. Addison shook her head at the schoolgirl grin the note brought to her face. While she would have preferred to lounge around this morning and have breakfast together—something she hadn't done with anybody in years—she knew Katie had an obligation to her family, and Addison would never stand in the way of that. It was true that her own father was often absent, but she knew if she needed him, he'd show up. She couldn't imagine what it must be like to have him nearby all the time but not be mentally present for much of it.

Rolling onto her back again, Addison stared up at the high ceiling of her bedroom and let herself reminisce about the limb-melting, toe-curling night she'd spent with Katie. Her grin widened as the thought occurred to her that Katie's cheerful enthusiasm in life also carried into the bedroom, where she was very much engaged and fun and completely open. Even better, Katie liked to snatch the upper hand from Addison—not something Addison was used to or allowed very often. But Katie had done so several times even after that first one. Once the clothes had all come off, they'd been on utterly equal ground—something new for Addison. She was used to being the boss, being in charge. But Katie Cooper had no problem playing that role, and surprisingly, Addison had no problem letting her. In her mind's eye, she recalled Katie above her on her hands and knees, looking down into her eyes. Telling her how sexy she was and then using her knees to push Addison's apart, almost roughly.

Arousal washed through her now as she recalled their third—or was it fourth?—time, Katie's hands on her thighs, holding her open as Katie's mouth, her tongue, did such sexy, erotic things to her, and a gentle, insistent throbbing began as she lay there in the morning light.

Addison reached for her phone and, before she could overthink, sent a text to Katie.

I want you. Right now.

Then she tossed the phone back onto the nightstand and let her memory have its way with her for a while longer.

When she got out of the shower a little while later, there was a text waiting from Katie.

The feeling is totally, completely, utterly mutual.

Addison couldn't keep the grin off her face. That is, until the next text came through fifteen minutes later. From her mother.

Family dinner tonight. 7 pm. Do not be late.

No preamble. No comments—good or bad—about last night. And just like that, Addison's lovely, carefree mood flew away to parts unknown. For a split second, she actually thought she could see it, that mood, sprouting wings and taking off from her shoulder, leaving her far behind while her usual worries and stress and intensity came stomping back in to take over. As if on cue, her stomach cramped for the first time in days, and Addison clenched her teeth as she bent forward slightly to ride it out.

It was kind of amazing how quickly her outlook could shift. Even Addison was aware of it, though she tried not to dwell. She did her best to shove Katie and their amazing night together into a corner of her mind so she could focus on the work she'd brought home on Friday. She spent most of Sunday on her laptop, returning emails, sending some out, doing research on James Lang and his complexes, even though she'd already learned everything she could possibly know about the man, from his age (fifty-seven) to his marital status (on wife number three) to his favorite sport (golf...of course) from him last night. And when she couldn't take it anymore, she sent a text to Katrina asking if her mother was mad at her for leaving the gala early. Her sister's return text came almost immediately.

She'll get over it. More importantly, HOW ARE YOU?

The capital letters made Addison chuckle, and before she could answer, another text came.

Did you and Katie leave together?

Addison gazed out the window at the light flurries as she thought about how to answer. If she should answer at all. It wasn't like they were subtle. They left the gala pretty much hand in hand and never returned. There really was only one conclusion anybody who had seen them could come to. Her phone beeped again with another text.

Addie, it's okay. Katie's great. You light up when she's around.

Was that true? Addison's brow furrowed as she pondered the words. Because the reality was setting in now. In the harsh light of day, the facts were suddenly clear. Katie was Addison's subordinate, and Fairchild Enterprises had a strict code about that sort of thing.

Won't matter to Mom, she texted back.

Katrina's response didn't come right away this time. Several minutes went by and Addison wished they were in the same room so she could see her sister's face, get a read on what she was thinking. Finally, the text came. *You never know.* Not exactly a super-positive response. More likely, it was Katrina trying to make her feel better. Which was nice of her, Addison had to admit. She was lucky to have such a great sister, even if she didn't always cop to it.

I'm sure I'll find out tonight.

The text exchange ended there and Addison got back to work for a little while longer before she had to change for dinner. She used to look forward to these gatherings, used to enjoy getting to spend time with her parents (when her dad was in town) and siblings. Now, though, it felt like that was a long, long time ago. Lately, the dinners just felt tedious. A lot of things felt tedious to her recently, and she wasn't sure why. The funny thing was, she'd never thought to examine it before. It never occurred to her to ask herself why. She simply accepted the feeling as something she had to deal with.

Addison stood and walked to the window she'd been staring out on and off all day. The traffic was light. The snow still fell softly, not sticking this time, though it would in the next week or two. The sun had set and dusk was creeping slowly in, dimming the lights and shading the sky in an indigo glow as the December days got shorter and shorter. She leaned her forehead against the cold glass of the window and tried to ease her racing thoughts. This was dinner with her family. It should be enjoyable, not something she dreaded.

Her phone beeped and she slid it from her back pocket and smiled. She couldn't help herself.

Katie.

Can I see you tonight?

Addison frowned. *Dinner with the fam. Maybe after?* God, was this a bad idea? She was so torn, but the thought of seeing Katie's face, of looking into those brown eyes, of watching them darken and hearing her breath hitch as Addison touched her…she wanted that again. So very much.

Sounds great. Text me when you're free.

In her head, Addison knew that this was going to cause nothing but problems.

In her heart, she didn't care.

CHAPTER EIGHTEEN

In the midst of the holiday season, Scartelli's was busy even on a Sunday night, and Addison had trouble finding a parking spot. The snow that hadn't been sticking earlier had apparently changed its mind and was now building up on roadways and sidewalks, making travel just the tiniest bit harder. In the lot, she picked out her mother's BMW as well as both Katrina's and Jared's cars, and irritation with herself at being the last one to arrive again settled in on her. Finally catching somebody leaving, Addison waited, parked, and headed inside.

The restaurant smelled heavenly, as it always did, the aromas of basil and oregano and simmering tomato sauce hanging in the air. Addison had decided long ago this must be the way every Italian grandmother's kitchen smelled. It was warm. Inviting. Comforting.

Nodding at the hostess behind her little podium, Addison headed to their reserved back room—absently taking note of all the glittering Christmas decorations—where she found all the usual suspects. Jack and Ed were both present again, their wives at their sides. Hellos went around the room as Addison took off her coat and hung it on the rack in the corner with everybody else's.

Her mother barely spared her a glance.

It's not like I didn't expect that. With a quiet sigh, Addison took her seat at the table. She'd talk with her mother privately after dinner.

Jared got everybody's attention, then picked up his glass of wine. "I just want to say what an amazing Christmas gala that was last night." Murmurs and nods of agreement went around the table. "We had a record number of guests and we raised—" He glanced at Katrina for confirmation. "Nearly three hundred grand?"

Katrina nodded, her smile wide and proud.

"Nearly three hundred grand for the hospital. I'd like to toast to that."

"Hear, hear," Jack said as everybody raised their glasses and clinked.

Big bowls of food were brought in and set on the table, and everybody talked amongst themselves as dishes were passed around. Addison's stomach was still sour—it had been all day and her mother's lack of eye contact didn't help—so while she made a show of filling her plate, she didn't eat much.

"You feeling okay?" Katrina asked her quietly as she leaned close.

"Fine."

"I'll pretend I believe you." She cut a meatball with her fork, popped a piece into her mouth. "I want to hear all about your night." That was said in a whisper, thank God, because Addison was not ready to address the subject of her night with Katie with the entire table.

"Later," Addison muttered.

"You two looked amazing together. Uh-*maz*-ing."

Addison fought the small grin that wanted to tug up the corners of her mouth. She lost.

"I meant what I said earlier," Katrina said, again leaning close, still so only Addison could hear. "I like you together."

I like us together, too, Addison thought, but there was no way she would say it out loud. She couldn't. That would be getting way ahead of herself. Way ahead of everything. No, she needed to maintain control of this, to relax around it. They'd had a wonderful night. That much was true. It was fun. It was exciting. It was sexy. Didn't have to mean anything beyond that, did it?

Any further trail of thought was halted by Meredith's voice, raised a bit to be heard over the hum of dinner conversation. "I'd like to speak for a moment, if you wouldn't mind giving me your attention."

Addison set down her fork and picked up her glass. As she took a sip, she made eye contact with her mother for the first time all evening. It was both a relief and a discomfort. Meredith offered her a barely visible smile, then moved her gaze around the table, her expression open and happy as she stood.

"I am so grateful to have all of you," she said, and the pride on her face was evident. She glowed. It made Addison's heart warm for her mom. "The holiday season always makes me a little mushy, so I hope you'll forgive me if I get overly sentimental." Soft chuckles went around the table as Meredith looked at each of her kids. "My three beautiful children." She shifted her gaze to Ed, then to Jack. "My right-hand men. I count on each of you every day, and you've never let me down. It's because of you that Fairchild Enterprises has been so successful and steady for so long. I owe each of you more thanks than I could ever give." As she did every year, Meredith pulled out her tablet and gave an overall "state of the businesses" report, telling the room how much of a profit each arm of F.E. made for the year, how much each gave to charity, and what was expected for the upcoming year. The numbers were excellent, which wasn't a surprise. Katrina's and Jared's stayed steady from the previous year. Addison's numbers went up, and she smiled as Katrina bumped her with a shoulder.

Setting the tablet back down on the table, Meredith looked to each of them around the table as she spoke. "So, with all the accounting put to rest, I think now is as good a time as any to make an announcement."

Eyebrows shot up. Eyes widened. Meredith was going to announce her successor. Here and now, at dinner, when none of them expected it. Addison's stomach revolted, her ulcer making itself known, and she clenched her teeth against the sharp pain that hit, felt a sheen of sweat break out across her forehead.

"As you all know, I am ready to retire." Meredith leaned forward with a little conspiratorial grin and added, "At least I think I am." Dutiful chuckles went around the room as she stood straight again. "Which means I'll need somebody to take my seat at the head of Fairchild Enterprises, to oversee it all. To run my kingdom." She winked to take any conceit out of the statement. "It wasn't an easy decision, but I believe it's the right one. Come January first, I will happily turn over the reins to my daughter, Katrina."

Addison blinked. She felt like the floor fell out from under her, yet she couldn't move. She just sat there. And blinked. Ed and Jack applauded supportively; clearly, they'd already known. Jared and Katrina and their spouses all looked as shocked as Addison must have. As shocked as she felt. Her hands clenched into fists in her lap. Unclenched. Clenched again. Unclenched. She blinked some more, too rapidly. Her stomach joined her fists in the clenching and it felt like her stomach was ripping her apart from the inside.

Air. What had happened to the air? She couldn't breathe. She had to get out of there.

"Addie. Are you okay?" Katrina asked quietly as she put a hand on Addison's upper arm. Addison shook it off.

"I don't...I don't understand," Addison said, and hated how timid and uncertain her voice sounded.

"Addison," Meredith said, and the sad smile on her face was too much. It was just too much for Addison. Meredith looked like she was about to explain something to a small child, and Addison couldn't stand that idea. Couldn't take it.

The warning cock of her head must have been enough for Meredith, because she stopped talking as Addison pushed her chair back and stood. She couldn't listen to the explanation, no matter what it was, because she was way too close to tears. The last thing in the world she wanted to do was start crying in front of her siblings, in front of Jack and Ed and their wives. But she didn't understand. She had so many questions that she just couldn't bring herself to ask without emotion taking over. No. She had to get out of there. Without another word, she grabbed her coat off the rack and pushed through the door of the private room, out into the bustle of the busy restaurant.

Her car was covered in light, powdery snow, but she didn't want to take too much time brushing it off in case somebody came out after her. She needed to escape. She keyed the ignition, quickly brushed off the rear window, then hit the wipers for the front.

"What the *fuck*?" she said out loud as she drove, then punctuated it with a couple of smacks to the steering wheel. That was supposed to be her job. *Her job*. Everybody thought so. Even Katrina, judging by the astonished look on her face. "What the actual *fuck*?" Addison had worked her ass off. For years, she'd been preparing to take over the family business. *For years*. She was the oldest. She had no distractions...no spouse, no kids, nothing to preoccupy her. She did nothing but work. Hell, she had the bleeding ulcer and the high blood pressure to show for it. How could her mother do this to her?

"It's because of Katie," she said into the empty car. "I knew it. God, I should've known better than..." She let her words trail off as she wondered what the hell she'd been thinking, dragging a woman out of the company Christmas gala and never returning. Not just a woman. Her *subordinate*. She'd broken her mother's cardinal rule and now she was paying for it. "Fucking A, Addison, what the hell were you thinking? You know the rules. You knew this would happen. You *knew* it!" She pounded the steering wheel again.

It was less than two weeks before Christmas and everything around Addison was so goddamn cheerful, she wanted to scream. White lights were twisted around the streetlight poles. Wreaths hung from the fronts of businesses. A car drove by with a giant red nose on its grill and antlers sticking up from each side window.

Addison hated them all.

It was only when she'd finally pulled into the underground garage at her building that she forced herself to accept that she shouldn't have run off in a huff like that. Made her look like a petty teenager. But she was so hurt and so freaking angry that she felt the only course of action was to get away from all of them, especially the ones looking at her with pity.

Her phone had pinged the entire ride home and did so again in the elevator. With an irritated sigh, Addison pulled it out of her purse. Three texts from Katrina asking if she was okay. One from her mother saying they needed to talk.

"Yeah, no thanks." She deleted that one.

The next was from Katie. *Hope dinner's going well. Can't wait to see you. Text me when you're done.*

"Goddamn it," Addison whispered out on a sigh. The elevator opened on her floor and she headed into her loft. She couldn't see Katie tonight. She was in no mood. In fact, she shouldn't see Katie again at all. Since the first day they'd met, she'd done nothing but cause turmoil. Addison had seen it immediately and yet she'd done nothing about it.

When the little voice in her head reminded her of their night together, how wonderful it had been, how sexy, how freeing, Addison mentally told it to shut the fuck up.

In her bedroom, she took off her dinner clothes, left them in a pile on the floor, and put on sweats but was unable to find her favorite blue hoodie. "Of course," she muttered, pawing through drawers. "Icing on the cake of this godforsaken day." She settled on a different shirt, pulled it on, and went out into the kitchen for something stronger than wine.

Whiskey would do.

She took the glass back to the bedroom, flopped onto her bed, and clicked on the TV, channel surfing for something mindless. Finding a cheesy horror movie with laughable special effects, she tossed the remote down and took a slug of the alcohol, which burned its way down her throat and didn't let up once it hit her stomach.

Her phone pinged again and she picked it up with an annoyed groan. Katrina again.

Are you okay?

Addison typed back quickly. *I'm fine. Leave me alone please.*

When she sent it, she saw Katie's text again and knew she needed to get ahead of it, so typed a quick response to her as well. *Not feeling great. Not up for company.* It was cold, yes, but Addison had nothing left in her to help with creativity. She honestly just wanted everybody to leave her the hell alone.

"I just want to get drunk," she said, then took another slug of whiskey. "I want to get drunk and..." A lump suddenly lodged in her throat as the words hit her brain. *...and wonder how my life ended up so...empty.*

A tear slid down her cheek.

CHAPTER NINETEEN

When Katie arrived at work Monday afternoon, she was surprised to find Addison's office dark. She took off her coat, got herself all set up, then buzzed Janie on the intercom.

"Hey, Janie? Is Addison at an off-site meeting or something?"

"No, she called in sick."

"She what?"

"She called in sick. Didn't she tell you?"

"She didn't. No."

"It's very unusual, that's for sure. I don't think she's ever called in sick since I've been working here." Janie sounded slightly mystified. "Maybe she's got that horrible flu that's going around."

"Maybe." Katie's brow furrowed as she thanked Janie, then scrolled through her phone to see if she'd missed a text. Nothing jumped out at her, so she quickly typed one out and sent it.

Everything okay? Janie said you're sick. What's up?

When no reply came right away, Katie sat down and got to work. When she logged into Addison's email account, she was surprised to see that Addison hadn't answered any of it. In fact, she hadn't even read it.

"Wow," Katie said softly, a hint of worry creeping in. "She must *really* be sick."

It was weird. While Katie didn't want Addison to be sick—of *course* she didn't—she found herself slightly relieved. After the abrupt, impersonal text from last night, a little ball of doubt had rolled in and parked itself in the pit of Katie's stomach. Because, let's be honest, they'd had sex the night before, and now it seemed quite possible

Addison was blowing her off with some lame excuse about not feeling well. At least the fact that she'd called in sick backed her up so that maybe it wasn't a lame excuse after all and Katie could relax.

Deciding it made more sense to simply sit at Addison's desk, Katie moved her things and got to work. The red light on Addison's phone was blinking and when Katie dialed in, she found six waiting voice mails.

"Who even leaves voice mail messages anymore?" she muttered as she listened to each one and jotted notes. She returned three of them. The other three were going to need input from Addison herself. Katie opened all the new email, responded to the ones she could, and flagged those that needed Addison's attention. Then she made a list of things they needed to discuss tomorrow, when she assumed Addison would return.

Between the phone calls—two of which came with fires that needed putting out—and the constant incoming emails, not to mention the pop-ins by various staff members, Katie's afternoon flew by. She only knew what time it was because Janie buzzed her to bid her good night. At six.

She hadn't heard her phone beep, but when she picked it up, there was a return text from Addison.

Fine. Just really sick.

"Oh, man," Katie said, then typed, *I'm so sorry. Can I bring you anything? Soup?*

The next response came immediately. *No. Probably contagious. Thanks anyway.*

Katie stared at her screen for nearly a full minute before putting the phone down without typing back. She didn't like the way it was making her feel, causing an uncomfortable churning in her gut, but she had no reason to think Addison wasn't actually sick. The woman never called in sick, according to Janie, so if she had, she *must be* sick. Right? It was the only thing that made sense. Unfortunate timing, yes, but Katie needed not to make it about her. This was about the sick woman and nothing else.

Wasn't it?

It took everything she had not to drive over to Addison's loft and check on her. But she was pretty familiar with Addison's demeanor, her short texts and to-the-point instructions. If she said not to come over, she meant do not come over. And while Katie did allow herself the leeway of thinking that, because they'd had sex, she could probably skirt some of Addison's rules, she wasn't 100 percent sure. She liked to think she knew Addison, but the reality was, she only knew what Addison showed her. Katie was a smart girl and she also understood that Addison was one of those people who ran very deep and complicated under that calm surface of hers and knowing her was not a quick and easy accomplishment. She had the feeling Addison was like a set of Russian nesting dolls and that every time you cracked through a layer, there was another solid one underneath.

But Katie wanted to know her. She wanted to know everything about her.

That was going to be a challenge. But it was one she was up for.

❖

It was Wednesday at noon and Katrina didn't bother knocking. Didn't call out a warning. No hello. She simply slid her key into the lock of Addison's front door and let herself in.

"What the—?" Addison sat up quickly from the couch, an expression of confusion all over her face. "What the hell, Katrina?" Her voice was sharp; her eyebrows dove into a V above her nose. "Haven't you ever heard of knocking?"

"Haven't you ever heard of being a goddamn adult?" Katrina snapped back.

She was done. She was *so* done.

Addison flinched as though Katrina had slapped her. "What?"

Katrina tossed her purse down on the chair, and her coat followed the purse. The television was blasting some cheesy infomercial about an indoor grill pan, and Katrina clicked it off, sending the room into silence. Then she parked her hands on her hips and stared down her big sister. "Seriously. Are you fucking twelve?"

Addison sighed and waved a hand at her, then settled back down onto the couch and reached for the remote on the coffee table. "Go away, Kat."

"Not until I say a few things." Katrina snatched the remote away before Addison could turn the TV back on. She'd almost said, "Not until I unload on you," but that seemed a little harsh, even for these circumstances. But it was exactly what she wanted to do because she'd had so much more than enough.

"Terrific."

Katrina took a seat in the chair across from the couch. She braced her forearms on her knees, folded her hands, and studied her sister. She looked like hell. Her hair was pulled up into a messy bun, but even that didn't hide the fact that it was dull and stringy. She had no makeup on, which only made the dark circles under her eyes stand out like she was about to take up her position in center field. Her sweatshirt was wrinkled, as were her yoga pants, as if she'd been lying on the couch for days in them. Which Katrina was pretty sure she had.

"What's going on with you?" she asked softly, surprising herself by taking a more gentle approach than she'd intended.

Addison turned to her, wide-eyed. "Really? Have you been away?"

Katrina frowned. "No, Addie, I haven't. I know what happened and I know you were upset by it. But what's—" She waved a finger around to encompass Addison's form. "What's all this? This isn't you. You don't...pout. You don't sulk."

"I'm not sulking."

Katrina tipped her head from one side to the other, then waited, but Addison didn't offer more. "Look. I get it. You expected to take over Mom's seat. Honestly, that's what Jared and I expected, too, but... have you even talked to her?" She already knew the answer. Meredith had called and texted several times since Sunday, and Addison hadn't answered. Meredith wasn't about to come over here. *I didn't get where I am today by kowtowing to anybody who doesn't like my decisions, you know*, she'd said to Katrina earlier in the week, using her usual bluster to cover up the fact that she was actually quite hurt by her daughter's cold shoulder.

Addison shook her head.

"Maybe you should."

When Addison turned to look at Katrina, there was no anger this time. No flash of ire. Only hurt. Pain. Confusion. "Why?" Addison asked quietly, her eyes welling up. "So she can tell me that working my ass off for pretty much my entire life, that forfeiting everything else so I could focus solely on her company, wasn't good enough? That all my dedication was for nothing?"

Katrina almost laughed then. She felt the chuckle bubbling up from her gut but forced herself to swallow it. This was not the time for teasing. It was a time for explanation. And she had to grudgingly admit to a tiny sliver of sympathy for her stubborn, often very black-and-white sister. Hands on her thighs, Katrina pushed herself to her feet and strolled over to the windows, gazed out onto the bustling street below, watched the people hurrying home early on one of the last shopping days before Christmas. "I have always admired you," she said without turning around. "From the time I was old enough to know you were my big sister, I've wanted to be just like you. We've both heard the stories of how, as a toddler, I followed you everywhere."

A small snort came from the couch. "You drove me crazy," Addison said, but there was nothing but fondness in her tone.

"In school, I tried to be like you. Tried out for the same teams and clubs." Katrina turned then, looked at Addison who, surprisingly, seemed to be paying close attention to her words. "I only made a few of them. I was never quite as good as you. At anything. Everybody knew it. And you know what? I was okay with that. You were my big sister and I have never been anything but proud of you." She moved back to the chair, took a seat as she contemplated her next words. "Lately, though…" She only saw that her words startled Addison because she was watching her closely.

"Lately what?"

"Lately, my pride in you has decreased because lately, my frustration with you has grown. Lately, Addie, you've become kind of…dense."

Addison's eyebrows shot up, as did the tone of her voice. "Dense? You think I'm dense?"

Katrina nodded. She knew this stung—though Addison would never admit to that—but she had to push on. There was no turning back now. Addison needed to hear it all. "I mean, you're stubborn. You always have been. That's not news. And it's served you well. I often wish I was as hardheaded as you, as focused. But I've never thought of you as so focused that you miss the entire big picture before."

Addison sat up now. Swung her legs around and mirrored Katrina's position. Her brows met in a V above her nose, and she was obviously puzzled. "What big picture? What is it that you think I'm missing?"

Her voice was low. Quiet. Katrina recognized it as her sister's you've-hurt-me-but-instead-of-saying-so-I'm-going-to-gather-information voice. She knew it well. Had counted on it, actually.

"*The* big picture. All of it. You're missing so much right now."

"Such as?"

"God, where do I start?" Katrina made a show of looking to the ceiling as if searching, even though she had the list right there in her head, everything she needed Addison to open her eyes and see. "First of all, how about *reasons* Mom might have for not choosing you to take over F.E. that maybe have nothing to do with your work? Think about that for a minute." She wasn't about to speak for their mother, but she had a pretty good idea why Meredith didn't choose Addison to step into a job that would make her feel like she had to work even harder than she already did now. "Second, what do you do for fun?"

The question seemed to catch Addison off guard, just as Katrina had hoped it would. "For fun? What do you mean?"

Katrina cocked her head. "The mere fact that you have to ask me what I mean when I ask you what you do for fun proves my point. Jesus, Addie, you used to have friends. You used to play soccer. You used to go to the movies with me. You used to throw dinner parties here. You used to *date*." She paused, gave the words time to sink in. "Now? All you do is work. You work at the office. You work when you get home. You work on the weekends. I've never said anything because I kept hoping it was just a phase, that you'd become exhausted and step back a bit, that you'd realize Fairchild Rentals isn't going to crumble around your ears if you put in a normal workday instead of one that's consistently ten hours or longer. But you didn't. And then you got sick. God, you got so sick they had to haul your ass to the hospital in an ambulance! You scared the shit out of us, do you know that? Sophie, who's the most stoic, levelheaded person I've ever met, was completely freaked out. We've talked about you regularly. And do you have *any idea* how worried Mom was after that? She was sure you were going to drop dead of a heart attack at thirty-one. *Sure of it.* She told me more than once. '*I'm going to walk in and find her dead at her desk, Katrina. I just know it.*' And I thought, 'Okay, *this* is it. *This* will get her to slow down.'" She shook her head slowly.

To her credit, Addison was not only listening, she seemed riveted. For that, Katrina was grateful. This conversation could just as easily have gone the other way, with Addison screaming at her to get the hell out and leave her alone. She hadn't done that, so maybe things were sinking in. She hoped so because there was one more card to play.

"But you didn't slow down. Not even a tiny bit. No, not you. Not Addison Fairchild, who has to be the absolute best at everything, even if it kills her. Which it almost did. And then..." Katrina broke their gaze, turned back to the window.

"And then?"

"I like to think the universe decided to give you one last chance."

"One last chance to what?"

Katrina shook her head with a frustrated shrug. "I don't know. To stop and smell the roses? To slow the hell down before your body does it for you? To fucking enjoy life?" She heard Addison swallow. "My God, Addison, that chance? It walked right into your office."

Addison's eyes brightened with clarity. "Katie."

"You're goddamn right, Katie. You resisted her. I know you did. I watched it happen. But she's just as stubborn as you are, and she was not going to be pushed around by you." Addison's entire face seemed to ease, to relax, so Katrina kept going. "She's good for you. And I don't know if you just don't see it or if you see it and you fight it or if you don't want to see it or what. But she...softens you. And I think you know that. And yet..."

Addison's gaze was on her hands. Her shoulders slumped, and Katrina knew she was hitting home with her words. If there was one thing she'd learned about her sister over the years, it was that, sometimes, the only way to make her listen was to hit her over the head.

"Do you know what Katie has been doing for the past three days?"

Addison shook her head.

"Running your office. And doing a damn good job of it, FYI." At the shock on Addison's face, Katrina furrowed her own brow, and a little bit of irritation crept into her voice. "Why do you look surprised? Did you think she'd just stop showing up? Come on, Addison, you know better than that. I don't know what happened between you two last weekend—though I have a pretty good idea—but you owe that girl *way* more than you've given her. You're barely answering her texts. You're crushing her. Forget the whole subordinate thing—that can be dealt with—but doesn't she deserve better from you than what you've given her?"

Addison didn't comment, but after twenty-eight years, Katrina could read her sister's face with alarming accuracy, and she knew she'd hit home. Addison rubbed her hands together slowly, her gaze aimed down. Her lack of defensiveness, of any argument at all, told Katrina her work here was done, and she pushed herself to her feet.

"I have to get back to work," Katrina said as she slipped an arm into her coat. Once it was buttoned up and she had her purse over her shoulder, she looked at her sister for a moment. Her voice much gentler than it had been, she said, "I love you, Addie, and I just want you to step back. Take a big step back from where you're standing. Hell, take two. And then look. *Really* look. At all of it. Look at me, because I'm going to need your help like you don't know. Look at Mom and give her more credit than you have been. And please, *please* look at Katie. She has picked up your very considerable slack all week, and I think it's time you ask yourself why. Don't you?"

Addison didn't mind the snow, especially when it fell slowly in big, fluffy flakes. The kind of snow that blanketed the world and made everything seem fresh and new again. Clean slate.

That's what Addison needed. Desperately. A clean slate.

She hadn't liked anything Katrina had said. Not a word of it. Seriously, who would? Who wants to be told by their baby sister that they're a mess? But she'd sat with it. From the time Katrina had left in the early afternoon and through the rest of the day, Addison sat on her couch, replaying the conversation, her sister's words.

There was a lot of validity. She could admit that, even though she preferred not to.

A couple parts had been harder than others for Addison. Those were the things she focused on as she lay on her couch, the daylight fading into the indigo of dusk and then deeper into night. She hadn't turned on any lights, just let the combination of the streetlights, the moon, and the falling snow give her enough to see by.

What do you do for fun?

Addison had snorted out loud when she recalled that question. Mostly because there wasn't an answer. She did nothing for fun. Not a thing. There was very little fun in her life. Katrina was right. Addison used to do things. She threw dinner parties at least once a month when she'd first moved into the loft. Small ones. Intimate gatherings of five or six people, close friends she'd since lost touch with, drifted away from, Sophie being the only one tough enough to remain. And even that made Addison wonder why. That Sophie and Katrina had been talking about her with each other was surprising news.

She'd poured herself a glass of water—after considering a glass of wine and deciding against it...Katrina had her thinking about her health now—and sat down at her kitchen table, continued to gaze out into the cold winter's night as she contemplated her life. And then that made her snort because, really, was it normal to sit around and contemplate life at thirty-one years old?

What do you do for fun?

Addison took a sip of her water, felt the cool of it slide down her throat, and tried to remember the last time she'd actually had fun. She narrowed her eyes as she searched her mind, but she didn't have to go far. Only to an animal shelter, a little pen full of goats, and a beautiful woman watching her and smiling like she was having the best day ever.

Katie.

She...softens you.

God, Katrina had batted a thousand with her accuracy today, because even Addison knew that was the truth. She felt it when Katie was around. Well, she *finally* felt it. After *allowing* herself to feel it.

What the hell do I do about Katie?

That was the big question now. It really was, Addison realized with startling clarity. The job thing sucked, and she still needed to talk to her mother. She'd go see her first. Say her piece. Give her mom a chance to explain. She had to. She needed to. And her mother deserved respect, even if Addison was pissed off, so she knew she owed her mom an apology. A big one. She'd acted like a child, a fact that now embarrassed her beyond words. But after that...she had some sorting to do. In her head. In her heart.

Now it was after dinner on Wednesday evening and Addison, having finally showered, was back at the kitchen table. She rarely sat here, and now, as she looked out at the snow, the lovely view of the city, she wondered why. It was a beautiful spot; she remembered thinking so when she'd purchased the place a few years ago. *I'll put a table right here so I can sit with my coffee and plan out the day.* And she had. For a while. And then…

What had happened to her life? And why had she allowed it?

Addison wrestled with that for a while as she watched the softly falling snow. When she'd stepped out of the shower a little bit ago, she'd gazed at her reflection. Stared at it. Stared into the eyes of a woman she barely recognized anymore. And for the first time in her life, Addison Fairchild didn't like what she saw.

That was a wake-up call. One she'd probably needed for a while now.

With a slow intake of breath, she stood and pushed her chair in. Her coffee cup went in the dishwasher, and then she moved toward the front door, donned boots, a coat, hat, gloves, and felt a little bit like she was putting on her suit of armor.

She was a mess. Her head was a mess. She was confused and hurt and…confused. But she needed to deal with it all, get her shit together and buck up. She'd created the mess, and now she needed to figure out how to handle it.

It was time to face the music.

❖

Addison was taking a chance assuming her mother would be home. Most people would be, as it was late evening in the middle of the week, but Meredith Fairchild was not most people. Not by a long shot. So finding the driveway plowed and the garage door open with her car parked snugly inside was a little bit like finding an Easter egg in a video game: a possibility, but a happy surprise when you actually discover it.

Addison slid her gearshift into Park and sat in the driveway for a moment. Getting her bearings. Gearing up. Gathering courage. All those clichéd things you did before heading into a discussion that would most likely be uncomfortable.

"Suck it up, Fairchild," she muttered and pushed herself from her car. She was halfway up the freshly shoveled front walk when the door opened, and Meredith Fairchild stood there, arms folded across her chest, her expression a combination of relief, anger, and satisfaction. When Addison reached her, she simply stepped aside to let her enter.

"Finally," she said, her voice hard, steely.

"Sorry," Addison said, and meant it.

They closed the door and Addison slid off her boots.

"I was about to make myself a cup of decaf," Meredith said, her way of asking if Addison wanted some, too.

"Okay."

After shedding her winter attire—and feeling slightly naked without all that padding to protect her—which was silly, she knew—Addison followed her mother into the kitchen where a fresh pot had just been brewed, judging by the rich aroma in the air. No words were spoken by either of them as Meredith filled two thick, black stoneware mugs, then set them on the island counter as Addison took a seat on one of the four barstools lined up there. A sugar bowl came next, followed by two spoons and a quart of half and half—Meredith had always used actual cream, and when she decided she needed to cut back on calories and fat in her daily life, the cream was the first thing to go. To wean herself off it, she'd backed it down to half and half, and that's as far as she got. "Why should I have to give up *everything* I like?" she'd asked Addison one day.

They doctored their cups in silence, spoons clanging gently against the stoneware, and Meredith took the stool next to Addison. They sipped in tandem, then set their cups down, like it was choreographed, and Addison would've found it amusing if she wasn't so nervous.

No, maybe nervous was the wrong word. She wasn't nervous to talk to her own mother, but she was hesitant. Along with that came a sliver of shame.

Clearing her throat, Addison turned to look at her mother, who gazed back at her with blue eyes Addison had inherited, and said simply, "I'm sorry, Mom."

"Mm-hmm," was all Meredith said, then sipped. She gave a small nod, and a beat or two went by before she sipped her coffee again without saying anything.

That was Addison's cue to elaborate. "I acted like a child. I embarrassed you. I ignored your texts and calls. I sincerely apologize."

Meredith nodded again, letting Addison know she was on the right track. "Mm-hmm."

Addison would've preferred a few more…words. The lack of them only made her feel like she was ten years old again, trying to explain some sort of failure. She watched her mother's face, as Meredith made eye contact, clearly waiting. Addison bit the bullet. "Can you tell me why, Mom?" she asked quietly.

"Happily." Meredith turned slightly on her stool so she was facing Addison, almost like she'd been waiting for her daughter to ask the question. Addison wondered if she had. Her face remained stony and no-nonsense, so her next words startled Addison. "I'm worried about you." She slashed a hand through the air suddenly. "No. Scratch that. I am *terrified* for you." She focused on Addison, who was pretty sure she could feel it boring into her, and Addison was astonished to see her mother's eyes well with tears. "You *terrified* me. When Sophie called me to tell me she'd had to call an ambulance for you? And I got to the hospital and saw you? God, Addison, you looked like death. Pale. Skinny. You work yourself to the bone and it scares me. Do you understand that? Can you? *You scare me.*"

Addison had never heard her mother's voice sound like that: high-pitched and shaky with worry, and she immediately felt terrible. Guilty. She nodded slowly.

"I was sure it would be the wake-up call you needed to slow down. When they let you out of the hospital with strict instructions, I was actually relieved. Relieved that something had finally gotten your attention." She sighed. "But that was short-lived, as we both know."

An unexpected lump formed in Addison's throat as she realized the full weight of what she'd put on her mother, on those who loved her.

"Why on earth do you think you need to work so hard?" It wasn't a rhetorical question. That was obvious from Meredith's tone, from her expectant eyes focused so intently on Addison's. "What is that?"

Slowly, Addison shook her head, not ready to get into this particular subject. Her voice wasn't much more than a croak as she answered, "I don't know."

A grimace crossed Meredith's face as she turned back to her coffee. "Well, maybe you need to think about that."

Maybe I do, Addison thought, picking up her own mug.

Silence reigned for several moments, the two women sipping their coffee, both lost in thought. Finally, Addison said as she stared into her mug, "So, that's why you chose Katrina instead of me? My overworking?"

"My worry about your overworking," Meredith stressed. "Yes."

In an instant, though, the concern on her face melted away and was replaced by a sternness that used to make Addison's stomach flip when she was a kid. Still effective. "And you did *not* handle it well."

Addison braced.

"I mean, really, Addison. Since last weekend. What on earth have you been thinking?" Her face registered massive distaste as she went on. "Leaving the Christmas gala with your assistant in tow for everyone to see? Calling in sick for three days because you're angry at my business decisions?" Addison must have looked surprised because her mother scoffed. "You think I don't keep track of what goes on in my company, young lady?"

Yup. Ten years old. Just like that. Addison looked into her cup, found her coffee very interesting.

"All you've done is convince me I made the right decision."

Ouch.

That one was rough.

And while Addison understood that she'd had this coming, it didn't make it any easier to stomach. She felt ill, stopped her mug halfway to her lips, and set it back down again.

"I think you've got some thinking to do," Meredith said, her voice slightly less harsh, as if she realized the effect her words were having, had intended it, but felt the tiniest bit bad about it. But only the *tiniest* bit.

CHAPTER TWENTY

When Katie was on her way down the hall toward Addison's office on Thursday morning and saw the lights on, the mix of emotions she felt was a bit overwhelming. The first was relief and it was big. It flooded in like water, running through her veins, warming her up from the inside. *Addison's better! Good! I didn't like the idea of her being sick.* The second was surprise; she'd actually expected to be on her own again. The third was more relief because she'd been handling more than her share of things and was starting to worry about the job she'd been doing. Flying blind, her mother had called it.

"You're back," she said cheerfully, as she entered the office.

"I am." Addison watched her enter, which was unusual. On top of that, her expression was...cool. All business. That was the only way to describe it, and a small seed of worry parked itself in the pit of Katie's stomach.

"You feeling better?"

"I am."

If asked later, Katie would have no explanation how she knew what was about to happen, but somehow, she did. She didn't cross to the little round table. She didn't even unsling her bag from her shoulder. She simply stood there and looked at this woman. A woman she'd slept with less than a week ago. A woman she'd *very much enjoyed* sleeping with, and she was pretty sure the feeling had been mutual. A woman she thought she'd clicked with, that she'd hoped to spend more time with, get to know. She stood there and was certain she could feel all those could've beens disintegrating around her.

A beat of silence passed. Two.

"Just say it," Katie finally whispered. "Get it over with."

A small flash of surprise actually zipped across Addison's face before she caught it, cleared her throat, and went back to all business. "I appreciate all you've done for me and for Fairchild Rentals, but I don't think we'll be needing your services any longer."

"My services."

As if realizing how maddeningly robotic and unfeeling she sounded, Addison quickly added, "We'll be giving you a generous severance package, of course, and I'm happy to give you a reference."

Knowing something was coming didn't necessarily prevent it from punching you in the gut. Katie learned that little fact in that very moment. She stood there, absorbing, willing her brain to focus on the anger and not the hurt. Not the pain. Not all the possibility that Addison had just ripped away.

"I understand," she said quietly, turned, and walked toward the door. Something stopped her, and before she even realized what she was doing, she'd spun on her heel, facing Addison once again. "I understand a lot. More than you, I imagine." She kept her voice low and calm for two reasons. First, she wasn't the kind of vindictive woman who, when scorned, thought the entire surrounding world should know about it; she'd keep their private business private. And two, she didn't want to give Addison the satisfaction of knowing exactly how hurt she was right then. "You're so worried about what others see, what others think, what your mother sees and thinks, that you've forgotten what it's like to actually think for yourself." She waved a finger in the yawning space between them. "We have something here. Something that could be amazing, and you know it. You feel it, too. I *know* you do." There was more to say, she was sure of it, but somehow, the words just dried up and left Katie standing there, staring at Addison. Who sat wide-eyed, infuriatingly still, and said nothing. Katie blew out a breath of defeat. "You're a coward."

Katie turned and walked calmly out of the office and out of the building, to her car, and headed home.

She didn't cry until she was safely out of the parking lot.

❖

You're a coward.

Those words sliced through Addison like a razor blade, so much more painful than anything her mother had said to her last night. And she'd been surprised by them. How was that even possible? Katie was absolutely right, and Addison realized it almost immediately, even though she'd done what she thought she had to, what was the best thing. Now? That certainty waned, damn it, and Addison wanted to spring out of her chair. To chase Katie down, to grab her, to pull her into a hug. To kiss her senseless.

But she didn't.

Instead, she'd sat there. Watched her go. Watched that wonderful, exciting, sexy, intriguing woman, her one last chance from the universe, walk right out of her life.

You're a coward.

It was true. She *was* a coward.

Slowly, as if she was in physical pain, she sat back in her chair as the air left her body like she had a slow leak, until she was slumped. Until she sat like a bored teenager in history class who wanted to make herself invisible. Small. Snow flurries had begun, tiny white dots blowing through the air, reminding Addison that life could be cold and unforgiving if she let it.

If she let it.

She squinted into the early afternoon, heard Katie's calm, factual voice.

We have something here. Something that could be amazing, and you know it. You feel it, too. I know you do.

To her own astonishment, Addison felt tears pool in her eyes. She had felt it. From the very first time she realized she'd wanted to kiss Katie, she'd felt it. Something. Something…strong. Something sure. Something solid. Oh, yes, she'd felt it. And she'd tried her hardest to ignore it, to swipe it to the side, to tuck it into a corner.

You're a coward.

"You're back. I'd hoped so."

Addison looked up in surprise to see Sophie walking into the office, her face a mask of concern and confusion. Addison swallowed hard, not trusting her voice.

"Why do you look like you're about to bawl? What happened?"

Addison propped her elbows on her desk and covered her face with her hands.

"Addison." Sophie's voice was firm. "Seriously, what's going on? You look terrible."

"I'm so confused, Soph. I don't know what to do anymore. I'm making shockingly bad decisions left and right."

Sophie dropped her purse and coat onto one chair and then sat in the other. Her expression shifted into lawyer mode, information-gathering mode. "All right. Tell me everything."

Half an hour later, Sophie knew everything she hadn't been privy to. Mostly details about Katie, the discussion she'd had with her mother the previous night, and the fact that she'd let Katie go.

"For fuck's sake, Addison." Sophie stood and paced. Profanity was par for the course when you were friends with her, but this was an angry-F bomb. Sophie was frustrated with her, and Addison could tell. "What the hell is the matter with you?"

"I don't know." It was the truth. It was the God's honest truth and she was so over it. She was ready to make some changes in her life; she could feel it in her bones. "Help me. Please."

"Help you what?"

"Fix the really stupid thing I just did."

Sophie continued to pace, her thinking face on. Addison knew it well from all the tests she'd helped her study for. Minutes ticked by. Addison waited. Finally, Sophie stopped her pacing, pointed at Addison, and said, "You need a grand gesture."

"A grand gesture?"

"Yes. Haven't you ever seen a romantic comedy? You need a grand gesture if you want to win back the girl."

"But…how? I can't…I fired her. I let her go. Told her we wouldn't be needing her services any longer."

"Jesus Christ, Addie, did you use those words?" Sophie's eyes went wide, and Addison cringed.

"I did."

With a loud groan, Sophie jerked her chin at the desk. "Get Katrina on the phone. We're gonna need reinforcements."

❖

Katie drove around for a while, giving herself time to pull it together before she headed home. Not too long, but long enough to let the tears flow, to cry it out a bit. The last thing she needed was to give her poor mother something else to worry about.

It was time to put Fairchild Rentals and Addison Fairchild out of her mind.

Yeah, she *needed* to put Addison Fairchild out of her mind.

What could only be described as a throaty growl emanated from Katie. A growl and wet, soppy tears. That was what she'd been reduced to.

It was still light out. It had been a while since the last time she'd driven home in the daylight, without being able to see the Christmas lights on the houses and trees in her neighborhood. Katie loved Christmas. Always had. This would be the first one with her dad sick and very possibly the last one they spent with him at home. That thought was so heavy, she was pretty sure she could feel it settle onto her shoulders, adding to everything that had happened with Addison, and press her down farther into the seat.

It was getting bad.

Katie and her mother both knew it, but neither wanted to talk about it. They needed to. They really did, and Katie understood that. But she didn't like to push her mother. While Katie could see it all happening, could see how quickly things were going south, she also knew she had no idea at all what it must be like to watch the love of your life simply fade away from you. So she did her best not to press her mother, not to force her into talking about something that had no good elements... but she was going to have to. Soon. There were things to discuss. To decide. Plans to make. Steps to be taken.

After more than an hour of driving aimlessly, she finally headed home. The second she slammed her car door shut, Katie could hear the shouting coming from the house, and she broke into a jog in the driveway, skidded a bit on the new fallen snow, hurried up the front steps and in, then stopped short in the entryway as she took in the scene of utter chaos.

The Christmas tree she and her mother had put up earlier in the week was lying on its side on the floor, ornaments strewn about the living room floor, broken glass from some of the bulbs catching the light from the TV and reflecting it out into the room in a display that might have been kind of dazzling if it wasn't for the rest of the scene. Liz and Rhonda were both in the room, Liz with her hands up in a placating stance, not saying anything, but her face a portrait of a woman about to crumble. Rhonda was calmer, of course, as it was her job to be, and she spoke in a gentle tone.

"David…just take a deep breath…"

The sight of her father made Katie's stomach clench. He was wide-eyed and looked terrified, his gaze darting around like a cornered animal who had no idea where it was, sweat beading on his forehead. He wore gray sweatpants and a black T-shirt with some sort of stain on the front. It was too early in the day for him to be sundowning, but it seemed like that was exactly what was happening. Which meant he was getting worse.

"I don't like it," her father said in a warning tone and pointed at the tree. "I don't like it."

"Okay," Rhonda said. "That's totally okay. We'll get rid of it for you. All right?"

Katie pulled the front door shut with a quiet click, and her father's gaze snapped to her. His eyes widened even more as his thick eyebrows raised up toward his stubbled scalp. "Who the hell is *that*?" he asked, his voice loud, his expression horrified as he shifted his arm to point in her direction.

"That's your daughter, David. That's Katie."

How Rhonda remained so calm, Katie had no idea. Simply *looking* at the situation made her stomach churn and her eyes well up.

"No," David insisted, as he glared at her. "I don't have a daughter."

That was it. She'd reached her limit. The way he looked at her—not only with zero glimmer of recognition, but also with such *disdain*—combined with the unfeeling dismissal from Addison, the pressure of having to find a new job as quickly as possible—it all just clobbered Katie fully, as if a mountain had collapsed onto her, burying her under its rubble of dirt and rocks and sadness and pain. The sob rose up from the depths of her and tore out of her throat before she could catch it. The last thing she wanted to do was add to her mother's grief, but she just couldn't keep it in. Her eyes welled up and the tears spilled over faster than she could even register.

"See?" David said, waving a dismissive hand at her. "Look at her. I wouldn't have a blubbering crybaby for a kid."

It was as if he'd reached down her throat and torn the sob from her body, it burst out with such violence. She couldn't take it. She turned, ripped the front door open again, and fled out of the house. She needed to escape. To get away from this day, this house, this life. So she ran. Down the steps. Along the front sidewalk, where she slid again.

Slid smack into another person.

Katie looked up. Into those blue, blue eyes. Those eyes that could undo her if she wasn't careful. This was *not* who she wanted to see right now, and she let Addison know it by slapping a hand against her chest, more in frustration than anything else. "Why are you here?" she managed to grind out, her tone an even mix of surprise and anger even as she continued to cry. She didn't really want an answer. Didn't really care. She just wanted to get around her, get to her car, get away.

But Addison grabbed her shoulders, held her firm as she dipped her head to catch Katie's gaze, and the concern in her own was plain, right there for Katie to see. Her light brow was furrowed, her eyes slightly wider than usual, confused, expectant. She brushed away a tear on Katie's face with her thumb, her voice soft and gentle as she asked, "Katie, what happened?" Addison Fairchild looked right at her, steady and solid, her hand strong on Katie's shoulder, the other on her face. She grounded her. Goddamn it, she grounded her. "What is it? Tell me."

Those eyes. Those godforsaken eyes held her somehow, even though that made no sense, and Katie felt all her defenses simply crumble and fall. Wash away like a sandcastle at high tide until there was nothing left but the real, undisguised version of Katie right in that moment. Her voice barely above a whisper, she said, "My father doesn't know who I am."

"Oh, no. Oh, baby." Addison pulled Katie close—Katie couldn't have resisted even if she'd wanted to. Which she didn't—and wrapped her in a hug. "That's got to be so hard. I'm so sorry."

And that was it.

Katie collapsed into Addison's arms and sobbed like she hadn't sobbed since she was a child. There was no way to hold it in. The dam had broken. She cried for her mother, who was losing the only man she ever loved in the most horrific way possible. She cried for her father, who had no idea anymore and never would again. She cried for herself, who was going to lose her father and, inevitably, a big part of her mother. She let it all out. All the pain. All the horror. All of it, sobbed into Addison's shoulder.

And Addison simply held her.

Addison held her.

CHAPTER TWENTY-ONE

When they entered the house, Addison noticed the curtains were drawn closed despite it only being midafternoon, and the living room felt deep and ominous, almost cave-like. To the left, a man sat in an easy chair, eating a sandwich and watching what looked to be some sort of fishing show on the television. He wore sweatpants and a dark, stained T-shirt, his face and head stubbled with gray, which made Addison assume he normally shaved both. A drop of mustard had fallen onto his shirt, adding to whatever had already collected on it. In the chair next to him sat a large African American woman in a paisley smock of some sort, knitting what looked to be a hat in the muted light of the floor lamp between them, the yarn a splash of cheerfully bright green in an otherwise gray and drab scene.

"Addison, this is my father, David Cooper, and Rhonda, Queen and Savior of All the Things." Katie said the second part with great fondness. The man didn't look at them at all, but the woman did, gave a chuckle and a small wave.

"Nice to meet you," Addison said, and crossed the room to shake the woman's hand. David Cooper's attention stayed riveted to the tube, so Addison didn't force her greeting onto him. Something crunched under her feet as she returned to the entryway and Katie, and she looked down at the floor, then up at Katie with worry.

Katie waved her off, as her eyes darted away. "Don't worry about it." She swiped at some remaining wetness on her face.

A woman appeared from the kitchen carrying a broom and a dustpan. She was inarguably pretty, though it was obvious that she was also exhausted and probably thinner than usual, judging from her rather sunken cheeks and the downward slope of her shoulders. While Katie was dark and the woman was light, it was still apparent that this was her mother; the almond shape of their eyes was the same, and when the woman caught Addison's eye and smiled, it was an exact duplicate of Katie's.

"Well, hello," she said, and Addison could almost see her mentally shift, rearranging the expression on her face from "completely drained" to "we have company."

"Mom, this is Addison Fairchild."

"Oh, the woman you work for."

"The woman who fired me, yes." Katie didn't look at Addison, for which she was thankful because she was pretty sure her face registered the instant embarrassment she felt. Reading Katie's tone was hard, especially given Addison couldn't see her eyes. Was she toying with Addison? Was she ashamed to have been caught crying? Both? More? Addison wasn't sure.

"Oh," Katie's mom said, making that one syllable carry surprise, curiosity, disappointment, and some Mama Bear protection all at once.

"Addison, meet Liz Cooper. My mother." She held out her hands. "Mom, let me sweep it up. Take Addison in the kitchen and maybe pour some wine? I think we all could use a drink."

Liz gave up her tools and gestured to Addison. "Follow me."

The Cooper kitchen was warm and cozy and inviting, even with all the paraphernalia that spoke of an ill person living there. On the counter was a tray filled with countless pill bottles and notes, a small stack of mail next to it, but there were no dirty dishes in the sink, and the small table in the middle of the room was clean, blue and white checked placemats marking three spots where meals were eaten. The only odd thing—and it was a very odd thing—was the Christmas tree propped in the corner near the back door. It was tipped so that it leaned against the wall, as its stand seemed not to be functioning properly, and several of its ornaments looked like they were broken or missing. Addison blinked at it.

Liz sighed. "My husband decided he didn't like the Christmas tree today. Even though he loved it when Katie and I put it up on Monday." She was trying to make light of it, Addison could see that, but she was falling just a little bit short. "So he threw it on the floor and broke almost everything on it." She shrugged as if to say, *what can you do?* Then she pointed at a cabinet door above the sink. "Grab some wineglasses from up there, would you?"

With a nod, Addison did as she was asked, pulling three off the shelf and setting them on the table. Liz retrieved a bottle of Pinot Grigio from the fridge, then gestured for Addison to sit down. She held up the bottle. "You okay with white?"

"Yes, ma'am."

"No. No ma'am. Liz, please. Ma'am makes me sound a hundred years old. And though I may feel like it lately, I'm not ready to age that much yet." She filled the three glasses, her eyes never leaving the sparkle of the liquid as she said, "So, you fired my daughter today, hmm?"

Addison was good under pressure. She always had been. In business. This? This was so different. So...unfamiliar. And navigating it was like walking on a cobblestone street in high heels. Every step, she was in danger of falling to the ground in a heap. She sat there under the penetrating gaze of a woman she'd just met and knew her eyes were slightly wider than normal. She could feel them, blinked several times to try and compensate. *Don't have crazy eyes in front of the mom.* Do not *have crazy eyes in front of the mom!*

This was so not the "grand gesture" she'd hoped for. Not even close. She'd planned to come here, knock on the door—thereby taking Katie by complete surprise—and grovel a bit. Then she was going to whisk her away to someplace quiet and grovel some more, tell her what she'd done, what she could offer, and how much she cared about her, how badly she wanted to give this thing a shot. It was going to be super sweet and devastatingly romantic. What she hadn't planned on was Katie already dealing with some huge emotional stuff and crying in her arms on the front lawn. What she hadn't planned on was sitting at a small kitchen table with Katie's mother, who was looking at her with a face that clearly said, "Go ahead. Give me a reason that will change my mind about killing you for hurting my little girl."

Addison stalled by picking up her wineglass and had to resist the urge to take a couple of *really* large swallows right about then. She was determined to salvage her plan—somehow—and make this work.

"I think I got it all," Katie said, entering the kitchen, *thank freaking God.* She carried the broom and a dustpan very full of shards of glass and colorful bits of what Addison had to assume were shattered and broken Christmas ornaments. She dumped the debris, put the broom and dustpan away, and took the third seat at the table. Wineglass in hand, she looked from her mother to Addison and back and asked, "What'd I miss?"

"Oh, I was just waiting for Addison here to elaborate on firing you." Liz gave a smile that didn't reach her eyes, and Addison's nerves jangled into even higher gear.

"Mom. Give her a break. I'm sure she had her reasons." Katie sipped, then turned her brown-eyed gaze to Addison for the first time since she'd arrived. Both Cooper women stared. Waited.

Addison swallowed hard. And loudly, which caused her face to heat up; she could feel it.

"Mom," Katie said finally, breaking the tense silence. "Could you give us a minute? Please?" A look passed between mother and daughter. Addison saw it, saw the unspoken conversation that happened right before her eyes.

"Sure." Liz reached over and squeezed Katie's hand. "I'll be right in the other room if you need me." She said that last bit while looking at Addison with a not-quite-glare on her face.

Wow. Do not *mess with the Coopers.* Addison swallowed again as Liz left the kitchen.

They sat there across from each other. Quietly. Katie had both hands on her wineglass where it sat on the table, and she spun it slowly with her fingers. Her gaze was fixed there, and Addison realized she was having trouble looking at her.

"Katie," she said softly, then waited.

The glass spun.

"Katie. Look at me. Please."

A gentle clearing of her throat, and Katie finally looked up. There was so much in her dark eyes right then. So very much. Pain. Hope. Fear. Exhaustion. Confusion. Desire. It all swirled around, blended together but also abundantly clear, each different emotion. Addison could pick them all out, individually.

"I'm sorry." Addison said the words, the words she should've said sooner. Much sooner. She *felt* them and did her best to make Katie understand that. She *meant* them.

Katie nodded slowly, her focus turning back to her wineglass.

"No. Listen to me." Addison reached across the table, closed her hand over Katie's forearm, waited for her to meet her eyes. "These past couple of months have been..." She searched for words, actually looked up at the ceiling. *Maybe they're there?* This wasn't like her. Addison Fairchild did not have trouble speaking. She did not stumble and stutter over her words. "They've been so many things. Brutal. Painful. Confusing. Scary. Exhilarating. Wonderful." Her head tilted to the side as she did her best to show Katie what she meant. To make her see into Addison's head. Into her heart. "Listen." She retrieved her hand, scratched at a nonexistent spot on the table with her thumbnail, focused on it. "I have made some really poor decisions lately. I know that. I've lost focus. I've closed myself off. I've...gotten away from who I am, and that started long before you entered the picture."

"And who are you, Addison?" The question lacked sarcasm. In fact, it seemed genuine, and Katie's expression had gone from shuttered to open as Addison met her eyes.

Well, if that isn't the million-dollar question.

"I used to know," Addison said honestly. "I was always sure. Always certain. I rarely questioned anything in life. I was in control, had my hands on the steering wheel. But..." She inhaled slowly, took a small sip of wine for strength—dealing with one's own inner demons could always benefit from a little liquid courage—and talked to Katie more openly, more truthfully, than she'd talked to anybody in a very long time. "Somewhere along the line, I confused my worth with my work, if that makes sense. I don't know exactly when it happened, but I started to base my own value on how well I did my job." She held up a hand. "Wait. No, that's not true. I do know when. I think, while it's always been a bit of an issue for me, it turned into a real problem when my mother announced last year that she was stepping down to retire and one of us would take over."

Katie nodded. "I remember hearing about that. When does it happen?"

"It happened last weekend."

"And when do you start?"

"I don't."

Those dark eyes widened in obvious shock. "What do you mean?"

"I mean she chose Katrina to take over. Not me." There. She'd said it out loud and the world hadn't crumbled around her.

"But...you're the oldest. The most dedicated..." Katie's voice trailed off as she seemed to search for the right thing to say. "Oh, my God, Addison." It was Katie's turn to reach across the table, close her hand over Addison's. "I'm so sorry. I know you wanted that. In fact, I kind of assumed it was yours."

"Yeah, so did I. That was a mistake."

"So…you weren't sick this week." It was a statement, not a question.

Addison shook her head. "No. I was sulking." A sarcastic chuckle escaped her lips.

"Of course you were. I would've, too." Katie gazed toward the window, her mouth a tight line.

Somehow, those words made Addison feel just the slightest bit better, and that gave her the strength to push forward. "So, here's the thing." She waited until she had Katie's attention again. "Katrina knows what she's doing. And if I'm going to be honest, she's actually a great choice. She balances work and home life much better than I do. She always has. I spoke to her before I came here today and…I have some things to say to you."

Katie's expression was suddenly unreadable, and Addison wondered if she meant it to be that way. If she was protecting herself from whatever words Addison might send in her direction. But she kept eye contact, stayed focused on the conversation, even as she continued to slowly spin her wineglass in her fingers.

Addison took a deep breath and continued. "I have worked my ass off at the expense of the other parts of my life. And by the time I realized I was doing it, I'd already pushed away almost everybody important to me. For a while, I thought that was fine. I didn't really *need* other people. I'd just work more. So I did, which, of course, helped nothing as far as those other parts of my life went. And after a little more time, they weren't just empty, they were dusty and filled with cobwebs."

The corner of Katie's mouth tugged up in a half-smile.

"But I was okay with that. I had my job. My work. I didn't need anything else. I was good. Even after my hospital scare and finding out I have an ulcer, my stress level was through the roof, my blood pressure was too high. Didn't matter. I was good." She paused, wet her lips, surprised at how nervous she'd suddenly become. "And then you came along."

Again with the half-smile, but this one had an edge of hesitation to it. Still, Katie remained quiet and seemingly enthralled.

"It didn't take long for my attraction to you to surface. And I fought it."

"Me, too," Katie said softly.

"In fact, I had just fired somebody for fraternizing not long before your arrival. My mom's big on not even a hint of impropriety at Fairchild Enterprises. She prides herself on it. So you were off-limits, plain and simple." The lump in her throat was unexpected, and it took two attempts to swallow it down. "But I couldn't. I couldn't do it. I couldn't resist. There's so much about you to like, Katie Cooper. So much. I just couldn't keep myself from crossing that line. And while I probably owe you an apology for that, I don't regret it. Not for one second." A snort. "Maybe I owe you an apology for that, too."

Katie shook her head, that half-grin still in place. When she opened her mouth to speak, Addison held up a hand.

"Wait. Let me get through this and then you can talk for the rest of the day as far as I'm concerned."

Katie's smile grew and she nodded but said nothing.

"When my mother announced—at a family business dinner in front of several people, which still stings, but whatever—that she'd chosen Katrina instead of me, I immediately assumed it was because of you and me. The way we left the gala."

"Yeah, we weren't exactly subtle, were we?" Katie asked, with a grimace.

"No, but that wasn't your fault. That was all on me. And I would do the exact same thing all over again. I know that now." Addison had never spoken truer words in her life.

Katie blinked at her, her eyes uncertain.

"I talked to my mother last night, got all her reasoning, most of which centered on my health, but a little tiny bit did focus on you and me. And instead of listening to my heart, I went with my head, went with what it would take to get my mother's approval in the situation, which has been my default for way too long. It's what I've always done: what my mom would want. Thus, letting you go. But I need you to know something." Addison paused there, let the words hang in the air while she caught her breath, tried to slow the pounding of her heart and the rushing of her blood. Again she reached across the table, took Katie's hand. "The second you walked out my office door today, I knew I'd fucked up. Royally. In the biggest way possible. That's why I'm here now. I want to make it up to you."

There. It was all out. All the cards on the table.

Well. Almost all of them.

Addison took in as much air as her lungs would hold, then let it out slowly. Being nervous was such a foreign feeling for her; she didn't like it. She didn't like the way her heart hammered in her chest, loud enough that she'd be surprised if Katie couldn't hear it. She didn't like the way the odd and uncomfortable wave of warmth coursed through her, like her blood was slowly simmering. She didn't enjoy the thin layer of perspiration that coated her palms...

She pushed on.

"I have a proposition for you."

Katie's eyebrows rose. "Okay." She drew the word out, her hesitation clear.

"Since I wasn't the one who hired you, I didn't see your original application, so I called it up. You have a degree in business administration and you started on your master's but dropped out. I'm assuming because your dad got sick?"

Katie nodded, and it was obvious from the look on her face that she wasn't quite sure where this was going.

"You had a job at a tech company but left it a couple months before you started working for me."

Katie's voice was soft as she explained, "They wouldn't let me work part-time, and I needed to so I could help my mom out."

"So you found the nanny position."

"Right. Not what I wanted to do, but the hours were flexible enough for me to look for additional employment, and I love kids, so..."

Addison nodded. "And it pays well?"

"Not as well as working for Fairchild Rentals."

"Touché. You like the nanny job?"

Katie seemed to think about it, tipping her head one way, then the other. "Yeah, it's okay."

"What if you had a job with a reputable company, that was in your field, paid you more than nannying, allowed you to have a flexible schedule so you could be available to help at home, and had opportunity for advancement and continued education?"

"I'd say that would be a dream come true." Katie cocked her head and narrowed her eyes. "What are you getting at here, Addison?"

They sat at that kitchen table, directly across from each other, gazes held tight. For the first time since they'd begun talking, Addison could hear the TV from the other room, somebody shouting excitedly about something—she imagined a very large fish. Without breaking the intense eye contact they were sharing, she sat up straighter, lifted her arms, put them on the table, and folded her hands.

"Katrina would like to hire you."

Katie's eyes widened. "What?"

Addison nodded. "In her new job, she's going to need somebody she trusts. Her current admin wants to stay where she is, so Katrina is looking for somebody new. But she doesn't just want an admin."

"What does that mean?"

"She wants somebody with business savvy. Somebody who will shift and grow along with the business, because she's got plans. If you start here, you'll have lots of chances to advance up the ranks of Fairchild Enterprises. In addition, my mother has always been a big advocate of education, and I know she expects that to continue on even in her retirement. So, I'm sure there would be plenty of opportunity to continue toward your master's degree."

"Addison, I..." Katie shifted in her chair and gave off the appearance of being both excited and uncomfortable. "I feel like you engineered this to make up for firing me, but...I'm a big girl. I don't need charity. Or a consolation prize. No matter how ideal it is."

"Oh, I'm not just doing this for you," Addison said, allowing a small smile as she tread carefully forward. "I have some selfish reasons."

"Such as?"

"Well, I've just kind of poured my heart out telling you how I feel about you."

A slow nod from Katie.

"And I'm plowing forward even though I'm not sure if you feel the same."

"Mm-hmm."

Yeah, she's not going to help me at all here. Addison had to admit she kind of admired Katie's toughness, even if she was the recipient. "And if you work for my sister at F.E., you're not working for me."

Katie's eyes narrowed.

"Which means you're not my subordinate anymore."

Addison saw the exact moment Katie understood and her smile grew wide as Katie's eyes did the same. "Which means we could date, and it wouldn't matter," Katie said, her pitch raising to a higher note. Addison chose to believe that was caused by excitement.

"Which means we could date, and it wouldn't matter." Addison waited a beat while the facts hung in the air between them. She could almost see them hovering over the center of the table, and she cleared her throat. "I mean, if you want. If you'd want to. Date me. Totally up to you. Totally." She cleared her throat again, mortified by her utter lack of finesse when it came to Katie. She sighed and said, with only a slight whine in her voice, "You know, I really am smoother than this. I don't know what you do to me, Katie Cooper, but…" She turned her hands palms up and shook her head, letting Katie know she was at a loss.

Katie's gentle laugh was like music, melodic and happy. "So, is the stoic and poised Addison Fairchild asking me out on a date?"

The reality of their situation struck Addison then, and she couldn't help the chuckle that bubbled up. "She is. Since we did things completely backward, I thought maybe we could go back to the beginning and start where we should have. With a real date."

"A real date, huh?"

"A real, actual date. Katie Cooper, would you have dinner with me?"

There was a beat of silence before Rhonda's booming voice startled them both with, "Girl, if you don't go out with her, I will!"

And then there was laughter. Addison and Katie and Rhonda and Liz all broke into peals of happy laughter. Addison couldn't remember the last time she'd felt so warm. So comfortable. And while she didn't want to wait any longer for Katie's answer, she was also sad to let this moment end.

"Yes," Katie said softly then. That rich, brown gaze of hers snagged Addison's and held it. "I would love to have dinner with you." She lowered her voice, let her head drop a little toward the table as she added, "And maybe after that, we can go back to your place."

Addison feigned a gasp, pressed her hand to her chest in mock horror. "Why, Ms. Cooper. What kind of woman do you take me for?"

It only took a split second for Katie's expression to turn absolutely serious. Addison saw it happen. "I take you for the kind of woman I could have a future with." Then her eyes went wide and she stage-whispered, "Oh, God, was that too much too soon?"

Addison's heart melted—she was certain she could feel it—at the cutest face of worry she'd ever seen. "No," she said with endless affection. "Not even a little bit."

"Oh, good. Okay, stand up." Addison did as she was ordered. Katie stood as well. "Come over here." Addison rounded the table until she stood face-to-face with Katie, whose voice dropped to a whisper. "I don't know what this is exactly or where it'll go, but I'm willing to hop on and take the ride. Are you?"

Addison nodded, her heart filled to bursting, and reached out to lay a hand against Katie's face.

Katie leaned into the touch, let her eyes close briefly before opening them and whispering, "Now, kiss me."

And Addison did.

The world fell away. There was no sound of fishing boats, no teasing from health care aides. There were no jobs. No concerned parents. No worried siblings, no stomach pain, no clients. There was only her and Katie and the soft loving warmth of that kiss. Addison knew without one iota of doubt that she could stay right there. Forever.

Their lips parted, but they stayed close, remained in each other's arms. Katie looked deeply into Addison's eyes—Addison was sure she could feel it in her soul—and reached up to brush her hair aside. No words were spoken, but Addison was certain she knew exactly what Katie was thinking, because she was thinking it too: She wasn't ready to say those three words yet, but they were right there, just waiting, and it wouldn't be long.

This moment, this woman, was it. She'd never been more positive of anything in her entire life.

Addison leaned forward and kissed Katie again. With everything she had.

Because this was it.

This was it.

About the Author

Georgia Beers is the award-winning author of more than twenty lesbian romances. She resides in upstate New York, where she was born and raised. When not writing, she enjoys way too much TV, not nearly enough wine, spin class at the gym, and walks with her dog. She is currently hard at work on her next book. You can visit her and find out more at www.georgiabeers.com.

Books Available From Bold Strokes Books

All of Me by Emily Smith. When chief surgical resident Galen Burgess meets her new intern, Rowan Duncan, she may finally discover that doing what you've always done will only give you what you've always had. (978-1-163555-321-5)

As the Crow Flies by Karen F. Williams. Romance seems to be blooming all around, but problems arise when a restless ghost emerges from the ether to roam the dark corners of this haunting tale. (978-1-163555-285-0)

Both Ways by Ileandra Young. SPEAR agent Danika Karson races to protect the city from a supernatural threat and must rely on the woman she's trained to despise: Rayne, an achingly beautiful vampire. (978-1-163555-298-0)

Calendar Girl by Georgia Beers. Forced to work together, Addison Fairchild and Kate Cooper discover that opposites really do attract. (978-1-163555-333-8)

Cash and the Sorority Girl by Ashley Bartlett. Cash Braddock doesn't want to deal with morality, drugs, or people. Unfortunately, she's going to have to. (978-1-163555-310-9)

Lovebirds by Lisa Moreau. Two women from different worlds collide in a small California mountain town, each with a mission that doesn't include falling in love. (978-1-163555-213-3)

Media Darling by Fiona Riley. Can Hollywood bad girl Emerson and reluctant celebrity gossip reporter Hayley work together to make each other's dreams come true? Or will Emerson's secrets ruin not one career, but two? (978-1-163555-278-2)

Stroke of Fate by Renee Roman. Can Sean Moore live up to her reputation and save Jade Rivers from the stalker determined to end Jade's career and, ultimately, her life? (978-1-163555-162-4)

The Rise of the Resistance by Jackie D. The soul of America has been lost for almost a century. A few people may be the difference between a phoenix rising to save the masses or permanent destruction. (978-1-163555-259-1)

The Sex Therapist Next Door by Meghan O'Brien. At the intersection of sex and intimacy, anything is possible. Even love. (978-1-163555-296-6)

Unexpected Lightning by Cass Sellars. Lightning strikes once more when Sydney and Parker fight a dangerous stranger who threatens the peace they both desperately want. (978-1-163555-276-8)

Unforgettable by Elle Spencer. When one night changes a lifetime… Two romance novellas from best-selling author Elle Spencer. (978-1-63555-429-8)

Against All Odds by Kris Bryant, Maggie Cummings, and M. Ullrich. Peyton and Tory escaped death once, but will they survive when Bradley's determined to make his kill rate 100 percent? (978-1-163555-193-8)

Autumn's Light by Aurora Rey. Casual hookups aren't supposed to include romantic dinners and meeting the family. Can Mat Pero see beyond the heartbreak that led her to keep her worlds so separate, and will Graham Connor be waiting if she does? (978-1-163555-272-0)

Breaking the Rules by Larkin Rose. When Virginia and Carmen are thrown together by an embarrassing mistake, they find out their stubborn determination isn't so heroic after all. (978-1-163555-261-4)

Broad Awakening by Mickey Brent. In the sequel to *Underwater Vibes*, Hélène and Sylvie find ruts in their road to eternal bliss. (978-1-163555-270-6)

Broken Vows by MJ Williamz. Sister Mary Margaret must reconcile her divided heart or risk losing a love that just might be heaven sent. (978-1-163555-022-1)

Flesh and Gold by Ann Aptaker. Havana, 1952, where art thief and smuggler Cantor Gold dodges gangland bullets and mobsters' schemes while she searches Havana's steamy red light district for her kidnapped love. (978-1-163555-153-2)

Isle of Broken Years by Jane Fletcher. Spanish noblewoman Catalina de Valasco is in peril, even before the pirates holding her for ransom sail into seas destined to become known as the Bermuda Triangle. (978-1-163555-175-4)

Love Like This by Melissa Brayden. Hadley Cooper and Spencer Adair set out to take the fashion world by storm. If only they knew their hearts were about to be taken. (978-1-163555-018-4)

Secrets On the Clock by Nicole Disney. Jenna and Danielle love their jobs helping endangered children, but that might not be enough to stop them from breaking the rules by falling in love. (978-1-163555-292-8)

Unexpected Partners by Michelle Larkin. Dr. Chloe Maddox tries desperately to deny her attraction for Detective Dana Blake as they flee from a serial killer who's hunting them both. (978-1-163555-203-4)

A Fighting Chance by T. L. Hayes. Will Lou be able to come to terms with her past to give love a fighting chance? (978-1-163555-257-7)

Chosen by Brey Willows. When the choice is adapt or die, can love save us all? (978-1-163555-110-5)

Gnarled Hollow by Charlotte Greene. After they are invited to study a secluded nineteenth-century estate, a former English professor and a group of historians discover that they will have to fight against the unknown if they have any hope of staying alive. (978-1-163555-235-5)

Jacob's Grace by C.P. Rowlands. Captain Tag Becket wants to keep her head down and her past behind her, but her feelings for AJ's second-in-command, Grace Fields, makes keeping secrets next to impossible. (978-1-163555-187-7)